CURSE CHASERS

A Dendera of Egypt Novel

LAURIE CHANCE SMITH

NATURA BOOKS

CONTENTS

This is a work of fiction. Names, characters, places, and incidents
either are the product of the author's imagination or are used
fictitiously.

Library of Congress Cataloging-in-Publication Data available

ISBN 978-1-7338961-1-5

Editor: Melanie Saxton
Cover Design: Isabelle Arné

For Luke and Joshua,
who love stories and heard this one first

Three ages marked time in ancient Egypt: the age of the sycamore, the age of the cobra, and the age of the lotus. Dendera lived during the age of the lotus, when some believed Seth to be as real as a rock, and others, a story told to knit fear into minds old and young.

ROCKING THE DESERT

The smooth red stone coughed and sputtered, concealed in Dendera's palm. She stroked the amulet. *Simmer down, will you?* As if on cue, the amulet quieted, then surged with heat. Dendera blew on the rock and bounced it between her palms. The rock retched, hiccuped, spat, and moaned.

Tetisheri, the old lady who took care of Dendera and her brother Zezi, glared. "That stone is cursed by Seth the Destroyer."

Dendera peered at Seth's face, carved on the front of the stone. "Seth can't curse anything. It's just a drawing."

Whether Seth was real or not, the amulet was the reason Dendera begged to come to the Beautiful Festival of the Valley. The stone screeched for three days until even Tetisheri bowed to its wishes.

Tetisheri's gaze shifted from stone to sky. The sun god Ra sailed his boat, carrying the sun across the azure horizon. "Ra burns. It is an unlucky day. We should be home."

"I wish Ra would take me on a boat ride." Zezi shielded his eyes.

There is no Ra, Dendera almost snapped. But since their parents died, Zezi wriggled further into her heart. She managed a smile. "At least there might be a breeze up there."

Dendera wiped the sweat from Zezi's face, and then wiped her own brow. Her fingers raked across the stubble where her eyebrows used to be. She groaned. *Why, by the waves of the rushing Nile, did Tetisheri make me shave my eyebrows to honor Zezi's dead cat? For our parents, yes. But for the cat?*

Dendera inhaled the sultry air, thick with impatience. How long could it take for two pharaohs to show up and get this festival started? Trumpets blared, and the crowd tensed like gazelles spotting a lioness. Pharaoh Hatshepsut, hands on her hips, appeared at the prow of an ebony boat. Seth's amulet squealed for a glimpse of pharaoh's entourage, but Dendera was barraged on both sides. Zezi bounced up and down to get a glimpse of Hatshepsut and landed on her toe. Dendera flinched and pushed him off.

Tetisheri elbowed her. "Look, Dendera. *Her* Majesty. 'Tis a lucky day, after all! Just look at the female king!"

Suddenly, Hatshepsut's voice rushed like the Nile River. "Amunet, guide us to your temple." This pronouncement brought whispers from the crowd.

"The rumors are true! Hatshepsut renamed the god Amun, and now we have Amunet." Tetisheri nodded her approval. "The pharaoh proclaims a return to tradition from ages past. All praise to Amunet!"

Rowers steered the pharaoh's fleet into the canals that undulated from the Nile, propelling the crafts through the desert and into the Valley of the Kings. The crowd shunted Dendera, Zezi, and Tetisheri alongside. Dendera sneezed as incense bearers wafted clouds of sweet frankincense and smoky myrrh about the boats.

On festival day, life was set aside. The flax in the shade of Tetisheri's house would not be ground. A farmer Dendera often saw working the fields had thrown down his sickle to watch pretty priestesses dance. Dalila, her neighbor, had forgotten her cooking and cleaning. Dalila's daughter yelled "Figs!" and plucked a juicy fruit from a priestess's basket abandoned on the ground.

Dendera clutched Seth's amulet and spied Hatshepsut's escorts. Dendera both blended and stood out from the crowd of commoners. She was tall, slim, and robed in a simple white shift. While many Egyptians shaved and wore wigs, Dendera grew her own hair, a braided copper crown. Her face was memorable not only for her missing eyebrows, but for the pyramid-shaped mole forever etched on her cheek. Mother told Dendera she was "lucky" to have such a mark of beauty. Mother also said Dendera's sand-gold eyes hadn't been seen in Egypt since the Dawn of Ancient.

As Dendera noticed a painting of goddess Hathor on the side of Hatshepsut's boat, a memory stabbed her chest: Her mother, when she was alive, visited Karnak Temple to admire columns honed into the likeness of Hathor's jaw-dropping figure.

"Hatshepsut favors the picture of Hathor," Dendera said. Seth's amulet whistled.

Tetisheri stared daggers at a man who hovered behind Hatshepsut, his head bobbing like a vulture. Next to Dendera, Dalila whispered, "That's Senenmut, pharaoh's steward."

Another boat carried statues of three deities. Several priests guarded the statues and sang. Tetisheri pierced the priests with her Eerie Eye.

Dendera squeezed Seth's amulet as each attendant passed. *Is he the one? What about her?* The stone hummed, as if on the lookout.

Zezi ducked under an old woman's walking stick, grabbed Dendera, and pulled her toward the food bearers who carried bowls of bread, dates, long sprigs of herbs, and dripping honeycomb. They weaved through rows of pirouetting acrobats. Temple leopards slinked in and out of the dancers as tame as house cats. One grazed Dendera's leg, and she ran a finger along its spotted tail. A tiny baboon, riding the leopard's back, shot Dendera a haughty look.

"They should have sacred snakes." Zezi gave his black braids a shake so they slithered like serpents over his shoulders. Dendera grimaced.

Tut, tut. Tetisheri glowered at a somber priestess. "It's a shame that one sold her soul to the temple."

Tetisheri always warned, "Be wary of the temple," but her admonitions no more curbed Dendera's obsession with Karnak Temple than they crushed her fear of snakes. Seth's amulet performed a backflip. Dendera *couldn't* steer clear of the temple. The stone pulled her toward it.

The priestess, her eyes warm as cinnamon, rattled a sistrum, a wooden musical instrument carved with Hathor's face. "Let not your heart be troubled," she sang.

Seth's amulet vibrated. *Which one?* Dendera rubbed Seth's face on the front of the rock. She turned the slick stone on her sweaty palm. The backside was carved with a hieroglyph Dendera's father taught her to fear moons ago. *Hwt–ntr.* Temple.

But Dendera wasn't afraid now. She was determined, even more determined than the time she chased her father's milk goat to the northern mountains after it escaped.

Since the moment Seth's amulet leapt from the black earth outside Dendera's home and into her hands, she hadn't had enough rest to suit a scorpion. She coddled the rowdy rock and balked at Seth's image, but resolved to complete the task it demanded for one reason: It meshed with her own plans. The spitting stone was the single grain of sand Dendera sought across all of Egypt. The rock could identify a killer.

Scores of priests and priestesses paraded before

Dendera. She knew one of them had owned Seth's amulet, but who? The culprit dropped the stone when they torched her home and murdered her parents. After the fire, the amulet found *her*. Seth's amulet wanted to oust the killer. When it did, Dendera would avenge her parents. She swore it.

"I bet that's him," Zezi said, pointing. "Benu Brain." To crown himself Karnak's leader, the high priest had slathered his bald head with gold makeup. The priest's sable-brown body capped with his golden head mimicked the Gyldan Benu Bird soaring wide-winged overhead. "Did Seth's amulet belong to you?" Zezi rubbed the stone on Dendera's palm.

"Put that away." Tetisheri could name more reasons for them to ditch the amulet than there were grains of sand underfoot. She snatched at Dendera's palm.

Dendera clamped her fingers shut, needing only one reason to keep the amulet: The stone would redeem her parents. She hated the stone's antics, but she'd die before losing this irrefutable clue. "All signs point to the temple. *Hwt–ntr* on the amulet. My dream last night."

"Dreams don't mean anything," Zezi said. "That's your mind playing tricks. The amulet though — that's foolproof."

Tetisheri shook her head. "What if the one who dropped the amulet sees you found it?"

"They might try to get it back," Zezi said, "and we'd know it was them."

"We have to find the killer *before* they find us."

Dendera's eyes swiveled between Zezi and Tetisheri. "The amulet says the murderer will return for Zezi and me."

"Let them try." Zezi's eyes brimmed with determined fire like they did the night their parents died.

"That amulet has *heka*." Tetisheri eyed the amulet as if it might burst into flames. "It harbors magic older than sand." Seth's amulet stilled. "You have less chance of finding the killer than you do finding a diamond in a goose egg," Tetisheri added. "Bury the amulet under a dune and forget it."

The amulet yelped. Several people turned to stare. "I will not." Dendera clenched her teeth to dam the tide of words she wanted to spew at Tetisheri. Suddenly, the tiny baboon chattered up her leg and landed on her shoulder. Dendera winced and rubbed her shoulder. "Watch it, little one."

Tetisheri's laugh rattled her worn body. "That's the smallest baboon I've ever seen."

"He's smaller than a green monkey." Zezi sniggered.

The baboon placed a finger on Dendera's left cheek. She cringed.

Tetisheri tipped her head to the baboon. "He likes your pyramid."

"My beauty mark, Mother called it." Dendera flicked the beast's hand from her cheek and outlined her pyramid with a finger. It was the one part of her body she wished to hide, but instead of hiding, her pyramid-mole gleamed from her cheek. Mother always said it reminded her of Sothis, one of sky goddess Nut's stars that beamed at night.

"Perhaps the little monkey can interpret Dendera's dream." Zezi smirked. "The priests claim he is an oracle."

"I know why I dreamt of Mother in a river of flames," Dendera said. "She and Father died in a fire. I wish he would tell me why, in my dream, Seth carried Mother's burning body to a crumbling temple." Dendera opened her palm to reveal the cursed amulet and craned her neck to question the baboon. "You live at Karnak. Who does this amulet belong to?"

The baboon didn't answer. He swiped the amulet from Dendera's palm, skipped to the ground, and vanished amongst the crowd.

"No!" Dendera scrabbled for the baboon, but Tetisheri grabbed her arm. Zezi was quicker. He zigzagged through the crowd. People chuckled as he darted under their arms and dove between their legs.

"Let's find Zezi." Dendera pulled Tetisheri toward Djeser-Djeseru, Hatshepsut's desert temple, looming like a stairway to the heavens. Pharaoh's boat docked. Hatshepsut dismounted and strode toward a copse of trees. Dendera scanned the crowd.

"Senenmut was the architect for Djeser-Djeseru." Tetisheri gabbled a running commentary designed to distract. "Those are myrrh trees Hatshepsut procured from Punt. It's a faraway land. Hatshepsut sent a team of explorers long ago. They sent back more gifts to Pharaoh Hatshepsut than a king of Egypt has ever received before."

Why, oh why, did I show my amulet to that mangy beast? Dendera tugged Tetisheri past Senenmut, who doddered to his knee, bobbing his head, and muttered "my goddess" to the vulture-topped statue of Mut. Dendera made a mental note. *Senenmut looks mean enough to torch someone's home.*

They passed a priest clad in spotted leopard skin. He slid a tambourine from his kilt, the muscles in his arms rising and falling like sand dunes, and sang, "Khonsu, sky walker." Other priests carrying the statues of Amunet, Mut, and Khonsu strolled through the Valley, allowing goddesses and gods to visit and bestow blessings on past kings — all male — resting in their tombs. Pharaoh Hatshepsut, her crown twinkling in Ra's sunlight, raised her arms. "All honor to Amunet."

A baboon babbled and Zezi appeared, dragging the beast by the arm. Zezi lifted the baboon to a stone sphinx. "Give Dendera her stone," Zezi said through clenched teeth. Prattling, the baboon examined the crimson rock.

Dendera extended her hand. "Give it back!"

Satisfied, the baboon held out the amulet, and Dendera snatched it.

Tetisheri groaned.

"Who is Osiris again?" Zezi pointed to the god's green face on one of Djeser-Djeseru's columns. "There's so many to keep up with."

"Osiris, god of resurrection, was both husband

and brother to goddess Isis." Dendera knew Egypt's religion by heart. Mother had seen to it. "Mother said they are all One." She shrugged. "Father said they are old stories people tell to pass time."

Pharaoh Hatshepsut glided up the sphinx-lined stairway. Pharaoh Thutmose III descended his boat and took his place behind his aunt and stepmother, Hatshepsut.

Zezi whispered, "No wonder the soldiers call Thutmose the war god Montu. Look at him!" Thutmose's eyes were gray pebbles, each of his muscles as taut as a bowstring launching a death arrow.

Next to Dendera, a farmer said, "The throne of Egypt belongs to Thutmose."

Dalila scoffed at him. "We've had nothing but peace and prosperity since the Queen took the throne."

It was true. Dendera had heard stories of war from long ago, but Egypt had known peace for as long as she could remember. She gazed up at the massive stone sphinx carved with Hatshepsut's face.

Dalila continued, "The queen's prerogatives are art and peaceful exploration of other lands, both of which give jobs to our people."

The farmer looked from Dendera to the sphinx. "The last thing we need is another statue memorializing the queen." He pointed at a distant statue that depicted Hatshepsut as a beefy, muscular man. "Or king."

"Shh," Tetisheri said. "They'll throw you in jail for such insolence. Remember the rumors."

"The Dethroners are active once again." Dalila nodded. Seth's amulet wailed.

"Who are the Dethroners?" Dendera and Zezi demanded, but Tetisheri shushed them.

"They're a secret society," Dalila said under her breath as she watched a priest beating a tattoo on his drum. "Through the ages, they've overthrown pharaohs, but no one knows when they'll strike next." Hatshepsut, a female pharaoh, was epoch-making. She'd bucked tradition to claim the reigns of Egypt when Thutmose was young. Near Dendera, an acrobat froze on bent arms with her legs curled over her head, a human-sized scorpion preparing to sting.

Hatshepsut's daughter descended her boat. "By the feather of Ma'at," Princess Neferura mouthed, staring at the mountain of steps she was expected to climb. Dancers, musicians, and incense bearers whirled around her. Neferura neared the sphinx avenue, and her breath slowed to jagged gasps.

"Maybe a Dethroner got her." Zezi elbowed Dendera.

The princess was notoriously delicate, but Dendera wondered if someone had poisoned her. Neferura's charcoal eyes rolled to white. She crumpled in the sand with a soft flump.

Ra's boat paused in the sky.

The baboon's eyes flickered between Neferura and Dendera. Zezi and Tetisheri froze. Shock rippled through the crowd. Hatshepsut marched on, unaware her daughter had fallen.

Seth's amulet quivered. It told Dendera to act, but touching a royal was taboo. Did she dare? Sweat drenched Dendera's back. She swallowed the grit coating her throat. The crowd's noise swam under Nile water to reach her ears.

The amulet prodded Dendera's palm. She plucked a handful of berries from her waist sash. She crushed the berries, squatted down, and held them under the princess's nose, careful not to graze her. She clasped the amulet, and Neferura's eyes flickered.

"Neferura." Senenmut snapped his fingers, and two guards jumped to attention. Senenmut pointed at Dendera. "Seize her!"

𓃭 2 𓆓

DREAM NIGHT WITH THE DEAD

The guards stomped down the staircase. With one swipe, Hatshepsut shoved them, Senenmut, and Thutmose from her path, ordering, "Send a physician."

Dendera dropped the berries on Neferura's chest, lowered her head, and bolted between Tetisheri and Dalila. Zezi shouted "Wait!" at Dendera's back, but she couldn't stop. She weaved through the crowd, and someone whispered, "The princess fell? Did a Dethroner get her?"

Royal guards threw prisoners in the Thebes prison and forgot them. Senenmut saw Dendera's face. *By the Nile, they might feed me to the crocodiles,* Dendera thought. At fifteen, she wasn't ready to die, to go to the Field of Reeds, wonderful as Tetisheri described the place where her mother and father lived now.

In the distance, clappers resumed their tune, and tambourines jingled. Dendera became lost in the crowd. The further she traipsed into the desert, the more people were harried about getting near the temple. No one whispered about the fallen princess.

Dendera held her palm flat. Seth's amulet spun, pointing toward a cluster of boulders. She dashed through an opening in the rock wall, a tomb under construction, and leaned against the cool stone, chest heaving, sweat dripping from her chin.

"Running away, are we?" A shriveled old man appeared inside the tomb. His hand rested on top of a black panther's head. The panther flicked his tail. "Mudada won't bite," the man said, rustling the panther's fur.

She reached out, and the big cat sniffed her hand. She rubbed his ears, and the panther purred so loud it muffled the sound of sandals slapping on sand. Zezi slung himself through the tomb opening and then stopped at the sight of the man, the panther, and Dendera. Gasping, he leaned over and clutched the stitch in his chest.

Sparing a glance for Zezi, the panther tamer asked Dendera, "Why did you run?"

"The princess fainted," Dendera said. "When I helped her, Senenmut ordered two guards after me."

"I don't think they're coming after you," Zezi said. "Dalila told the pharaoh you helped Neferura." He indicated the old man. "You met Gazali, I see."

Dendera accepted a date Gazali produced from a cloth sack. "How do you two know each other?"

"We're friends," Zezi said. "Mother introduced us."

"I met your mother shortly after I came to Egypt," Gazali explained.

"Where are you from?" Dendera asked the man, gaping at the kilt he had sewn together from cobra skins. Black panther fur draped his shoulders. It resembled the fur on the living panther beside him.

"My homeland is Punt." Gazali nibbled a date.

"You're from the same place Hatshepsut got those trees," Dendera said.

"When Senenmut traveled to Punt for Hatshepsut," Gazali said, inclining his head, "he asked me to return to Egypt with him. I was a shaman and healer in my own country."

"Then you must go to Neferura." Dendera pointed. "Hatshepsut called…"

"Pharaoh prefers her Egyptian physicians," Gazali said, "though they will not help her daughter."

In the distance, harps twanged, and flutes whistled. Dendera stepped outside the tomb. The sun sank, bathing the desert in streaks of Nile green. The royal boats carrying Hatshepsut, Thutmose, and Neferura glided along the canals. The Festival was over.

When she turned to tell Gazali she and her brother must leave, he was gone. Zezi was gone too. In the distance, inside the rock corridor, torchlight flickered. Gazali, the black cat, and the boy padded straight through the belly of the mountain.

Dendera ran to catch up and grabbed Zezi's arm. "It is Dream Night, remember? We have to sleep with

Mother and Father tonight, in their tomb." Zezi gave her a look that said it would be more fun to face a pack of wild jackals. Dendera agreed. When she imagined the bodies of her mother and father in their cold tomb, and that she would soon join them, beetlebumps popped up along her arms. She said to Gazali, "It is tradition after the Beautiful Festival. We must go." She pulled Zezi back toward the tomb opening.

"This will also lead to their tomb," Gazali said. "I know the place, near the tamarisk tree." Gazali pointed into the dark tunnel. "This is a hallway through the mountain, built before the age of the sycamore."

"Tetisheri took us over the Theban Mountains to get to the burial grounds." Dendera pointed at the stony roof overhead. The tunnel's air seemed squeezed out by the weight of the ancient rock enveloping them.

Zezi grabbed her hand and pulled her further into the darkness. "It's a secret passageway," he said. "The torch gives enough light." Zezi whispered to Gazali, "She hates the dark."

Dendera gave Zezi a withering look and asked Gazali, "How did you meet my mother?"

"I live in the forest outside your home," Gazali said.

Walking through the mountain was quicker than Dendera and Zezi's route with Tetisheri had been, but the darkness was absolute except for the flares of light the torch threw on the wall. Zezi crisscrossed from one side of the tunnel to the other, making shadow animals in the torchlight on the walls. Footsteps on sand were all that broke the silence until Gazali asked, "What treatment did you choose for the princess?"

"Juniper berries." Dendera clasped Seth's amulet and decided to leave off telling Gazali that the stone told her what to do for Neferura.

"A wise choice," Gazali said. "Tetisheri has trained you well. Perhaps you are the healer Hatshepsut seeks for Neferura."

"I doubt I'll ever see her again," Dendera said, and Seth's amulet sighed. Dendera exhaled, hoping Gazali would think it was her. "The princess and I live in two different worlds."

Gazali narrowed his eyes. "You are not happy with Tetisheri. Is she good to you and Zezi?"

"She is kind, but I do not want to live the way she does," Dendera said.

"The people of the countryside revere her," Gazali said.

Dendera nodded. "Tetisheri is our rekhet, our healer."

"Your mother was also a healer," Gazali said. "She would have been the next wise woman. Tetisheri's job falls to you now."

"I could never," Dendera spluttered. "Tetisheri will surely live a long time."

"Let us hope." Gazali placed his finger between his eyebrows to bless the wish. "The healing gift is not to be wasted. What do you wish to do with your life?"

"I have no idea," Dendera blurted and caught Zezi's eye. *How did Gazali know so much about her family? Why should he care what she did with her life? For Shabti's sake, she never had time to think about it.* Dendera's waking hours, and even her dreams, were consumed by her quest. Eating, sleeping, small pleasures, plans for the future — these were secondary to the drive to find the killer. Seth's amulet directed her life's course. Zezi responded with a look that said, *me too.* He was right. The amulet sucked Zezi into the quest right alongside her.

Gazali tossed a date, and Mudada caught it with his teeth. "Has Tetisheri taken you to the temple since your parents died?"

Dendera gave a short laugh and shook her head.

"It's complicated," Zezi said.

A gust of wind extinguished Gazali's torch. Amber streaks of evening seeped into the opening. When they exited the tunnel, the sky turned mauve. Twilight proved Gazali's eyes greener than a wild forest cat's.

"The ancients say Dream Night will bring you answers." Gazali pointed to the towering tamarisk which marked the opening to the family tomb. "This is where I leave you."

"Where will you sleep?" Zezi asked.

"Under a star, but do not worry." Gazali stroked his panther's head. "Mudada will protect me from the night's wild jackals, and you will be safe underground." He turned to Dendera. "Guard that amulet in your hand. It holds answers for you, perhaps more than you will find in the tomb of your parents."

Dendera glared at Zezi.

"I didn't tell him."

"One last thing," Gazali said. "I must warn you both to stay away from Senenmut."

"Why?"

"He enjoys causing pain," Gazali said without heat. He and Mudada turned toward the mountain pathway.

Dendera stared as the pruny-skinned, panther-clad man and his stalking panther disappeared in the black tunnel. She turned to her brother. "I'm not sure Mother and Father would want you spending time with Gazali. He's strange."

"Mother wanted you to meet Gazali," Zezi said.

"Mother — what?" Dendera said. "Why?"

Zezi shrugged. "Maybe she knew what was coming. Maybe she knew we'd need help."

"We've got help." Dendera held up Seth's amulet.

A sandstorm blew howling winds from the north, pushing Dendera and Zezi further into the desert. Sand slapped their bodies and pebbles whacked their ankles. They attempted to steer around the shifting dunes while tracking the distant tamarisk tree. Dendera slipped and fell face-first into a depression of soft sand. She grabbed Zezi to right herself but yanked him down too. When they climbed out, spitting sand, Ra's light sank in pink rivers along the horizon, and the desert sands cooled. Dendera wished for Gazali's panther skin shawl to shield her from the piercing, grainy wind. The sandstorm quieted. The tamarisk tree was a few feet away.

At the mountain's base near the tree, Dendera sank to her knees and sifted sand to the side, searching for the small limestone slab that enclosed the tomb opening. A sudden gust blew her sideways. Her shoulder slammed into something solid, the rock. A few feet away, next to the twisted tamarisk trunk, the vicious sand twirled into the shape that haunted Dendera. A burning red figure, the desert god Seth, floated above the ground. His chiseled human body supported a crocodile head with blazing eyes. Dendera righted herself and scooped sand feverishly. It was bad enough that Seth filled her nightmares. Why was she seeing him in daylight?

Zezi watched a hawk dip and dive on its evening hunt over the desert. "Help me!" Dendera yelled. Zezi fell to his knees and shoveled sand over his shoulder.

"Do you see him?" Dendera asked.

"See who? Gazali left," Zezi said.

Seth gnashed the air, advancing on them. The amulet blazed so hot Dendera almost let go. *Cool down. I'll lose you forever in this sandstorm.* Her frantic fingers found the edge of the rock that blocked the tomb and heaved it aside. Diving headfirst through the black hole, she slammed into the hard floor. Zezi fell on top of her. Dendera scrambled from underneath him and shunted the rock to block them in. Hurling the amulet to the ground, she blew on her scorched palm. "It's pitch black in here," she said.

"And I know how much you like the dark," Zezi said.

"Where's the torch?" Dendera ran her shaking

fingers along the wall, grabbed the torch, and aimed it near where she'd dropped the scalding amulet. "Flammakhaten," she said. A ball of flame surged from the amulet. The torch caught fire, and light erupted around the tomb.

Zezi gawked. "When did you learn to do that?"

"Just now." Dendera placed the flaming torch back in its wall sconce. "I'm learning as I go."

"Tetisheri is right," Zezi said. "That amulet is dangerous."

Dendera stared at the amulet on the ground with revulsion. Seth's face on the stone, still surrounded by flickering flames, taunted her. "You didn't see him?"

"Dendera, who are you talking about?"

"Seth."

"I think the wind blew your brains out your ears," Zezi mumbled.

"Father said the gods are stories." Dendera doubled over and cradled her head. "He said they weren't real, but I saw Seth. He twirled up from the sandstorm. He had a crocodile head."

"Nobody sees a god in the desert." Zezi laughed but told his worry with his eyes. "Did the amulet make you see Seth?"

"Maybe." Dendera sighed. "You've understood this amulet since the first time I showed it to you."

Zezi glanced at the amulet, which was now coughing puffs of smoke, and back at his sister. "Something about you brings out that rock's power, sis, but I still wonder why we have to chase the killer. Isn't it bad enough our parents had to die?"

"What if Seth is real and came back for his amulet? It's his face on the stone." Dendera rubbed her temples. The stone made her think too hard. "What if Seth doesn't want me to find Mother and Father's killer?"

"Could even Seth stop you?" Zezi plucked two figs from his tunic and handed one to Dendera. He knelt at the shrine and placed his fig on the stone plate as the required offering to their parents. "Besides, if the sandal was on the other foot, Mother and Father would do it for us," he said.

Dendera ran her finger over a carving of Hathor. "Father would hate it here, with images of goddesses plastered on the walls."

"Mother would be happy," Zezi said. "Tetisheri said we should pray."

"Go ahead," Dendera said.

Zezi bowed his head. Dendera looked around the tomb. She touched the hieroglyphs for her parents' names: Beloved mother, Ramla; Devoted father, Baruti. She knew little of Egypt's artistic language, but Father had taught her the few glyphs he knew. Mother had once showed her how to mix paint from cornflower blossoms. Dendera had drawn their names in the tomb herself.

The walls were etched with seven scenes, depictions of Hathor, Mother's favorite goddess. Dendera hoped to feel closer to Mother and Father here where their bodies rested, but the tomb was empty. Mother and Father weren't here. Goddesses and gods weren't here. Etchings of Hathor were only etchings. There was no help to be had. She and Zezi were alone. Bowing her head, Dendera said her prayer straight to Mother and Father: "Give me a Seth-free dream, and lead me to the killer."

"I wonder if either of us will sleep tonight." Zezi patted the stone floor to gauge the comfort of his bed. "When we find the killer, what then?"

"The stone will tell us how to…" Dendera said.

"Kill them?" Zezi raked his fingers over his braids. "We've jumped to the Nile deep. The waves are over our heads. You realize that, right?"

"Whoever set that fire meant to kill our whole family," Dendera said. "It's them or us." She curled up beside Zezi, wondering what their parents would think if they could see the two of them now.

3

CROSSING A CROCODILE

Yellow light spilled overboard Ra's boat, staining the sky the color of persea fruit. Ramla and Dendera led two donkeys across a desert and entered a trampled barley field. A farmer stood in the middle of his ruined crop, shaking his fist as he watched a hippopotamus galumph toward the Nile. The beast turned his head, munching barley stalks that stuck out both sides of his mouth, and dove to the river bottom.

Daughter and mother neared the gates of Dendera, the great city Dendera was named after. Ramla nudged Dendera toward a temple's open doors. "Dendera is the city of dreams," Ramla said. The doors slammed shut. Dendera banged the knocker bearing Hathor's face, but a gust of wind knocked her to her knees. The door swung open, and a hippo bellowed, charging from the temple. She rolled sideways to clear a path. Too late! The beast lowered its snout and rammed Dendera's side.

Dendera jolted awake, rubbing her ribcage. Seven faces of Hathor ogled from the shrine. "What in the desert did that mean?"

"Eh?" Zezi rubbed his eyes.

"Dream Night, sleeping with our dead parents, was supposed to give us answers." Dendera sat up, nettled before the day even started. "Tetisheri promised me I'd dream my answers."

"What were your questions?" Zezi stretched.

"Why did they die? Who killed them? Who pulled me out of the fire?" Dendera stood. The hippo dream flopped flatter than a duck's neck on Wringing Day. It answered none of Dendera's questions and only gutted her with images of Mother. The way Mother had smiled when she nudged her — it was the same smile she gave Dendera on the day she turned twelve, the day she became a woman. Dendera brushed sand from her shift. If Mother were here, first thing in the morning, she'd tousle Dendera's hair with her feathery touch and hand her a fresh shift. "What did you dream?"

"Nothing." Zezi shrugged. "Dreams are a load of beetle dung."

Dendera plucked Seth's amulet from the dirt. "When will you answer my questions?" The stone gave a stubborn snore.

Zezi shoved the rock from the opening. Dendera snuffed out the torch light, and they climbed out of the tomb. The desert yawned in morning's bronze light. There was no Seth beside the tamarisk tree, no sandstorm, no Gazali. Dendera's ears had never heard such silence, only the occasional scuttling of a long-legged ant across cushy sand.

Reluctant to walk the dark tunnel without Gazali and Mudada, Dendera convinced Zezi to scale the pathway up the mountain. She peered over the sheer cliffs, and a hawk soared, calling for his breakfast. Dendera spread her arms and looked down to where Djeser-Djeseru sat cradled amongst the great rock wall, Hatshepsut's sacred of sacreds.

"Let's go." Zezi pointed toward the zigzagging river in the distance.

As they descended the cliff and wound their way through the sand dunes and toward the riverbank, Dendera wondered if the ferryman still waited on this side of the Nile. Ra's light revealed they had slept through half the morning, and if they had to wait for the second ferry, Tetisheri would not be a happy rekhet.

Near the banks, canals flowed, ingenious inventions of Hatshepsut's architects that carried water from the Nile through the desert to Djeser-Djeseru. Most of the boats that lined the riverbank yesterday were gone.

"Uh-oh." Zezi pointed to the ferry boat full of sleepy Thebans. The ferry was halfway across the river, carrying yesterday's festivalgoers toward today's chores. The ferryman rowed with his triangle-tipped paddle and serenaded the crocodile god Sobek, no doubt seeking protection from creatures lurking beneath the water.

The single boat left on the riverbank was large and crafted from ebony. *Hwt–ntr* was etched on its side.

A young woman leaned over the river, washing her face. A sistrum lay on the ground beside her.

"She's a priestess," Zezi whispered.

The priest wearing the leopard skin loaded the ebony boat with leftover festival baskets. The priestess, whose name was Annippe, plucked a creamy lotus from a reed basket and tucked the flower into her waist-length blond hair. She turned, and a flicker of recognition crossed her face. "Hail to you, daughter and son of the desert." Annippe's eyes were sky-kissed blue; it made Dendera think of her mother. The priestess searched the land behind them. "You two are alone. Do you need a ride?"

Zezi shrugged. "It beats waiting on the ferry."

"This is Ty," Annippe said as the leopard-clad priest slid his arm around her waist. Dendera and Zezi introduced themselves. Annippe smoothed Dendera's coppery locks and tucked a white lotus behind her ear. "My father, the priest Paheri, once mentioned the city of Dendera. Were you born there?"

Dendera shook her head. "My mother only liked the name, but she wanted to visit there." Dendera smoothed wrinkles from her shift. She felt like a country goose next to Annippe in her fancy priestess gown.

Annippe held a sistrum which was adorned with Isis's face. "You are clever and brave like Isis," she said to Dendera. "I saw what you did for the princess."

The leopard-skin priest took Dendera's hand and led her aboard the boat. "Why did you run away?"

Dendera sputtered, "Senenmut..."

"Senenmut is scary," Annippe said.

"He worships Mut," Zezi said with a grimace.

"Mut is the grandmother of Isis!" Annippe said.

"And people were whispering about the Dethroners," Zezi continued.

Ty shook his head. "The Dethroners aren't real." He escorted Dendera to a bench. "Those old folk tales are as silly as dust."

"Tell that to the pharaohs who've been turned to dust," Zezi mumbled.

"There are legitimate explanations for each pharaoh's death," Annippe said earnestly.

Ty pushed the boat into the water. A sistrum rattled on the floorboard, and Dendera picked it up. Hathor's face on the sistrum brought memories of Mother and Father and their ongoing debate over Egypt's deities. She's real. She's not. "Is this yours?" Dendera held out the sistrum.

"Keep it." Annippe patted Dendera's hand. "To remind you Hathor is with you."

"Can I row?" Zezi asked. Ty handed Zezi the oars, leaned back, and tucked his hands behind his head.

Zezi paddled them across the Nile, and Seth's amulet weighed heavy in Dendera's fist. She remembered her father's voice. *Priests and priestesses are not to be trusted. Stay away from the temple.* Seth's amulet barked.

"Was that a wild dog?" Zezi turned from his

rowing and glared at Dendera.

"They run rampant in the desert," Ty said, glancing to both sides.

Dendera took the amulet's hint; she was to gather clues. She blurted, "Who makes amulets at the temple?"

Ty and Annippe exchanged a nervous glance.

"Dendera wants one to keep away bad dreams," Zezi said to smooth things over.

"Ah," Ty said. "The high priestess Eshe is Master of Amulets."

"Was she the one who led the procession?" Dendera asked.

"She had cinnamon eyes," Zezi said.

"That's Eshe." Ty nodded. "She is Mother to All at Karnak. Here's her remedy for bad dreams: Pluck any stone from the Nile mud, rub it with rosemary leaves, and place it behind your ear before sleep."

"Humph." Zezi pointed to Annippe's forehead. "What's with the headband?"

She laughed and straightened the gold circlet topped with an arching golden scorpion.

"Annippe is Karnak's Isis expert," Ty explained.

Dendera shook the sistrum playfully. "What do you do, Ty?"

With a sly grin, he answered, "It's a messy job, but someone must do it."

Annippe shook her head, and Dendera knew she missed out on their game.

"I am in charge of mummification," Ty explained. "I am a sem priest."

"Yuck." Zezi stuck out his tongue.

"My friend Tetisheri and I mummified my father and mother when they died," Dendera said, shifting in her seat. "We used the herbs and linens we had on hand. I'm sure you do finer work at the temple."

Annippe gasped.

"Dendera wrapped them. I hid in the forest," Zezi noted.

Ty leaned forward. "It is mostly royals who use the temple's sem priest, but did it bother you at all? I mean, your own parents."

Dendera shrugged. "There was no one else to do it. It was my last gift to them." To avoid their stunned gazes, she examined the river's rippling face. *If Ty and Annippe know who my parents were, they hide it well.*

Small waves churned around the boat, and something massive thumped underneath. "Uh-oh," Ty said.

"We forgot to pray to Sobek!" Annippe clutched her seat.

Dendera rolled her eyes and said, "Go faster, Zezi." He slapped his paddle through the water, intent on the shoreline.

Two nostrils peeked above the water. "Watch it!" Dendera pointed, and the snout sank below the surface.

"Maybe it went away," Annippe whispered.

Ty wrapped his arm around Annippe. "Not to worry, desert dove."

The waters were still except for the slashing of Zezi's paddle, but then an armored tail lashed over the side, slamming into the boat. Annippe shrieked. Spikes hacked Zezi's arm, and the weight of the tail pulled him over the side. Ty snagged Zezi's legs before he toppled into the river. He righted Zezi and stretched his arms to each side of the quaking boat. "We've got to keep our balance!"

The crocodile surged free of the water, baring jagged teeth. It sliced the air as it hurtled toward Dendera. Seth's amulet pulled her arm in front of her face like a shield. Dendera shouted, "Begonacon!" The crocodile froze in midair, its eyes gleaming red like Seth's, and then somersaulted backward, plummeting into the river tail-first. As its jaws disappeared, it roared and chomped at the water. The splash arced high over their boat, and then fell, drenching them. Annippe and Ty goggled at Dendera, spluttering for air.

"What is it with you and crocodiles?" Zezi choked, and they all burst out laughing.

Dendera regained her composure first. "Let's go before it comes back!" She grabbed an oar and rowed.

Zezi winced, trying to pick up his oar.

"That crocodile skinned you," Annippe said. Zezi's arm was torn, jagged, and bleeding.

Ty helped Dendera steer them to shore. Annippe ripped cloth from her gown and bound Zezi's arm. Near the east bank, the papyrus stalks thickened. Using his oar, Ty poked the water charily before hopping in to pull their boat to shore. After he tied the craft to the ferryman's dock, he helped Annippe and Dendera step onto dry land.

"That was…" Annippe searched for the word.

"Interesting," Zezi said, cradling his arm. "I told you she has a thing about crocodiles."

"Let us take you to a healer." Annippe pointed toward the sphinx-lined pathway to Karnak Temple.

"Our friend Tetisheri is our rekhet. She lives in the country." Dendera looked toward the dusty path leading away from Thebes. "She will care for Zezi."

"It's not that bad." Zezi cinched up his bandages.

"How did you do that?" Ty appraised Dendera as if she were the goddess Bast, fresh from the Field of Reeds. "How did you knock back that crocodile with your hand?"

"Knock it back?" Dendera plastered innocence on her face. "I held up my hand out of instinct. The beast changed direction midair."

"You screamed something at it," Annippe said.

"I did?" Dendera prodded a pebble with her toe. Her heart beat faster than a priest's drum. Her amulet held Seth's face; Seth's eyes possessed the crocodile. Had the amulet hurled the crocodile into the river? What was happening to her? Seth in the desert, Seth in the river, Seth wasn't real.

"I'm beginning to see why you have bad dreams, Dendera." Ty wrapped his arm around Annippe's waist.

"It is a lucky day," Annippe said. "Sobek was watching over us after all."

"Yes, I suppose he was." Ty saluted Dendera by touching three fingers to his heart, a Karnak greeting among equals. "Until we meet again, brave one."

4

VENOMOUS

"Ty and Annippe are as innocent as ibises," Zezi said, wincing and shifting his arm as he and Dendera bustled along Main Street in Thebes.

"So, we've ruled out two from what — a hundred thousand priests and priestesses." Dendera kicked a rock in frustration.

A faint *ting ting* drifted from the doorway of Jingles and Jangles. Dendera spotted the jeweler inside, bent over his worktable and melding gold into a bracelet fit for a queen. She jumped as a farmer yelled from his horse and cart, "Fresh dates, all the way from the city of Dendera!"

Two boys raced down the street, playing snake and goose. A chariot whizzed by, and the driver brandished his whip, yelling, "Move aside!" A cloud of dust rose, and the boys threw themselves out of the chariot's path and into Sweet Temptations' open doorway. Dendera shook her head at their narrow escape. Birabi the baker yelled, "Away from the ovens!"

Further from town, square mud-brick homes lined up like desert ants. White-clad women stood in their courtyards, kneading bread dough. Flax fields stretched to the northern mountains, and farmers slashed the billowing tops for harvest, leaving the crunchy stalks as fodder for the pigs and donkeys. At the edge of one field, two out-of-towners set up a crude camp and foraged for food.

"What's our next move?" Zezi asked as they passed the leaning sycamore tree near Dalila's home.

"We start attending Temple each week," Dendera said and veered off the dirt path.

"Tetisheri ought to take that well." Zezi held back a branch and let Dendera pass through the cedar thicket.

Tetisheri's voice rang through the trees. She sang a hymn about the ancient gray benu bird whose cry was the first sound ever heard in their black land. A sparkling green scent grew strong. Tetisheri had gathered basil stalks to dry in the sun on her wooden table. "Did you two finally deign to come home?"

Dendera's shoulders bristled, but then she skidded to a halt. "Tetisheri, look behind you!"

A cobra slithered across the ground. Dendera brandished her Seth amulet, but Tetisheri yelled, "Don't you dare!" Tetisheri crouched and slunk around the far side of the table. She closed in behind the massive snake, pounced on top of it, and pinned its head to the ground. When Tetisheri did what she loved, she shed her age as a cobra sheds its skin. She shifted to her knees. "Dendera, grab a jar from inside. Dalila needs venom."

Dendera veered to the far side of the yard, ducked under the willow tree branches, and entered the house. When she returned with the clay jar, she kept her eyes glued on the cobra, placing the jar on the table and backing away.

Tut, tut. Tetisheri had no patience with Dendera's fear of snakes.

Zezi sidled up next to Tetisheri and stroked the snake's body with his unhurt arm. "This one's longer than your table."

"Hathor, help us, what happened to your arm?" Tetisheri clucked.

"We had a run-in with a Nile croc," Zezi said.

"Teeth or tail?"

"Tail." Zezi scowled.

"It is a lucky day," Tetisheri said.

"That's what Annippe said," Zezi said.

Tetisheri hooked the cobra's teeth on the inside of the jar. "Cobra venom has a surprising number of uses."

As Tetisheri began to enumerate the benefits of cobra venom, Dendera let her mind wander. Her first memory of Tetisheri was at this same wooden table. She was four and had fallen and scraped her knee. Ignoring Dendera's wails, Tetisheri pulled her up by the hand, walked her to this dilapidated table, and busied her with crushing poppy seeds into a pain-killing paste for her knee.

Learning herbal lore from Tetisheri had its advantages. Tetisheri's rose soap cleared the small red blemishes that dotted Dendera's face now and then. Better still, when Tetisheri told Dendera to stop eating cinnamon, her breakouts stopped altogether.

From a safe distance, Dendera marveled as the lethal liquid oozed from the cobra's fangs. She had no interest in snake-handling, but Mother did. Once, Father twisted his ankle plowing the field, and Mother sat under a tree until a cobra approached. She slid a wooden bowl under the snake's head, asked it for venom, and the snake spit in her bowl. Dendera never would have believed it if she hadn't been watching from the safety of a sycamore limb overhead. Father's ankle, of course, was better by morning.

Zezi edged around Tetisheri, planted one elbow on the table, and rested his chin on his hand. He and the cobra held each other's eyes while the snake's beaded-gold venom filled the jar. Satisfied with the amount of venom she'd collected, Tetisheri unhooked the snake's fangs.

Zezi asked, "Can I release it?"

Tetisheri allowed Zezi to grasp the snake's head with one hand. She then draped the snake's body across Zezi's shoulder. He marched to the edge of the forest, the snake's tail trailing the ground, and released the cobra.

When he returned, Tetisheri was mixing poppy seeds with a dash of cobra venom. She removed the blood-soaked cloth from Zezi's arm and dabbed the concoction over his skin. It sizzled and frothed. "Let that sink in," Tetisheri said. "How does it feel?"

Zezi sniffed. "Smelly, but better."

"Poppy seeds dull pain," Dendera observed.

"How long until it heals?" Zezi asked.

"Not long, it's a shallow wound." Tetisheri wrapped Zezi's arm in fresh cloth and began stripping basil leaves from the stalks. "Why did the ferryman not protect you from crocodiles?"

"We overslept in the tomb, and the ferry was gone," Zezi said, and shot Dendera a silent question. *Are you fessing up about banishing the crocodile with that amulet?*

"A priest and priestess from Karnak brought us home," Dendera said with composure, "Ty and Annippe."

Tetisheri cleared her throat. "They can't even steer clear of a crocodile."

"Did you know sem priests do mummification? If I'd known Ty when Mother and Father died, he might have helped us," Dendera said.

"We did a fine job on our own." Tetisheri tossed basil seeds into a wooden bowl.

"I'm glad I hid in the forest until it was over," Zezi said.

"Where under Nut's sky did you get that?" Tetisheri put her hands on her hips.

"The priestess gave it to me." Dendera jangled the sistrum, and Tetisheri frowned. The night Mother and Father died in the fire, Tetisheri brought Dendera and Zezi to her home and gave them each a strong draught of poppy tea to help them sleep. Hathor began visiting Dendera's dreams that night. Always, Hathor rattled a sistrum and sang, "You belong to me, child." When Hathor played the sistrum in Dendera's dream, something inside Dendera moved. She had an odd feeling it had something to do with Seth's amulet.

Each morning, the memory of Father's voice dismissed the feeling. *Stay away from the temple, Dendera. Trust yourself, not stories of Egypt's gods and goddesses.* If Hathor was a story, how did she get in Dendera's dreams? The sappy way Mother looked at paintings of Hathor in the temple confused Dendera more.

"Why don't you go to the temple?" Dendera asked. Seth's amulet let out a loud whistle.

"I told you to bury that in the desert." Tetisheri glared at the amulet and sighed. "Gods don't live in a temple. I carry my goddesses with me." She patted the ample cleavage over her heart.

"Zezi and I want to visit the temple each week to honor Mother," Dendera said.

"Your father forbade it," Tetisheri said. "Honor your mother by ditching that amulet and staying alive."

"Nice try," Zezi whispered.

"Listen to me, both of you." Tetisheri pierced them with the look she reserved for delivering the worst of news to one of her patients. "The temple is dangerous. Stories of the Dethroners are flying up and down the countryside."

"But isn't that just a rumor?" Zezi asked.

"Ha! They're a gang of killers as real as you or me," Tetisheri declared. "During pivotal points in Egypt's history, they've overthrown pharaohs and put people in power to do their bidding. Down through time, they've passed secrets, magic, and killing skills from follower to follower. They're known for gaining inside access to the royals through the temple and palace. There are whispers of death threats against both pharaohs. The princess's fainting fit put people in a dither. I implore you both to stay in the countryside. Do not go to town. Do not go near the temple. Your parents trusted me to keep you safe." Tetisheri pointed to a large wooden tub full of barley. "Use the pestle to grind the stalks to a powder."

We're not giving up, Dendera mouthed to Zezi and grabbed the pestle. Something black flashed near the edge of the forest. Gazali, draped in panther skin, stroked Mudada's head, picked a ripe fig, and turned toward the depths of the forest.

5

ORDERS, PHARAOH-STYLE

Horse's hooves clattered in the courtyard. Dendera stretched on her woven mat on Tetisheri's roof, the last tendrils of a dream escaping her mind. She and Annippe jangled sistrums aboard a boat on the Nile. For once, Dendera's dream was peaceful. She wanted it to stretch on and on. The day ahead held nothing more than brewing barley beer and baking bread in Tetisheri's stone oven.

Snorts and stomps shook the walls. Strange, none of Tetisheri's neighbors owned horses. Dendera rolled over, content to sink into another dream. Tetisheri's angry voice drifted up from the ground below, augmented by grunting.

Zezi kicked Dendera in his sleep. She shook off her dream and sat up, listening to Tetisheri's rant downstairs. Peering over the roof's edge, Dendera spied a royal guard in the courtyard, a pudgy man dressed in a red and gold uniform. He towered over Tetisheri. Dendera shrank back.

"What is it?" Zezi yawned.

"The guard, the one Senenmut ordered after me at the festival, he's here."

Zezi rubbed his eyes and peeked over the rooftop. "He came in a chariot," he whispered.

"He's after me! Who cares what he drove!" She peered downward again.

Tetisheri bellowed, "I'll answer none of your questions, so stop asking!"

The guard glanced toward the roof at the exact moment Dendera peeked. "That's her!" He pointed.

Another guard, this one thin and wiry, dismounted the chariot. "Princess Neferura requires an audience with you. Come down at once, and dress in your finest clothes." Dendera gawked. Impatient, the guard said, "The priestess Annippe told us you lived this way, and we've searched the countryside until we found you." He glanced at her pyramid mole and then at the other guard. "She's the one Senenmut described."

Dendera froze. The guard shouted, "Come! Quick!"

"You'd better go." Zezi prodded her with his finger.

Dendera climbed down the stairs and stepped into their bathroom, a tiny corner with a hole in the floor for the water to drain. *What could the princess want?* She leaned against the wall to steady herself. *I could be rotting in Thebes Prison by nightfall.* The front door was the single exit from Tetisheri's house, and the guards were standing in front of it.

There was no escape. Her solitary hope was to cooperate.

Dendera stripped off her clothes, rinsed off, and put on a fresh gown. Tetisheri stumped into the house, grumbling about priestesses or princesses. It was hard to tell which. She tapped Dendera's cheek. "I may never see you again."

"Thanks for the encouragement," Dendera snapped.

Zezi sidled up beside Dendera and shouldered her arm. "You'll be home before supper." His eyes told her, *don't leave me here.*

Tetisheri clomped to the kitchen and began punch-kneading a bowl of wheat dough. Zezi walked Dendera to the courtyard. The thin, wiry guard opened the chariot door.

"I'll follow behind on foot," Dendera said. Zezi groaned.

"The chariot is much faster," the guard said. "You'll see."

Dendera stalled. Seth's amulet shot a heat wave through her palm, telling her, *Ty called you the brave one.*

Fine, Dendera quipped and swung herself inside the chariot.

Zezi watched from the courtyard. *Lucky,* he mouthed and waved.

The guard settled into the driver's seat and clapped the reins. He wore a wrist amulet carved with a crocodile. Dendera gasped at the sight, and then held on for dear life as the wheels ground into the sand, flinging dust behind them. They flew through the streets of Thebes at breakneck speed, and Dendera knew for sure she'd have been better off walking.

"Who are they?" The wiry guard pointed to two hefty men who filled several baskets with bread from Sweet Temptations. Birabi the baker bounced on his toes, examining a gold ring one of the men handed him from a jeweled pouch. The men looked out-of-place on the Theban streets, but Dendera remembered them. She and Zezi had seen their camp in the countryside. Ivory amulets inscribed with a red hippopotamus shone against their black attire.

"I've never seen them in town before," said the pudgy guard. "They look like they're hoarding food for an army."

"Better report it."

They whizzed by the massive complex of Karnak Temple and arrived at the entrance to Hatshepsut's Mooring Place, her palace on the Nile. The gates flew open. Losing her grip on the seat, Dendera ricocheted between both sides of the chariot as they soared up the road and circled to a halt.

Dendera finger-brushed her hair and followed the guards through the bronze palace doors, down a hallway glimmering in gold from floor to ceiling, and inside a circular room, the Room of Treasures.

"Wait here." The guards left Dendera to stand alone, shifting foot to foot and trying to tamp down her nervousness by peering around the lavish room. A lapis lazuli throne sat centered on a dais with smaller thrones on each side. Paintings of Nut's stars adorned the ceiling. The tiled floor appeared to lap like the Nile, with bolti fish spouting their young straight from their mouths into the emerald water.

A door swung open. Dendera leapt back, expecting guards to seize her, but it was Princess Neferura. She made a beeline for Dendera and hugged her.

Neferura spoke into Dendera's shoulder. "It often takes me three days to recover from a faint, but not yesterday! My mother's physicians usually give me wormwood mixed with fenugreek. It's revolting! What kind of berries did you hold under my nose? And what's your name?" Neferura stepped back and sucked in a breath.

"I'm Dendera, and they were juniper berries." She closed her fingers over Seth's amulet. "You were having trouble breathing, and I thought the smell of juniper might help."

"No one knows what's wrong with me." Neferura clasped her hands. "I was born sick. Mother orders me to stay in bed except for festival days. Ma'at, help me." Neferura was as wispy-bendy as a young eagle. Dendera thought she needed coaxing toward open sky.

The door flew open again. This time, Dendera sank to her knees and stretched her hands along the floor.

"Rise, child," Hatshepsut thundered and took her throne. Dendera's legs quavered like strands of papyrus in the Nile.

"Mother, this is Dendera," Neferura said. Steward

Senenmut tottered after the pharaoh, head bobbing, and hovered near Neferura. Dendera recalled Gazali's warning that Senenmut enjoyed causing pain.

"Dendera, I want to thank you for helping Neferura." Hatshepsut held her crook upright with a steady hand. "Her recovery was quite extraordinary. Where did you come by your gift of healing?"

Senenmut pursed his lips.

"Pharaoh, my friend Tetisheri teaches me herb lore," Dendera said. "My brother and I live with her in the country outside Thebes."

"Where are your parents?" Pharaoh asked.

"They died in a fire not many moons ago," Dendera said, and her stomach burned. Saying it out loud to a stranger somehow made it more real.

Neferura gasped. "Dendera, I'm sorry."

"Thank you." Dendera bowed to the princess.

Hatshepsut sighed. "Dendera, in my temple, all the healer priests are men."

One of them killed my parents, Dendera thought, and Seth's amulet hissed. Dendera coughed to cover the noise, squeezing the stone as if to clamp its mouth shut. "Excuse me, Majesty."

"What course of healing do you suggest for Neferura?"

Dendera stared at pharaoh's crook, stalling. *If Tetisheri were here, she'd rattle off a healing regimen without blinking. Think! Think! What would Tetisheri say? Juniper helped at the festival. That was a good place to start.* "The princess should drink juniper tea three times per day." She also thought it must be hard on

Neferura to stay in bed day after day. "Egypt's land itself might be a cure, Majesty. The princess should walk outdoors as much as possible."

"Ridiculous." Senenmut bobbed his head. "Neferura is not strong enough."

"Dendera's suggestion will do no harm." Hatshepsut pointed her crook at an attendant. "Send the order to Physician Puky." Senenmut clenched his jaw. Neferura stood silent as her mother made decisions for her.

Hatshepsut paused. Her gaze traveled over Dendera, searching out her deepest secrets. "I wonder if she is the one," she mumbled and rubbed her temple. When Pharaoh Hatshepsut made up her mind to do something, no storm of Seth could stop her. Years ago, she made up her mind to rule, even though every court official told her only men could be kings. She ignored them and seated herself Queen upon the high throne of Egypt. There in the Room of Treasures, Hatshepsut made up her mind about Dendera. "It suits you to use your talent in the temple. You will train to be a healer priestess at Karnak."

Senenmut held his tongue no longer. "Gracious Pharaoh, this young girl cannot enter the temple. She is…" His face grew sour as he contemplated the full measure of Dendera's inadequacy. "Unsuited."

Hatshepsut's face became stern. "She will go through rigorous training. She will be tested. It will be up to Dendera to succeed or fail."

"But Your Majesty…" Senenmut argued.

Hatshepsut swung her crook at Senenmut, stopping shy of his nose. He dropped silent.

Dendera said, "Majesty, I may not be right for work at the temple. I don't believe in Egypt's deities."

Neferura choked, and Senenmut sneered. Tetisheri always said, think before you speak; you don't have to say everything out loud. But Dendera needed to know how far she could push the pharaoh. Queen Hatshepsut was also Head of Karnak. How did the pharaoh feel about Egypt's pantheon? Would Hatshepsut punish someone who didn't revere goddesses and gods, someone like Father?

"It is my duty and honor as Queen to train more women, to draw more women into the temple." Hatshepsut tapped her crook. "Your time at Karnak will bring you answers. Report there for training. When you are ready, I will arrange your Priestess Test."

Dendera's mind raced. She didn't know what kind of test that might be, but she had bigger problems. "Forgive me, Majesty, but what of my brother? I am his family, and Tetisheri, the friend we live with, is older. She cannot care for him on her own." Zezi could be a nuisance, but he was also her biggest supporter. From the first moment Zezi saw Seth's amulet in Dendera's hand, he'd believed in her quest to find their parents' killer.

Hatshepsut asked, "What skills does he have?"

"My father taught him to farm." Dendera shrugged.

"What is his age?"

"Twelve, my Queen."

"Bring him to the temple," the pharaoh commanded. "He too will be tested. If he possesses other skills, we will find use for them. If not, he can join Karnak's gardeners." The audience over, Hatshepsut stood to leave, and Dendera genuflected. Hatshepsut dropped a bracelet onto Dendera's outstretched hands. "Accept this gift of thanks. Come, Neferura."

Senenmut glared at Hatshepsut's back. Neferura rose from her throne and knelt beside Dendera.

Dendera sat up and clasped Neferura's hand. "Stay well, Princess."

Tears fluttered on the edges of Neferura's eyelashes. "I've never had a girl friend before."

"You do now." Dendera patted Neferura's hand.

"Good luck at Karnak," Neferura said.

Senenmut, his lips curled into a snarl, pulled Neferura from the floor.

"Visit me when you can," Dendera said.

Neferura nodded as Senenmut steered her from the room. *It's no wonder she doesn't soar toward open sky,* Dendera thought. Hatshepsut and Senenmut both clip Neferura's wings at every turn.

Seth's amulet rang like a hand bell, reminding Dendera it directed her life. The stone orchestrated the events that brought her here before Hatshepsut, and now… now Dendera had Hatshepsut telling her where to go and what to do. The temple, she was to live inside the temple.

Father's words sprang to her mind: *Stay away from the temple*.

Obey, the amulet countered.

The stone was right. To defy pharaoh's orders was death. Hatshepsut gave Dendera no choice, and through her order, Hatshepsut handed Dendera the chance she was looking for. What better way to find the arsonist, the owner of Seth's amulet? She would live amongst them and uncover the truth.

Dendera pushed herself from the floor, left the throne room, and walked into a man whose every muscle was a poised bowstring. She stuttered an apology and caught sight of his striped nemes headdress and Montu amulet. Dendera sank to the floor, again.

Pharaoh Thutmose heaved her to her feet. "Are you the one who helped Neferura at the festival?" Thutmose dug his fingers into Dendera's arms.

"Yes," Dendera stammered. One would think Thutmose would be grateful. She saved his future wife! All of Egypt knew he and Neferura were betrothed, but he seemed ready to throttle Dendera before another drop of the water clock fell! She tightened her grip on Seth's amulet, thinking she might be able to knock him back like the Nile crocodile.

He relaxed. "Did Hatshepsut thank you?"

Dendera nodded. "She ordered me to train at Karnak."

Thutmose took in Dendera's pyramid mole. "I

thank you also, pyramid girl." He kissed her hand and strode down the gilded hallway.

As Dendera watched him go, an epiphany dawned. Hatshepsut defied Egypt's ancient system to claim the throne. Who would she have to defy in the temple to find her parents' killer? If she found proof, could she convince Hatshepsut to punish the guilty one, or would she take matters into her own hands? Dendera opened her palm. The amulet jeered. *One step at a time.*

Dendera set her jaw. *Fine, I'll play this game your way, for now.*

✤ 6 ✤

GATE TO THE UNKNOWN

Hathor turned her mirror on Ra's boat, and broad sheets of light splayed down to highlight the wrinkles on Tetisheri's face.

"Thank you for taking care of us these past moons." Dendera slipped Pharaoh's bracelet from her wrist. Forged of finest gold, perhaps in Jingles and Jangles on Main Street, the bracelet was inlaid with lapis lazuli in the pattern of stars. It looked like Nut, the sky goddess Tetisheri loved, the sky goddess Father mocked. Dendera kissed the bracelet and tried to hand it to Tetisheri. "We couldn't have made it without you."

Tetisheri clucked and waved the bracelet away. "How can you even think of going to that temple? They say a hundred thousand people work there." Tetisheri gestured around her solitary home as if its merits were obvious.

"Hatshepsut ordered it," Dendera said. "She didn't offer me a choice."

"Do I get to ride in the chariot?" Zezi tugged Dendera's elbow.

"The priestesshood is a perilous path. Your mother wouldn't want..." Tetisheri's voice trailed off.

"Mother loved the temple," Dendera said.

Tetisheri changed course with the speed of the rushing river. "Your father hated it."

"I will find who killed my parents." Dendera opened her hand to reveal Seth's amulet. "Maybe I'll discover why Father despised the priests. Maybe that's why they killed them."

Tetisheri paced. "Dendera, you must not go. Dethroners are known for infiltrating the temple."

"Ty and Annippe don't believe in the Dethroners," Dendera said.

"Unbelief is why the Dethroners are adept at infiltrating." Tetisheri sighed. "Child, you are a gifted healer. The people of the countryside will need you when I am gone. Why go to the temple to jangle a rattle at festivals? You have important work to do."

Dendera bristled. "Hatshepsut intends for me to be trained in the healing arts."

"I train you to heal." Tetisheri slammed her hand on the table.

"I'm grateful." Dendera stared at Seth's face on the stone. "I told Hatshepsut I don't believe in Egypt's deities. She ordered me to Karnak, to her service."

"Think how you want people to remember you and live that way," Tetisheri said. "Follow your heart, not another's direction."

"Pharaoh's direction, Tetisheri. I cannot refuse our

queen." Dendera walked away but then turned back. "How many times have you asked me how Hatshepsut will be remembered in eternity? Will people down through time remember Hatshepsut only as Egypt's female king? Will people remember you only as rekhet? Will people remember me only as a priestess, if I become one? Each of us is more than one thing. Look." Dendera twirled Hatshepsut's bracelet on the end of her finger as Ra's light streamed in prisms from the lapis lazuli stones. "Inside," Dendera touched her heart, "each of us has myriad colors. I don't care about becoming a priestess, but Hatshepsut handed me the one thing I do care about — a chance to find out who killed my parents. The temple holds the answer, and I'm going to find it."

"Nonsense," Tetisheri said. "You're walking into a trap."

"Then I will spring the trap. I can't rest, I can't live, until I find the killer." Dendera put Hatshepsut's bracelet on the table and walked in the house.

Tetisheri followed Zezi inside, needling him. "You must help with the harvest. You can stay here."

Zezi swapped his look of horror to determination. "Tetisheri, I'm going to Karnak with Dendera."

"Pharaoh ordered him to come," Dendera said. "We will both visit and help you when we can."

Tetisheri slumped down on the stool in her kitchen.

Since Tetisheri's house was one room, Dendera claimed a tiny corner for her own space. She spread out a woven papyrus mat and folded three linen sheaths inside it. On top of these, she placed a small but beautiful ammonite. This rock was her last visible reminder of Mother and Father. Dendera traced the spiral on the stone, remembering the touch of their hands on hers. One bright spring day, the three of them had walked along the bank of the Nile. Dendera was young at the time. Zezi hadn't even been born. When Mother spotted the ammonite on the riverbank, Father picked it up and called it Dendera's Treasure. Dendera could still hear the herons calling overhead and feel the soft black earth squishing between her toes. Father placed the stone on her palm. "May kindness guide you... always," he said. If Father had a religion, it was kindness.

By the time Dendera finished packing, only a few drops of Tetisheri's water clock had fallen. She turned to help Zezi finish packing, but he'd already slung his stash over his shoulder.

"You've been a blessing from my goddesses, both of you." Tetisheri stood. "Be careful. Listen to the voice of Goddess inside you. If you feel uneasy at the temple, come home." Tetisheri turned and busied herself with washing grapes.

Zezi and Dendera exchanged shrugs.

Dendera had never heard Goddess' voice inside her, no matter how many times Tetisheri told her to listen. Zezi looked solemn as he sauntered out of Tetisheri's house and then let out a wild "Whoop!" as he flew up the steps to the chariot and begged the driver to let him drive. The pudgy guard chortled and budged over to make room. After Dendera hunkered down in the chariot, Zezi snapped the reins and leaned over the side to watch the bronzed wheels turn. His braids dusted the ground, his arm, peeled by the crocodile, forgotten.

"Lean back inside, Zezi!" Dendera called. "You'll fall out!"

The guard heaved Zezi to the seat. "Your sister's right. We want to deliver you to Karnak in one piece."

"Woo-ooo-oooo!" Zezi grinned, his braids flying, and steered them down Main Street.

Dendera stewed. Why had Zezi chosen to drive the chariot instead of sitting with her? They needed a plan of attack. Dendera spotted the same two boys playing snake and goose near the doorway to Sweet Temptations. They chased after the chariot while Zezi flourished the reins and yelled, "This is amazing!" Dendera scowled.

When the chariot wheels ground to a stop, Dendera stepped onto a long stone walkway. Annippe, crowned with her scorpion headband, stood waiting to welcome them to Karnak. "You drove?" she asked Zezi. "How is your arm?"

Zezi, windblown and grinning, hopped from the chariot and unraveled the bandage. "Better. You can't let a crocodile get you down."

Annippe laughed. "Hail to you both. Hatshepsut sent the happy news. Dendera, when you held my sistrum on the boat, I sensed the priessthood calling you." Annippe touched Dendera's pyramid mole.

Seth's amulet banged around Dendera's waist

sash, and Dendera cleared her throat to cover. She pressed her fingers over the stone. *I remember why I'm here.*

"Nah," Zezi said to Annippe. "She got lucky. Good things always happen to her. She's the one who found the am…"

Dendera stomped Zezi's toe. "He means I'm the one who found the juniper berries to help the princess."

Annippe ushered them past a line of human-headed sphinxes. Karnak Temple loomed in the distance. Dendera thought each sphinx, carved to appear wise, saw through her game, knew that she wasn't meant to be here. Part of Dendera wanted to bolt straight back to Tetisheri's, to what felt safe and familiar. The other part of her knew that answers hid here at Karnak.

Zezi was in his element. Priests and priestesses worked like bees in a hive, and Zezi buzzed amongst them all, making friends. In the garden, workers pruned frankincense trees, plucked figs, and hauled jars of water to douse the blue lotuses in a lotus-shaped stone pool. Under a massive sycamore tree, scribes bent over writing tables, dipped feather tips in palettes of black and red ink, and copied ancient texts on fresh papyrus scrolls.

"Do you read?" Dendera asked.

"Not much, but I've learned a sign or two by gardening near the scribes." Annippe pointed to a sign on a stone column. Painted in black, the picture had a straight line across the bottom and three humps on top.

"It means 'gate to the unknown,'" Annippe translated.

"Is it a gate?" Zezi asked.

Seth's amulet made a rippling sound. "It's Nile water rising and falling," Dendera said.

Annippe cocked her head. "I see the waves too." She smiled. "All things are open to interpretation."

A baboon swung from the lowest branch and hopped onto Dendera's shoulder.

"That's the tiny baboon from the festival." Zezi pointed. "He tried to tell Dendera something."

"I never understand Ipi." Annippe shook her head.

As they passed the sacred lake, the waters swelled to a massive wave, and a flock of geese took flight in a chorus of honking. Ipi shrieked and jumped to a tree, swinging branch to branch until he was near the top.

"Why did the waters rise?" Dendera asked.

"The sacred lake is connected to the Nile." Annippe pointed to the canal that stretched to the river. "The workers from Aswan have arrived with more of Hatshepsut's building projects."

More boats than Dendera could count were linked together, carrying two massive obelisks between them. The men from Aswan argued in their drawling southern accents about how to best deposit their onerous cargo. Hatshepsut's steward Senenmut stood on the shore, overseeing the project. His head bobbed as he yelled instructions to the workers.

They passed a massive statue of Hatshepsut. "Why do they make her look like a man?" Zezi scrunched his nose.

"I suppose to make her look powerful." Annippe was a chatty and informative tour guide, leading Dendera and Zezi past the Red Chapel where several carvers chiseled hieroglyphs onto stone walls. "They are installing artwork to honor the Princess Neferura," Annippe said. "Hatshepsut wants her daughter to become more involved in the royal court and temple celebrations."

A bald priest with a gold-painted head emerged from the doorway to the Red Chapel. This was the one Zezi suspected a culprit and dubbed Benu Brain during the Beautiful Festival of the Valley.

"Hail to you, Hapuseneb." Annippe bowed. "This is Dendera."

Hapuseneb appraised Dendera with tomb-black eyes. "I am high priest, and Hatshepsut commands I welcome you to Karnak." He smiled, revealing gold-capped teeth to match his gilded head. "Be warned. We train without mercy. Annippe will show you to your quarters."

He's vexed I'm here, Dendera thought. Nonetheless, she bowed to thank Hapuseneb, and there in plain sight, dangling against the pure white of his kilt, was a wooden amulet bearing Seth's face.

✿ 7 ✿

SOUL SISTERS

Dendera masked her face with serenity. Inside, she screamed, *He's the killer! No! He's the high priest! I bet he ordered our home torched!* Hapuseneb's wooden amulet held no resemblance to the carnelian Seth amulet Dendera found after the fire that killed her parents, but if Hapuseneb honored Seth...

The high priest turned to Zezi. "The pharaoh asked that we assess your skills and find work for you in the temple."

"I want to work with temple snakes, and I want to drive chariots," Zezi said, as if that settled it.

Hapuseneb chuckled, and Annippe jumped back, startled that the high priest was indeed capable of laughter. "I'll deliver you to Omari for assessment." Hapuseneb clapped Zezi's back. "You two may proceed to your quarters." He waved away Annippe and Dendera as if they were bothersome flies.

Annippe led Dendera along a walkway lined with

ram-headed sphinxes, and Dendera looked back. Zezi stared at her before following Hapuseneb inside the Red Chapel. Dendera hadn't expected to be separated from Zezi right away. "Is Zezi going to be safe with that…" She stopped herself from saying "Benu Brain."

"He'll be fine," Annippe said but cast a worried glance at Hapuseneb.

They entered a courtyard framed by massive columns where masons and carvers filled the air with rainbow-colored dust. Ra's light poured into the temple from a cerulean sky. A tall priestess approached, her cinnamon-toast eyes looking Dendera up and down. "Dendera," the priestess said, smiling. "I am Eshe, high priestess of Karnak. Let not your heart be troubled. We welcome you."

Dendera bowed. She thought she'd never seen a more elegant woman. Eshe was cloaked in an elaborate white-and-gold beadnet dress, wore a menat necklace that stretched shoulder-to-shoulder, and her wrists and fingers were adorned with colorful bracelets and rings. The high priestess towered over everyone in the courtyard and yet carried herself with more grace than a benevolent sphinx.

"What should I call you, high priestess?" Dendera asked.

"Call me 'Mother' for I am Mother of Karnak." Eshe gestured the two young priestesses trailing her. "Meet Jamila and Khay, twin daughters of the priest Omari."

Jamila and Khay each touched three fingers to her own heart. Dendera mimicked the gesture, trying to feel comfortable amidst temple formalities. Khay jabbered away. "We're twelve years old, but we've lived at Karnak since we were young. I hear you brought your brother with you." Jamila erupted in a fit of giggles.

Ignoring this, Eshe led Dendera to a garden bench under a towering frankincense tree. "Dendera, let us begin your time at Karnak with song." Beside the tree, several crocodiles swam in a small pool. One beast cracked his jaws wide, and a small white bird hopped in to clean his teeth.

Dendera whispered, "We play in front of everyone?"

"Sometimes." Annippe handed her a sistrum.

Artists working nearby put down their brushes to watch. Dendera wished they wouldn't. Their eyes bore into her hands. She'd never heard the hymn Eshe sang, never rattled a sistrum other than the one Annippe gave her on the boat. Zezi appeared alongside the priest Omari. When Omari placed one finger on his proffered mouth, he resembled Ipi the baboon. This made Dendera remember a story Mother once told about a magical baboon. Her hand slipped on her sistrum.

Zezi snickered as Dendera tried to catch up with the tune. Eshe put down her sistrum and bent over Dendera. "Raise your hand higher on the handle." Even the turquoise beads of Eshe's menat necklace chinked in tune. "When you play your sistrum, you move energy. Play with intention. Focus on your deity of choice."

For love of the black land, Dendera thought, but she only said, "Thank you, Mother of Karnak."

Annippe kept perfect rhythm and sang like Isis:

Our Lady lives, there is no sorrow.
Our Lady lives, Ra's light shines on.
Our Lady lives, rich soils sustain us.
Our Lady lives, rivers run strong.
Our Lady lives, ever I praise her.
Our Lady lives, all life goes on.

J amila and Khay circled the courtyard, dancing and playing tambourines. Other young priestesses arrived and joined the twins' procession. Zezi wedged himself between Jamila and Khay and danced like he'd heard the song sundry times before. When the lesson ended, Eshe's cinnamon eyes flashed to where Hapuseneb stood watching. "Practice in your room, Dendera. The Opening of the Year draws near. Give no one cause to deny you the right to participate."

Two men approached Hapuseneb. One pulled several gold rings from his beaded pouch. "I offer a gift for the temple. I need an amulet for..." Hapuseneb, gold head gleaming, waved Eshe over.

Annippe took Dendera's elbow. "Mother, I'll show Dendera to her room now."

"Who are those men bringing gifts to Hapuseneb?" Dendera whispered to Annippe. The amulet buyers were the same ones who'd traded with Birabi for loads of fresh bread. They camped near the flax fields.

"I've never seen them before. Perhaps they are travelers seeking amulets for good fortune, although they already wear hippo amulets." Annippe led Dendera past the Temple of Ptah where an artist sat chiseling a cobalt-capped image of the craftsman's god.

"Why does Hapuseneb wear a Seth amulet?" Dendera asked.

"Seth is Strength," Annippe explained. "Hapuseneb thinks he is strongest of the priests."

Behind the temple, one story mud-brick homes lined up like a walking maze. A mother cat slinked amongst the trash bins, snatching scraps to take back to her mewing kittens hidden in a bush. Dendera scratched her eyebrow stubble, still miffed that Tetisheri made her shave for Zezi's cat.

"The priests don't mind the wild cats from the forest. They keep rats and snakes out of the grain houses." Annippe pointed to a row of sunburned houses. "Zezi will squeeze into Ty's home, amongst the priests' quarters." A stone walkway led to a home with a keep-out face. "Mother Eshe lives there, with Jamila and Khay." She indicated a sleepy cottage. "Older priestesses retire here."

Annippe stopped in front of a soul-sister home. "You and I have this palace all to ourselves." Annippe led Dendera through the entryway. Open windows welcomed cool breezes and shafts of light. Dendera swept through the turquoise-tiled sitting room and brushed her fingers over bright paintings adorning the walls.

"Our bedroom is this way." Annippe pointed through an arched doorway. A second room nestled two lion-headed beds cushioned with barley stalks, each equipped with a wooden headrest. Annippe slipped a sistrum from a drawer on a carven table. Dendera pointed to Annippe's necklace, an oyster shell painted with Isis's face. "Did you make that?"

"No," she said. "It was my mother's."

"It's lovely."

"Thank you," Annippe said, fingering the shell. "Isis is brave. Who is your goddess?"

"I don't believe in any of them." Seth's amulet made a soft *zing*, and Dendera wished she could reel back the words. Annippe was devout. To discover her parents' murderer, Dendera needed to hold her tongue and play the part of a priestess. When she looked at Annippe's face, however, she didn't see even a trace of judgment.

"Karnak is the right place for you," Annippe said, nodding. "Truly, there is one Divine, with lots of ways to glimpse it."

Dendera stood stunned. Moons ago, Mother had explained Egypt's pantheon of deities the same way.

How odd that Annippe used the same words. Seth's amulet yowled.

"What was that?" Annippe asked.

Dendera looked out the window. "Sounded like a cat to me."

❧ 8 ❧
THE FORBIDDEN AND
REMEMBERED

Dendera's first days in the temple blurred like the sandstorms that blew across the breadth of the Nile. She clung to Annippe as tight as the rock in her hand, forever grateful that Annippe accepted the barrel of excuses she gave for her amulet's racket. Annippe offered food and drink for Dendera's "gurgling stomach, hiccups, and coughs" but remained blasé about the numerous noises that emitted near Dendera's body.

To memorize the layout of Karnak would take a lifetime. The temple was a maze of houses, shrines, storage huts, sculptures, gardens, secret passageways, hidden staircases, and underground tunnels. Dendera would have been ever-lost without Annippe who had a handy map in her head which always led her right. Dendera and Zezi had nil time to speak, much less compare notes on the complexity of Karnak and the gaggle of people living there.

One lucky day, Dendera woke in her temple home

and looked out her window. The sky appeared fresh-painted by a purple heron's feather. Night's cool air vanished with a pop, and she slipped from bed to watch Annippe add a new scene to her Isis mural.

"Do I visit Neferura today?" Dendera asked.

"I believe you visit the princess in two days." Annippe ticked off the days on her fingers. She made it a habit to know Dendera's schedule. Most days were packed with temple lessons and duties. Several days per week, Dendera attended Sema, an exercise class where she contorted her body into poses that supposedly mimicked Egypt's deities. Other days, Pharaoh Hatshepsut called Dendera to the palace to tend Neferura in her sick bed or to take a walk with her.

"Omari sent for you," Annippe said. "I'll walk you to the House of Life."

Dendera pulled on her priestess robe. "What is a House of Life?"

"It's where you will take Scribera lessons. You'll learn to read and write hieroglyphs." Annippe turned her back.

"How about you? Do you get Scribera lessons?"

"No," Annippe said. "Each priest and priestess receives lessons according to their skills. My skills are music and art. You are still being tested to determine your strengths."

"Your devotion to Isis is also a gift." Dendera picked up a feather brush and pointed at Annippe's painting. "I like Isis on the throne of Egypt. Your ability to paint the deities seems just as important as the language, the hieroglyphs." She dipped the brush in Annippe's yellow paint and crowned Isis's head with the moon. "Do you want me to teach you?"

"Teach me what?"

"Hieroglyphs, as I learn them," Dendera said.

Annippe gasped. "I'd love to learn."

After their breakfast of eggs and cheese, Annippe and Dendera hiked past the priests' drab houses, the sour-and-sweet smelling Apothecary, and stopped before Karnak's smallest shrine. The stone sanctuary sat sulky and neglected as if everyone had forgotten it stood beside the tallest tree in Thebes. Dendera pushed aside the cobwebs stretching across the shrine's slab-door, shaking the sticky strands from her fingers. It begged her to enter, but no matter how she pushed and cajoled, the door wouldn't budge.

"We are forbidden from entering the House of Sycamore," Annippe said while Dendera rammed the door. "It is Hathor's temple, but it has been locked since the age of the sycamore."

Dendera massaged her shoulder and leaned against the towering sycamore tree. Her pyramid mole twitched. She rubbed it and gazed skyward. Its branches were a labyrinth leading inward, the trunk its center. "The tree is ancient."

"And sacred to Hathor," Annippe said. "It is said Hathor waits at the edge of the Field of Reeds in…"

"A sycamore tree," Dendera finished. "My mother told me that story more times than the leaves dancing on these limbs."

Annippe smiled. "May I ask? How did your parents die?"

"They…it was…" Dendera fumbled for words. "I'd rather not talk about it." She couldn't tell Annippe she was hunting a killer and decided it was better to cut off talking about her parents than to start chatting and end up spilling secrets she didn't intend.

"I understand," Annippe said. "You have a new life, here at Karnak."

A stone pyramid, a cubit taller than either girl, sat between the sycamore and Hathor's abandoned temple. Dendera traced her fingers across the pyramid's hieroglyphs, glad she would soon be able to read them.

The staircase to the House of Life rivaled Djeser-Djeseru's in the desert. When Annippe and Dendera reached the top, gasping for breath, they pooled their strength to heave open the wooden door. Inside, the walls of a cavernous room were lined with shelves holding dusty papyrus scrolls, all of Egypt's ancient wisdom sequestered here.

Dendera remembered the magic book Mother mentioned, the one with the baboon on its cover. "I once heard that Karnak's library is filled with scrolls of magic and power."

The priest who resembled an aged baboon emerged from the maze of shelves. This was Jamila and Khay's father Omari, the one testing Zezi. He said, "You are Dendera."

Dendera bowed in respect. "Could Annippe stay for the lesson?" Annippe glowed.

Omari gestured toward a wooden table with three chairs. "I planned for your brother to join us, but he is late. Annippe may take his place."

"Has Zezi already started lessons with you?"

"This was to be his first," Omari answered, licking his fingers to open a scroll.

Dendera worried why Zezi would be late. She couldn't shake the amulet's warning that the murderer would be back for her and her brother. Once they were seated, Omari pierced Dendera with a steady gaze. "Pharaoh Hatshepsut directed me to teach you healing, in other words, the Secrets of Wisdom. You come to Karnak seeking magic and power. Is this wise?"

"Uh…no." Dendera wanted to kick herself. "I meant no disrespect, Omari." She took a deep breath. "Please tell us: What do these ancient texts hold?" A chattering baboon leapt onto the table and pounded his chest. They all laughed. "Ipi knows how to break the tension," Dendera said, and the baboon sniffed her hand.

"Ipi is an idiot," Omari said, "but if he's taken a liking to you, he can't be all bad."

The little baboon swung onto Dendera's shoulder, content to stay for the lesson. "Will Ipi grow any larger?" she asked, pulling the baboon to her lap. "The baboons in the Temple of Thoth are enormous compared to him."

"Ipi is a runt," Omari said, "and runts, in theory, make the best oracles. The power they would otherwise use to grow outwardly turns within. Ipi, however, fails at showing even the slightest oracular abilities." Omari unrolled the scroll they were to study. "Do you know any hieroglyphs, or do we start from the beginning?"

"My Father taught me the few signs he knew," Dendera said.

"Me too," Zezi said, pulling up a fourth chair. "Sorry I'm late, Omari. My snake lesson ran long. I was learning to handle a viper, and its fangs kept getting in the way."

"Excused." Omari proffered his lips like Ipi.

Annippe pointed to a spell of Isis. "I want to learn this one."

"A wise choice," Omari said.

Dendera smiled at Isis's image. Annippe bore a striking resemblance to her goddess, but where Annippe wore a headband topped with a golden scorpion, Isis's headdress held seven live and lethal scorpions.

Over a lunchtime salad of lettuce, cucumbers, onion, and garlic, Omari taught them hieroglyphic basics. Seth's amulet purred in tune with Dendera's breath, and she found learning Egypt's artistic language to be a breeze of Nile wind. Zezi and Annippe struggled to keep pace with her.

"You are the most advanced scribal student I have ever taught." Omari placed a quill in Dendera's hand. Before the afternoon sun sank, Dendera deciphered the text in which Isis's spell cast out the fatal poison of a scorpion. She even copied the hieroglyphs, rewriting the spell on a fresh scroll.

"This garlic would keep away scorpions." Zezi waved the pungent bulb. "A spell to neutralize snake venom would be more useful."

"Another lesson, perhaps." Omari straightened his Thoth amulet, which was inscribed with a baboon, and then four things happened in quick succession. Ipi's eyes darted from the amulet to the priest's face, telling Dendera with his eyes that the two bore a striking resemblance, but how could Ipi tell her anything? Seth's amulet raised a din in Dendera's sash. Annippe banged Dendera's back, thinking she must be choking. Zezi doubled over, feigning his own coughing fit to cover the amulet's noise.

The memory rattled into place like a sistrum's bead: Mother spoke of a book with a baboon. The baboon was a symbol of Thoth, god of scribes, scribes like Omari. Mother had said, "The *Book of Thoth* brings magical wisdom. It will answer any question, *if* you can put your hands on it," and winked. At the time, Dendera thought her mother was telling a simple bedtime story. Had Mother prepared her for this quest? Dendera realized she was grasping for a silver pearl in a barrelful of barley, but she needed hope. If she found the *Book of Thoth*, could she ask who the killer was, and then use her evidence — Seth's amulet — to prove the killer's guilt?

Dendera pointed to Omari's baboon amulet. "Omari, is there a *Book of Thoth*?"

"The *Book of Thoth* is under the protection of Seth," Hapuseneb said in a stiff voice. He emerged from the scroll shelves, sweat smearing his gold makeup. His

Seth amulet banged his chest. "I forbid you from seeking information on the *Book of Thoth*. It is," Hapuseneb's eyes sized up Dendera, "too advanced for your abilities." He turned to Annippe. "Eshe requires your help in the Sanctuary of Song." Annippe jumped from her chair, and Hapuseneb swept her from the library.

Ipi clutched Dendera's hand. "Child, Her Majesty sent you here to learn healing," Omari said. "The gods of Egypt share their magic with the worthy. Keep to the scrolls of Hathor and Isis; they will be your greatest guides. The *Book of Thoth* teaches power, yes, but all those who have sought power over the gods of Egypt have gone mad, taken their own lives, or otherwise perished in various degrees of misery."

❧ 9 ❧

TEMPLE TALENTS

Omari ushered Dendera and Zezi from the library, their arms weighted with study scrolls.

"I'm sorry I couldn't warn you about Hapuseneb," Zezi said.

Dendera stopped and turned to her brother. "He was hiding behind the shelves for the whole lesson?"

"Act natural." Zezi pulled Dendera further down the dirt path. "I don't think he trusts you."

"But Benu Brain trusts you?" Dendera asked.

"We better not call him that anymore." Zezi peered side to side, as if someone might be listening. "You have to find something in common with these people. He and I both like snakes."

"Do you recall why we're here?"

"Course I do. We've got to drum up clues, and by the way..." Zezi dumped his stack of scrolls into Dendera's arms. "Your job is sifting through this stuff. I'm not bent on hieroglyphs."

"We need to look for the *Book of Thoth*," Dendera said.

Seth's amulet hacked until it retched.

"I don't think your amulet likes that idea." Zezi laughed.

"We need a clue, a plan, something real," Dendera said. "Mother told me a story about the *Book of Thoth*."

"She never told me," Zezi said.

"She said the *Book of Thoth* will answer any question," Dendera said. "Zezi, all we'd have to do is ask the book."

"People often tell stories to pass time," Zezi said, imitating Father's voice. "If you think the *Book of Thoth* is real, do you think gods and goddesses are real?"

"Believing a helpful book might exist is different than worshipping deities," Dendera said.

Zezi frowned.

"We need hope," Dendera said. "Promise me you'll help me look for the book."

Zezi groaned.

"Another thing," Dendera said. "The amulet told me the murderer will come back for us. What if Hapuseneb arranges for a poisonous snake to bite you? You aren't being careful."

"Course I am," Zezi said. "Hapuseneb looks shifty, but he's only power hungry. You have too much clout with Pharaoh Hatshepsut, and Hapuseneb doesn't want to be shown up."

The thought of Benu Brain, his unfair treatment of her, and his favoritism for Zezi gnawed at Dendera as they navigated the maze of houses, gardens, and pathways. Annippe was already home and stood in their doorway with Ty. He looked at Annippe in a way that made Dendera's skin shrink. Dendera thought of Ty as a sister would, but why was he leaning over? *No.* Seth's amulet cooed. Ty whispered "desert dove" and kissed Annippe. Not wanting them to know she'd seen them, Dendera searched for a place to hide. There wasn't a grain bin or a juniper shrub in sight.

Zezi called out, "Can't you two find someplace private?"

Ty glanced over Annippe's head and laughed. Annippe ducked under Ty's arm and slipped inside. "How are your hieroglyphs coming along, Dendera?" Ty grinned.

"Better than yours," Dendera teased.

"Better than mine too." Zezi punched Ty's arm, and they headed toward the priests' quarters.

Inside, an evening meal was set at a low table. Annippe bustled around, avoiding Dendera's eyes. "Eshe wasn't even in the Sanctuary of Song," she said.

Dendera slathered sesame paste on barley bread. "Hapuseneb hates me."

Annippe paused. "He doesn't hate you, but I'll admit you aren't his favorite."

"Thanks, but that doesn't make me feel better." Dendera handed Annippe some almonds. "He was not pleased that you studied hieroglyphs with me."

"Perhaps I should not," Annippe said. "I do not want to dishonor the high priest nor shame my father.

He taught me to follow temple rules without shirking. There are steep penalties for those who read the temple's scrolls without authority. Some priests have been executed." Annippe offered a cinnamon stick for Dendera's Bouza, or wheat beer.

Dendera put up her hand, remembering Tetisheri's advice. "No cinnamon for me." So, the temple had no qualms about disposing of those who disagreed with the rules. She wondered if she should tell Annippe about the danger lurking at Karnak. Seth's amulet shot off warning sparks; Dendera walked toward the window to extinguish the singe marks on her sash.

"Someone must have started a cook fire," Annippe said, sniffing the air.

"Yes," Dendera said, wafting smoke from her waist sash out the window.

Annippe was loyal to the temple, to her goddesses, and to the high priest and priestess. She'd lived her life tucked safe at Karnak. Whoever torched Dendera's home and killed her parents had changed her life forever. The night of the fire, life stabbed her in the gut.

Seth's amulet gabbled, and Dendera banged her cup on the windowsill to muffle the noise. *Yes, it is strange*, she told the amulet, *to trust a stone more than people. Be quiet.* Dendera couldn't confess her inner hauntings, so she wheeled the conversation around to Annippe. "Ty is not as old-fashioned as Hapuseneb." Dendera arched her eyebrows.

"No." Annippe wound a blond lock around her finger. "He and I...we're both interested in alchemy."

"Alchemy?" Dendera flopped down across from Annippe.

"The melting and rebuilding of ... things." Annippe fiddled with her oyster shell necklace.

"Ty does mummification," Dendera said, frowning.

"After a body breaks down, Ty rebuilds it, makes it a mummy," Annippe said. "Of course, Isis is the Mother of Alchemy."

"Isis was a metal worker?"

"Alchemists don't just rebuild metal," Annippe said. "Isis rebuilt her husband's body. She made Osiris a spiritual body that would endure. I'd love to get my hands on the Tincture of Isis."

"Do your parents approve?" Dendera stood to clear the dishes.

"I haven't told my father," Annippe said. "Ty and I have been meeting in secret since the Beautiful Festival."

"What about your mother?" Dendera wondered which of the priestesses might be Annippe's mother.

"I never knew her," Annippe said. "She left when I was a baby. Father doesn't talk about her, but he says he loves me enough for both of them."

"I imagine he does," Dendera said, thinking Annippe had it harder than she did. Dendera's parents were dead, but she knew they both loved her. It sounded like Annippe's mother had abandoned her.

Dendera lit the bedside lamp, shifted the mountain of scrolls on her bed, and sat. The chariot wheels in her mind spun while Annippe sang a hymn to Isis.

To master reading, Omari had given Dendera the *Basics Scroll*. It expounded upon their earlier lesson. She placed the *Basics Scroll* beside the scroll she wanted to read, *The Dreams of Isis*, and decoded one hieroglyph at a time. Seth's amulet vibrated at an even pace, the same as it did during Omari's lesson. Dendera caressed the amulet and wondered if it accelerated her reading skills. The stone purred like a kitten.

"Mother Cat must be teaching her kittens to hunt," Dendera said and looked out the window.

"What are you reading?" Annippe stopped playing her sistrum.

Dendera held up the scroll. "*The Dreams of Isis.* It's an index of dream symbols." Beside the hieroglyph for the word desert, she cracked this code and read to Annippe: "Whosoever dreams of taking a journey across the desert desires to reach a life goal. This goal may be finishing the harvest on time, learning a new job skill, or procuring that special one as your beloved. Bear in mind …" When Dendera and Zezi spent the night in their parents' tomb, she dreamed she and Mother crossed a desert on their way to Dendera Temple. Dendera wondered if trying to locate a killer was considered a life goal.

"Your life goal is to become a priestess," Annippe said.

"Right," Dendera said and flipped to the final

pages of the scroll. Here were the exercises Omari asked her to perform.

"Do you want to decode one of your dreams?" Dendera asked, handing a blank sheet of papyrus to Annippe. "Draw a scene and tell me about it." She pulled writing feathers and ink bottles from her bedside table. *What did the hippo mean in the tomb dream?* The beast had destroyed the crops in its path. She flipped through the animal section and looked for clues, even though she didn't want to write about the tomb dream for the paper she had to turn in to Omari. She'd have to come up with something else for her assignment.

The bedside lamp's syrupy, sesame scent filled the room, and Dendera fell asleep staring at the snakes, scorpions, hawks, and crocodiles that adorned the pages of Isis's scroll. She dreamed of a temple where priestesses studied together. Annippe stood before an image of Isis, reciting an ancient goddess teaching before a group of students. Jamila and Khay were well-versed in scribal arts and recorded Annippe's oration of *The Parables of Isis*.

"Get up!" Annippe shook Dendera awake. "My father Paheri is waiting outside the door."

Dendera slit open one eye. Burnt-orange light jabbed it closed again. "Then go talk to him."

"Get dressed." Annippe tossed Dendera's priestess gown on her bed. "You are to observe Father's work this morning."

"No one told me." Dendera rolled her head on her wooden headrest to ease out the kinks.

Annippe slipped out while she dressed. Dendera had adopted the habit of wrapping Seth's amulet in a cloth before depositing it in her sash to muffle its noisiness. After this ritual, she found Annippe and her father sitting and holding hands on the garden bench. They looked content with each other, not saying a word. Paheri tapped the walkway with an ebony staff topped with a black jackal's head, a sure sign of Anubis, the Great Protector. Sleepy, Dendera blurted, "I did not know I was needed in Amunet's temple so early."

Paheri's ears perked up like the jackal's ears on his staff. "Adopt the habit of rising early, Dendera, to center your devotion on Egypt's deities."

Pfft. Seth's amulet echoed Dendera's thoughts.

"I'm off to work in the gardens with Zezi," Annippe said, handing Dendera a steaming loaf of bread. "He's handy to have around if a snake turns up."

Dendera wished for time in the sunshine too, but Paheri led her away from the gardens. She nibbled her breakfast bread, which was cinnamon-free. Annippe must have told Karnak's baker. Dendera and Paheri passed Mother Eshe, and she offered to assist Paheri during their lesson. Dendera hoped Eshe would tag along, but Paheri declined.

The priest stopped at the side door to Amunet's shrine. "Hatshepsut requested that you hear the petitioners' requests. I chose this morning for your training." He sighed and tapped his Anubis staff.

A long line of people clamored outside the main

entryway. It was Sun Day at Karnak, which explained why Ra splattered the sky titian. On Sun Day, commoners attended temple to ask the gods for a boon or the answer to a burning question. Dendera followed Paheri inside the shrine. Stone walls were carved with luminous scenes of Egyptian gods. Ipi lounged beside a statue of Hathor but hopped to Dendera's shoulder as she entered.

Paheri scolded Ipi. "Go back to your perch."

Dendera tried to wrench Ipi loose, but the baboon clung tight, chattering. Paheri shook his head. "The baboon is incoherent as ever."

Seth's amulet swayed in Dendera's sash, and underneath Ipi's screeches she heard, *You will understand. He never does.*

Paheri pried Ipi's paws and then threw up his hands. "Sit in the chair." He indicated a golden stool swathed in linen. "When a petitioner asks a question, I will interpret Ipi's answer."

Dendera perched beside Amunet's statue. She'd read a few pages of *Oracles to Remember* for Omari but was excited to see a priest act the prophet. Paheri burned a handful of frankincense resin in a marble bowl.

Goddesses love frankincense because it purifies the air. The memory of Mother's voice wafted through Dendera's mind. Paheri placed the smoking bowl on a stone slab near Amunet's feet, muttering. He offered figs and dates to Amunet's statue, pulled a fresh cloak from another drawer, and shrouded Amunet in new clothes. Paheri was skilled in secrecy; Dendera tried to glimpse Amunet's face without success.

As Paheri finished his ritual, Hapuseneb entered the temple with Senenmut bobbing alongside him. They each appeared to be praying that Dendera would disappear with a puff of frankincense smoke.

"Get out of the priest's chair!" Hapuseneb demanded, dabbing his sweating golden head with a cloth.

Instantly, Dendera came to standing and the conclusion that Hapuseneb and Senenmut were up to no good.

"We require use of the temple," Senenmut said, "and the runt." He sneered at Ipi.

Bwaaaa-uh. Seth's amulet howled. Dendera froze.

A BALANCING ACT

She was about to be found out, surrounded by three men, and each seemed to loathe her.

"Bwaaaa-uh." Ipi mimicked the amulet's sound.

Bwaaaa-uh.

"Bwaaaa-uh."

The amulet and Ipi barked back and forth until Hapuseneb screeched, "Enough, Ipi!"

Ipi hopped to his perch beside Amunet's statue. Dendera wiggled her fingers to get her blood flowing again. No one seemed to think a thing; Ipi had covered for her. The men thought it was only the baboon barking nonsense. She bowed to Hapuseneb. "We were told to hear the petitioners' requests. A mob of people from Hatshepsut's lands are waiting."

Senenmut leered. "Pharaoh Thutmose requests an answer from Amun…Amunet on a matter concerning all of Egypt. He is more important than you or them." He flapped his arms, vulture-like, to shoo Dendera and Paheri from the temple. Paheri waved away the disgruntled petitioners and escorted Dendera toward the courtyard, his staff clinking on each stone.

Dendera asked, "Will Ipi act the oracle for Hapuseneb?"

Paheri perked his ears.

"Do Senenmut and Hapuseneb meet often?" Dendera knew it was brazen to prod Paheri, but she'd never find the killer by acting as meek as a mummy. Paheri shushed Dendera.

At a nearby table, Eshe sat carving hieroglyphs onto an amulet. Two men waited next to Eshe. These were the men Dendera had seen trading with Birabi the baker. *They'd already bought amulets! How many could they need?* One of them placed a jangling bag on the table.

"Karnak thanks you," Eshe said.

"Who are those men?" Dendera whispered.

Paheri took Dendera's elbow. He led her down a secluded walkway and tugged her behind the lion-headed statue of Sekhmet, warrior goddess, so they were hidden from view. "Dendera, too many questions will cause trouble for you." He bowed his head. "Your mother was a beautiful woman, and I was sorry to hear of her death."

"How did you know her?" The last person Dendera wanted to suspect was Annippe's father, but he was the only person who admitted knowing her mother.

"She often visited Karnak. Honor her memory by keeping your head down and attending your studies." With that advice, Paheri turned toward the priests' quarters.

Dendera stared after Paheri and made a silent pledge to share this news with Zezi, post haste. She entered the courtyard where workers were raising Hatshepsut's obelisks and spotted Ty chatting with Neferura. The princess wore a resplendent blue robe, but her cheeks were paler than chamomile's yellow flowers. Next to the princess, Thutmose stood rigid with his muscly arms crossed over his bare chest.

"Dendera is due for her lesson with me, but I'll excuse her for Your Highness." Ty beamed at Dendera, bowed to Neferura, and left.

Thutmose looked ready to throttle Ty.

Dendera bowed to Neferura. "How are you feeling today?"

"I am strong enough to come and visit you, my fr…" Neferura said.

Thutmose interrupted, "Senenmut and I have business with Hapuseneb. I am pleased to see you, pyramid girl." He pulled a papyrus stalk from the Pool of Tefnut's Tears, fashioned a pyramid from it, and handed it to Dendera.

Neferura frowned and tugged Thutmose's elbow. "Meet me at Ma'at's temple when you are finished."

Dendera fingered the papyrus pyramid, looking between Neferura, so frail and bendable, and Thutmose, so severe and rigid. Now that she knew the two of them, she had a hard time picturing two people more wrong for each other. The last thing Neferura needed in her life was another person ordering her around. She already had Senenmut and Hatshepsut for that.

After Thutmose left, Neferura and Dendera strolled past the sacred lake and entered a garden where Annippe and Zezi were pruning wild rose bushes. The three girls settled on a bench outside the aviary and watched the ducks paddling along the lake. Zezi squelched through the mud alongside three large gray herons. A spoonbill scooped a tasty snack from the lakebed.

Before Dendera could devise a plan to whisk her brother away to share what she'd learned about Paheri, Neferura said, "Mother's physician, Puky, stopped by this morning." She grimaced. "He prescribed fenugreek."

"You have lost weight," Dendera said.

Neferura lowered her voice to a whisper. "Thutmose is here to ask Amunet about a plot to unseat the pharaohs. They've heard rumors. Puky fussed over me so I wouldn't hear." Neferura smirked.

"Are there rumors of the Dethroners?" Zezi asked.

"Who?" Neferura asked, but Annippe cut in. "Let us hope Amunet returns the answer that Egypt and her pharaohs have favor."

Neferura turned to Dendera. "Thutmose likes you. Do you know my mother wants me to marry him?"

Annippe clenched her hands. Zezi stuck his finger down his throat. Seth's amulet gagged.

"He's only grateful because I helped you with the berries." Dendera tucked the papyrus pyramid in her sash. "Do you want to marry him?" Again, Dendera imagined their union as disastrous, but she was sure Hatshepsut had political reasons for wanting the two married.

"What Mother orders, I do." Neferura folded her hands in her lap, resigned. "Would you marry him?"

Zezi froze. A quick glance at Annippe told Dendera the correct answer for a priestess: *Veil the truth with a gracious response*. Dendera smiled at the secret Annippe and Ty were keeping and said, "My life is the temple."

"You are fortunate," Neferura said. "I wish I had the luxury of making my own choices."

Dendera almost blurted that Neferura's own mother pegged her for temple service, but she held her tongue. Annippe's manners were rubbing off on her. "What would you choose?" Dendera asked.

"Mother doesn't give me a chance to know." Neferura sighed. "I ask her if I may stay home from festivals. I hate parading myself."

"Does Hatshepsut know that you hate it?" Zezi asked reasonably.

Neferura imitated her mother's decisive voice. "You are a royal. You have no choice. This is your duty."

Annippe rubbed Neferura's back for lack of something helpful to say.

"Perhaps it won't matter. I may die before Mother orders my marriage." Neferura pulled an ostrich feather from the grass blades at her feet. "I believe in Ma'at's laws." She balanced the feather on her finger.

"Ma'at has forty-two laws, did you know? They are all good. Ma'at is good. When I pass into the afterlife, Ma'at's feather will tip in my favor. She will bring me justice. My life in the Field of Reeds, at last, will be fair."

"You are too young to think of dying," Dendera said, wrapping her arm around Neferura like a protective wing.

Is there ever enough time? Seth's amulet whispered in Dendera's mind, and Dendera agreed: *Mother and Father were too young to die too.*

"We will find a way to heal you," Dendera said.

"I've never been well." Neferura shook her head. "I've never been free."

Annippe slid her arm over Neferura's shoulders, twining her arm with Dendera's. Zezi sat at Neferura's feet, placing his hands on her knees. Dendera squeezed Neferura.

"Thank you for your good intentions." Neferura bowed her head. "It is time to meet Thutmose."

Leaving Annippe and Zezi to their gardening, Dendera walked Neferura toward Ma'at's Temple. Seth's amulet *wisp-wisped, wisp-wisped* back and forth like a feather ready to tip out of balance, but for once, Dendera ignored her stone.

SAID IN STONE

Next morning, Dendera thought of Neferura while Eshe moved stones and shells on her table like pawns on a senet game board. She challenged Dendera to choose the correct amulet for a family who wished to protect a loved one in the afterlife.

"I wish an amulet could make Princess Neferura stronger in this life, Mother of Karnak." Dendera plucked a turquoise stone off the table and bounced it on her palm.

"You are a natural at Amulet Aptitude." Eshe patted Dendera's back. "Perhaps one day you will find a stone that suits the princess."

Only two other priestesses, Lapis and Akil, took amulet lessons with Dendera. On Hatshepsut's command, Eshe, Master of Amulets, procured a rare copy of *Abrasax Maximus* for Dendera. In the scroll, Dendera discovered that the spells placed on amulets were more varied than the magicians who cast them.

A deep understanding of the scribal art was crucial: Inscribing hieroglyphs onto the amulets transferred magical power.

Lapis favored working with her namesake stone, and Dendera had to admit that the lapis lazuli amulets seemed to work best when Lapis cast the spells upon them.

Akil breezed through the lessons in *Abrasax Maximus*, which Dendera shared with both priestesses. When Dendera commented on Akil's knack for academics, Akil simply explained, "My parents named me to excel." When Dendera looked nonplussed, Akil explained, "My name means 'brains.'"

Smiling, Dendera turned to Eshe. "Did you take scribal lessons at Karnak?"

"I learned to scribe long before I arrived at Karnak." Eshe waved her hand, banishing the memory. "You must be a daughter of Seshat. You have taken to reading and writing as a spoonbill to water."

"The myths say Seshat invented the scribal art, right?" Dendera tried to picture the page on which she'd read the story.

"It is not myth but *truth* that Seshat invented hieroglyphs," Lapis said.

Dendera sighed.

"Let not your heart be troubled," Eshe said. "All will make sense in time." Eshe chose an amethyst gemstone for their next spell; her long fingers moved like a spider's legs spinning its web. "Many men and women come to the temple asking for love amulets, or meri stones, spinning their own webs to catch the admiration of the one they desire," Eshe said. "Did you ever see your mother with a meri stone?"

Dendera shook her head. "My father forbade amulets in our home."

"That is a common problem in households." Eshe nodded as if she knew all too well. She held up the amethyst and taught them to speak the meri word of power. "In some cases, women hide amulets on their person, especially during pregnancy."

"Is that why you're called Mother of Karnak?" Dendera asked.

"Childbirth amulets are only one of my specialties." Eshe spurred Dendera and the others to imbue magic to amulets of wood, clay, gemstones, and shells. "Remember, the spell spoken over an amulet coincides with the magician and the needs of the amulet wearer. Speak each incantation unique."

Seth's amulet breathed in rhythm with Dendera; it seemed to know she was striving to decipher the spell placed upon it. If she could break its code, perhaps the stone would tell her who killed her parents, and then she wouldn't have to keep searching for the elusive *Book of Thoth*.

Thinking of Neferura, Dendera turned to the herbal rubrics in *Abrasax Maximus*. Eshe peered over her shoulder. "You are also a natural healer."

"I learned from my mother's friend, Tetisheri," Dendera said. "No one knows more about herbs than Tetisheri."

"Admirable," Eshe said and soon assigned

Dendera the task of collecting the stores needed for the Apothecary.

The priestesses of Karnak came to depend on Dendera for moon-time help, and she dispensed frankincense when available, stockpiling wild celery as an alternative. When Khay succumbed to a fever, Dendera and Annippe scoured the fields for the hairy stems of the chicory plant to help her body release the heat.

"Chicory is easy to find," Annippe said, smelling the sweet blossoms. Dendera warned that the blue blooms closed at noon and to search instead for the plant's bristled, oblong leaves.

❧

One lucky day, gentle winds passed over Karnak, and Dendera asked Eshe if she and Zezi could visit Tetisheri. Her purpose was two-fold: She did want to check on Mother's old friend, but she also needed to compare notes with Zezi. Their hectic schedule had never allowed her to tell him what she'd found out.

Eshe loaded their arms with baskets of food. "Let Tetisheri's heart not be troubled. Show her we take good care of you."

"You're becoming the temple rekhet," Zezi said as he and Dendera strolled down Main Street. "And you found out something." Zezi looked sideways at his sister. "Spill it."

"Paheri knew Mother," Dendera said. Ipi hopped

to her shoulder.

"Annippe's father?"

"He said she was a petitioner," Dendera said, "but he was hiding something."

"You think everyone is hiding something," Zezi said.

"They are," Dendera said.

Zezi bumped Dendera's shoulder, sending her stumbling. "Ask Annippe."

Dendera righted herself, rebalanced Ipi, and shoved Zezi. "We can't let anyone know what we're looking for."

"We need allies," Zezi said. "Annippe might know how her father knew our mother. She knows the temple upside-down. Ty does too. We can trust either one of them. Maybe that's the reason we met them first."

"Have you found any clues about the *Book of Thoth*?" Dendera said to change the subject.

Zezi shook his head. "Not one. Don't you trust Annippe?"

"I have a hard time picturing her father burning down our house, but we don't know anything for sure."

"You have to trust somebody someday, sis."

As they passed Dalila's home, two black-clad men emerged from the forest — the same men Dendera had seen buying bread from Birabi and amulets from Eshe.

They bowed deferentially to Dendera, as she was robed in a priestess's gown. "Good day to you both," she said. Dendera had never glimpsed their faces up-close before. One of the men bore a jagged red scar that crisscrossed downward from his left eye to his chin. The other man had lost his right eye. He rubbed his empty eye socket.

"Is he yours?" The scar-faced man pointed to Ipi.

"He lives at Karnak," Dendera said.

"But he's attached to my sister." Zezi thumped Ipi's head.

"I often see you at the temple," Dendera said.

"Yes… we…" The scar-faced man stammered.

His one-eyed companion said, "We have need of mag…many amulets."

Ipi swung onto the one-eyed man's back, snatched a fig from his backpack, and zipped back to Dendera's shoulder.

"We'd better get back to camp while we still have provisions." The scar-faced man laughed; the sound mimicked a hippo gnashing its teeth.

They parted ways, and Zezi and Dendera climbed through the cedar thicket to enter Tetisheri's courtyard. "You love that baboon as you never loved the family cat," Tetisheri said by way of greeting.

"She never forgave Viper for scratching her," Zezi said.

"I still have the scar." Dendera rubbed her forearm at the memory. Zezi had rescued the wild cat, the miw, from the forest, but there had never been any love lost between Viper and Dendera.

"Were those men visiting you?" Dendera asked.

Tut, tut. Tetisheri followed Dendera and Zezi

inside. She nosed through the baskets they dumped in her kitchen. "Since you two went to the temple, people up and down the countryside want to know what happened to your parents. Where were they when we needed help?"

"They're not from around here," Zezi said.

"They're out-of-towners from who knows where and desperate for food. I gave them what bread I could spare."

"They buy bread from Birabi." Dendera put her hands on her hips.

Tetisheri shrugged.

"And they buy amulets from the temple." Dendera handed Tetisheri a fresh bundle of thyme.

"They could use an amulet or two," Zezi said. "What happened to their faces? Scar and One-Eye."

Tetisheri grunted. "I see your eyebrows grew back."

"I made an eyebrow amulet." Dendera smoothed each eyebrow with a finger.

"You what?" Tetisheri spluttered.

"Annippe sculpted a clay eye for me, and I used a spell from *Abrasax Maximus*. It regrew them once and for all." Dendera stocked the pantry with dates and figs sent by Eshe.

"I don't need all this food." Tetisheri scowled.

"You just gave all yours away," Zezi said.

"Give some to Dalila. She has three children." Dendera placed a single pomegranate on Tetisheri's palm, trying to appeal to Tetisheri's love of goddess.

"Annippe plans to sing a hymn to Isis at Wep-Renpet. You should come."

Tetisheri balked. "I'll sing to myself."

Dendera began lining loaves of bread on Tetisheri's table and bumped into Zezi. Tetisheri's house was tiny, cramped. Dendera had grown used to Karnak. It felt strange to be here. Tetisheri's wasn't home anymore.

"I take it *you* still aren't singing to the goddesses," Tetisheri said.

My home is a temple, Dendera thought, *and I don't believe in goddesses and gods. I don't belong at Karnak. I don't belong at Tetisheri's. Where do I belong?*

"Karnak gardeners plant rosemary next to cucumbers," Zezi said, thinking he could distract Tetisheri with a gardening trick.

"You should be here helping me," Tetisheri said.

"I'll help you now." Zezi stole outside and toiled in Tetisheri's yard, harvesting, washing, and lining the vegetables across her wooden table to dry.

Dendera continued rearranging the baskets of food in Tetisheri's tiny kitchen. She rubbed Seth's face on her amulet. "Hapuseneb follows Seth, Tetisheri. He's the high priest. I may break into his office to try to find clues."

"Don't you dare!" Tetisheri shrieked. "You're in enough danger holding onto that cursed amulet!"

"Do you know Paheri?" Dendera asked. "He's a priest. He knew Mother."

Tetisheri stumped toward Dendera and took her hand. "Stay here. Don't go back to Karnak."

"We have to go back," Dendera said. "Pharaoh's orders, remember?"

"You are too comfortable at the temple." Tetisheri snorted. "Servants prepare your meals, wash your clothes, clean your room. When you walk through the Theban streets in a priestess's robe..."

"There is nothing wrong with feeling respected." Dendera slipped her hand from Tetisheri's. "Zezi and I should go. I have lessons this afternoon, and I must visit Neferura." She hugged Tetisheri and walked outside.

Tetisheri followed. "At least put some marshmallow root in that princess's tea."

Dendera looked back and nodded. *No matter how Tetisheri hurt inside, she never stopped healing others.*

12

KARNAK'S HEALER

After music lessons with the other priestesses, Dendera trimmed sycamore limbs in the gardens alongside Annippe and Zezi and then harvested supplies for the Apothecary: rose hips, wormwood's silvery leaves and yellow florets, and marshmallow's pink blooms.

"Tetisheri recommended marshmallow root for Neferura," Dendera explained to Annippe as she eased a marshmallow plant sideways, still rooted in the earth, and brushed soil from the thick, squishy roots.

"It was a lucky day for you to visit Tetisheri," Annippe said. "I have no doubt you'll find a way to help Neferura."

"Tell Annippe the story with the mouse and Mother," Zezi urged.

She knew Zezi was goading her to confide in Annippe, but Dendera saw no harm in telling the story. "Once, my mother and Tetisheri took Zezi and me deep in the forest behind Tetisheri's home. I wandered off because I spotted some pink flowers I wanted to pick for Mother. When I got near the plants, I screamed because a mouse was hiding underneath the hairy leaves. Mother and Tetisheri came running. They told me it was good fortune to find a mouse protecting the marshmallow root. After I calmed down, the vermin let me pick him up."

"I took him home and made him my pet," Zezi added.

"I picked the flowers," Dendera said, nodding at Zezi. "Tetisheri dug the root, and Mother boiled the root for Dalila's tea when we got back to Tetisheri's. Dalila's head cold was better by evening."

"You must both miss your mother," Annippe said. "My father told me your parents died in a fire. I am sorry for your loss."

How did Paheri know Mother and Father died in a fire? Dendera wondered.

Zezi nudged Dendera, but she shook her head. She was trying to figure out how to ask Annippe how her father knew so much about Mother without also telling Annippe that she and Zezi were at Karnak to stalk a killer. Annippe tucked a marshmallow flower behind Dendera's ear, awaiting a cue to continue the conversation.

Dendera glanced across the fields and pointed. "Look."

A man crossed from Pharaoh's Mooring Place to Karnak. He walked with a purposeful stride, clothed in a waist-down shift. His nemes headdress swayed in the breeze as he drew near. Dendera stood and dusted earth, herb leaves, and roots from her shift. "Priestess Dendera," he said.

"Pharaoh Thutmose." Dendera bowed.

"You plan to visit Neferura this afternoon." Thutmose swung his arms.

"Yes." Dendera looked skyward to check the position of Ra's boat. "It is early, but..."

"I would walk with you." Thutmose straightened his Montu amulet.

Dendera stooped and cut off part of the marshmallow root. She covered the marshmallow plant with soil, nestling it back in the earth, and then opened her sash. Seth's amulet sniveled, but Dendera stuffed the marshmallow root over the stone. "I am ready, Pharaoh."

Thutmose offered Dendera his arm, and Annippe and Zezi walked alongside. The pharaoh escorted them to the palace's outdoor kitchen and seated himself on a stool.

Having visited Neferura often, Dendera knew her way around the palace kitchen. She set a pot of water to boiling and showed Annippe where to find a serving tray, cup, and spoon.

"What type of tea will you make for Neferura?" Thutmose pulled a papyrus stalk from his belt and began weaving it into the shape of a flower.

"Marshmallow." Dendera rinsed the root before dropping it into a cup. She poured hot water in the cup and prodded the marshmallow root with a spoon.

Zezi poked Thutmose's arm. "How many chariots do you have?"

"One hundred chariots await my command at the Mooring Place alone," Thutmose answered, weaving with his hands and staring at Dendera.

After Annippe prepared the tray to take to Neferura, Thutmose bowed to her and knuckled Zezi. He handed Dendera a realistic-looking papyrus lotus bloom.

"Thank you," Dendera said, spinning the flower on her palm. "Where did you learn to make these?"

"I taught myself. Warriors spend a fair amount of time waiting, especially under Hatshepsut's reign," he mumbled.

"It's beautiful." Dendera tucked the lotus in her sash.

"I enjoyed our walk, pyramid girl." Thutmose kissed Dendera's hand, and she nodded.

As Dendera followed Annippe and Zezi upstairs and into the palace, she glanced back at Thutmose.

He stood warrior-like with both fists planted on his hips, but his eyes looked hopeful.

He wishes the marshmallow tea would finally cure Neferura, Dendera thought. *Her whole family has waited long for her to heal.*

There was one thing Dendera couldn't figure out though. She whispered to Annippe right outside Neferura's room. "Why, by the desert sands, did Thutmose come to walk us to the palace?"

Zezi stuck his finger down his throat.

Annippe knocked on Dendera's forehead. "He likes you."

Dendera scrunched her eyebrows. "He's marrying Neferura. He must be thanking me for helping her." She pushed open the door as Zezi and Annippe exchanged an exasperated glance.

Senenmut was reading to Neferura. "No visitors for the princess."

Dendera bowed to Senenmut. "Pharaoh Hatshepsut asked that I visit Neferura."

"Let them stay." Neferura propped herself against her headboard.

Senenmut sneered. "Only for a moment."

Dendera walked to Neferura's bedside and handed her the tea. "Is your vulture bracelet new?"

"It was a gift from Senenmut." Neferura turned the bracelet on her wrist.

"Don't drink this now, my dearmut." Senenmut took the tea from Neferura, handed it to a servant, and waved her away.

"Tetisheri recommended marshmallow root for you, Neferura," Dendera said, looking between Senenmut and Neferura. "Your mother wishes you to have herbal teas."

"Yes, we know," Senenmut snapped.

Dendera wondered if Senenmut blocked other healing measures Pharaoh Hatshepsut ordered for her daughter.

Neferura folded her hands in her lap and played with her fingers.

Annippe, hoping to mollify Senenmut, pulled a

sistrum from her pocket. "Shall I sing a hymn for Mut?"

"Absolutely not." Senenmut pushed Annippe toward the door. "Neferura needs rest." He pulled Zezi by his braids. "Get out."

As Senenmut lunged toward Dendera, she wrapped her hand around Neferura's wrist. "I will check on you soon." Neferura's vulture bracelet throbbed as Seth's amulet thrashed against Dendera's waist.

Neferura's mother might be overbearing, but Dendera believed Pharaoh's intentions were good. Senenmut was another story. He hovered over Neferura like a vulture, like an omen of evil.

Senenmut wrenched Dendera from Neferura's bed, put his foot in her back, and kicked her out of the room. Dendera stumbled to the hallway floor but caught herself with one hand. She turned fast enough to glimpse Neferura watching Senenmut as if she were in a trance. Then Senenmut flapped his arms and slammed the door.

Seth's amulet asked, *Do you still think the right herb or a simple healing amulet is going to fix the princess?*

Dendera had bigger questions. *Was Senenmut cursing Neferura? Was he controlling her with the vulture amulet he gave her? If Senenmut was cursing Neferura, who or what else had he cursed?*

13

TWO SIDES OF THE SAME STONE

The season of harvest stretched long, and the storage houses overflowed with the farmers' hard work and goodness from the black land. Dendera dreamed of ripe-smelling earth and her father toiling his own plot in the Field of Reeds. He looked up, leaned on his spade, and said, "Leave the temple." The dream shifted to Hathor at the edge of the Field of Reeds, calling to Dendera from her sycamore tree, "You belong to me."

Dendera woke bolt upright, unease hard and round in her stomach as if she'd swallowed a fig whole. She couldn't leave the temple against Hatshepsut's orders, and how could she belong to Hathor when Hathor wasn't real? If Hathor was real, Dendera reasoned she would be helping her find the killer, helping her understand Seth's amulet, helping her heal Neferura. She clenched her head in both hands, gritted her teeth, and sat up.

Annippe was nowhere to be found. Ra's

climbing boat spurred Dendera to dress, eat, and hurry toward her first lesson. She passed a small house with a front door inlaid with jewels and precious stones: triangular rubies, rough-cut diamonds, obsidian squares, wedges of turquoise, and oval sapphires. Nearby, Ty and Annippe sat on a garden bench, wrapped in each other's arms, laughing, and with eyes only for each other. Dendera stopped.

"Ah!" Annippe looked up. "Hail to you…"

Ty hugged Annippe to his side, grinning.

"Good morning, you two." Dendera winked and turned down a side path. She'd seen Mother and Father laughing with each other that way. It relieved her somehow, to know that life and love carried on for others, consumed as she was with her solitary task.

At Omari's request, Dendera settled herself under the grand fir trees outside the House of Life to begin deciphering and copying hieroglyphs onto fresh scrolls. Reading was another activity that eased Dendera; to her, Scribera lessons were bliss. Ipi sat on her shoulder, a constant reminder of Omari's preference for the baboon-god Thoth who favored writing, wisdom, and knowledge.

As Dendera read, Seth's amulet purred like the wild cats that stalked Karnak's grain bins. The amulet egged her toward specific scrolls in Omari's collection: astronomy, geography, mathematics, law, the interpretation of dreams. The rock also produced reading scrolls of its own. These magical scrolls appeared beside Dendera's headrest, in her sash, and under a rock near the cornflower field.

With the amulet's help, Dendera became Omari's most devoted student, and he invited her to join his Advanced Scribera class. Omari relied on Dendera for fresh copies of *The Book of the Dead*, a wise and ancient funerary text that Karnak sold to its wealthiest parishioners. There were medical texts in Omari's collection, which Dendera scoured for ideas to help Neferura, but Tetisheri's knowledge of herb lore far outweighed Karnak's healing literature. Besides, the amulet hinted that Neferura's healing wouldn't come through simple means, whatever that meant.

Zezi stopped joining Dendera for Scribera lessons. Both he and Omari admitted the scribal art was not his gift. "Your brother knows his strong points," Omari said, "snakes and farming."

"And chariots," Dendera added.

Dendera found Karnak's library lacking entirely on one subject: the fabled *Book of Thoth*. She remained hopeful that the book containing all answers could help her find the killer. Omari refused to discuss the *Book of Thoth* but told Dendera his favorite story, "Thoth's Birth." Dendera gagged when she pictured Thoth springing full-fledged from Seth's forehead.

"Thoth was wisest of the gods." Omari tapped his nose. "He was also peacemaker amongst the gods."

"How could a peacemaker come from Seth?" Dendera asked.

"Not every question has an obvious answer," Omari said.

Omari trained Dendera to read aloud the ancient stories of Egypt's deities. In *Favorite Spells of King Khufu*, she recited the story of the 110-year-old magician Djedi, who murmured a spell to rejoin a goose's severed head to its body. Djedi performed this advanced magic in Pharaoh Khufu's court. "Did Djedi ever learn the number of secret chambers in the Temple of Thoth?"

"Doubtful," Omari said with a pointed edge. "Djedi counseled King Khufu to put aside his obsession with the *Book of Thoth*."

She wondered if Djedi had lived and worked magic, or if he was made-up in the same way Father claimed Egypt's goddesses and gods were stories. The scroll said Khufu wanted to duplicate the Temple of Thoth for his own burial tomb. "Djedi ate a hundred loaves of bread and drank a hundred jugs of beer a day," Dendera recited, and Ty plopped down beside her.

"How much did he weigh?" Ty bantered. Dendera flipped through the adjoining pages looking for an illustration of the old magician.

"He owned enough magic scrolls to fill a boat," Dendera informed Ty. She whispered, "Where's Annippe?"

"In her Decoramun lesson," Ty whispered back.

"She would like the story of Djedi," Dendera said, planning to take the scroll to read to Annippe that night. She, too, had stopped joining Dendera in Scribera lessons because Hapuseneb disapproved. But tucked in their home with bits and pieces of spare time, Dendera continued teaching Annippe to read and write.

Ty read over Dendera's shoulder. "It says here that Djedi wrote a secret scroll that many have searched for but never found."

"Next, memorize the spell of the ancient benu bird." Omari steered Dendera onto what he deemed a more suitable course of study. He opened a scroll entitled *This Pure Chapter*, licking his fingers to flip the pages.

"Let me find it." Dendera took the scroll. Omari's finger-licking habit annoyed her.

Omari stuck out his lips, Ipi-like. "Be prepared to transcribe it for me tomorrow morning."

She plopped the scroll on top of her large stack of study materials and strolled through the Gardens of Seshat, arms sagging.

A priest leaned against a chariot parked on the stone pathway. He chewed a barley stalk, removing it and twirling it between his fingers as Dendera drew near. "Heavy load," he observed, throwing the stalk on the grass. "May I help?" He extended his arms as if to take Dendera's books for her.

Dendera shook her head. "I've got this."

Zezi crawled from underneath the vehicle with metal tool in hand.

"Just tinkering with the wheels," he said in answer to Dendera's burrowed eyebrows. "This is my friend Shay." Zezi pointed to the priest.

"I am Dendera." She inclined her head.

"Like the city?" Shay asked.

Dendera nodded. "Shay? Like the god of destiny?"

"I was my mother's seventh child. She wanted me to be unique." Shay clipped his thumbs on his belt.

"What's destiny?" Zezi asked.

"People all have their own destiny, something they have to do in life," Shay said. "Your shay is supposed to give you purpose."

Zezi snatched *Favorite Spells of King Khufu*. "What was Khufu's shay?"

Dendera seized back her scroll. "We need to talk about our shay. Nice to meet you, Shay."

Zezi scooped the entire pile of scrolls from his sister's arms and dumped them in the chariot's storage box, the one reserved for weapons. "Let's go for a test drive. See if I fixed the wheel that was out-of-round." After Zezi hitched the chariot to two horses, the pair took off. When Zezi drove, Dendera felt easier in a chariot. Even she admitted her brother was a smooth driver.

"You seem happy at Karnak," Dendera observed. She hadn't noticed as much worry in Zezi's eyes since they'd come to the temple.

"It's good to be busy." Zezi flicked the reigns and looked sideways. "What about you? Have you found any hobbies to distract you?"

Dendera dug Seth's amulet out of her sash. "Is amulet-taming a hobby?"

"Some things never change." Zezi smirked and then grew solemn. "I haven't found any clues, Dendera. Nothing. Nobody knows anything."

"We need to find the *Book of Thoth*," Dendera said.

Zezi rolled his eyes.

"You promised to look…" Dendera said.

"*You* promised I'd look." Zezi sighed. "I'm not sure this is our shay, sis. The *Book of Thoth* is like trying to figure out your dreams. It's dust in the wind. We need clues, something real."

"We're not finding anything real," Dendera said. "The *Book of Thoth* is at least a hope."

"If it is a hope, we need help." Zezi pulled on the reins to slow the horses. "Everything about Karnak is too much. Too many people. Too much information. We need someone who knows the system to help us figure this thing out. Don't you want to know how Paheri knew Mother?"

"Yes," Dendera said, "but…"

"He's not going to tell you himself," Zezi said.

Dendera shook her head. "I know where you're going with this…"

"We can trust Annippe and Ty. That's the one thing I am sure of." Zezi parked the chariot. "Ask Annippe."

Dendera shook her head as Zezi helped her carry her scrolls inside. Ty was visiting Annippe, and the foursome decided to have a picnic in the gardens. Ipi dropped from a fig tree, snatched a date from Zezi, and bounded to Dendera's shoulder.

"These were my mother's favorite fruits," Zezi said, shoving a handful of dates into his mouth. Dendera glared at her brother. He was so predictable. "One year, Father and I harvested so many dates, the storage house door wouldn't shut." Zezi laughed, heading off into other stories about farming with his father.

Once Dendera relaxed into the conversation, she enjoyed listening to Zezi's stories, remembering.

"...and Mother liked to sleep with a baby grass snake coiled around her ankle." Zezi chuckled. "One time, Father screamed so loud, I bet you could hear it here at Karnak. You heard, didn't you?"

Ty and Annippe leaned shoulder-to-shoulder, laughing and slapping each other's knees.

Why not ask her? The amulet prodded Dendera's waist.

When they caught their breath, Dendera turned to Annippe. "Your father remembered my mother."

"He did?" Annippe asked, wiping happy tears from her cheeks.

"Her eyes were as blue as the sky, like yours," Zezi said.

"Ah! I remember her now!" Annippe touched her temples. "It is a memorable eye color. She and Father spoke in his office for a long time."

"About what?" Dendera held her breath.

"I didn't ask." Annippe shrugged. "Father is a great counselor. Many come from afar to ask his advice."

"My father did," Ty said.

"Who was your father?" Zezi asked.

Ty laughed. "My father is Omari."

"Then Jamila and Khay..." Dendera said.

"...are my sisters." Ty nodded.

"We attend Omari's lessons together." Dendera sat up straight. "You never told me."

"Why don't you call him 'Father'?" Zezi asked.

"I did when I was younger, but now that we are both priests of Karnak," Ty said, "this is easier."

"Where did your father travel from to ask Paheri for advice?"

"Nubia." Ty popped a fig in his mouth. "I was born there. After my mother died, Omari wanted a new life for my sisters and me. He said Egypt was the birthplace of magic and the place to be. He learned to scribe in Nubia, and his skills secured his spot at Karnak when we arrived. It was easy for him to learn Egyptian hieroglyphics with his background. But we digress from the subject of your parents. I must ask, how did the fire start at your house?"

You could have heard a hoopoe feather drop, the four became so quiet. Ty had asked the question Annippe was dying to have answered but never posed for fear of causing pain. Zezi gave Dendera his *come on, sis* look, but Dendera remained unconvinced. In Dendera's sash, Seth's amulet rolled back and forth, nodding.

Dendera closed her eyes and exhaled. "Someone threw a burning cedar branch through our window."

"No." Annippe's hand flew to her mouth.

Ty shook his head. "Forgive me if this is indiscreet, but you mentioned that you and Tetisheri mummified your parents' bodies. If they were burned, I'm interested in how that worked, from a professional standpoint, of course."

Tears streamed Annippe's face. Zezi left on the pretense of picking figs from a nearby tree.

"Zezi and I shared a room at home, and Mother and Father must have gone there to see if they could help either of us escape. We found them barricaded between the two beds in our room. It shielded them from the flames, and their bodies weren't burned."

"Ah. Then they died from smoke inhalation," Ty said. "You are stronger than I realized, brave one."

Dendera called Zezi back. She pulled the amulet from her sash. It hummed. *If you say so*. Dendera blew out her breath. "I found this outside our house. We think whoever dropped it was the arsonist and our parents' murderer."

After exchanging a horrified look with Ty, Annippe said, "May I?" She turned the stone to its back and mumbled, "*Hwt–ntr*. Temple. Karnak?"

Ty took the amulet from Annippe and looked on its front. "Seth."

"With a hound's head," Dendera said. Ipi barked.

"He looks regal," Annippe said.

"For a dog," Zezi said.

"He's usually a crocodile," Dendera said.

Ty turned the amulet to its backside. "Wait. These were not inscribed by the same artist."

"What?" Dendera, Zezi, and Annippe crowded around Ty.

"The symbol for Seth is old, perhaps ancient," Ty said. "See how worn it is? *Hwt-ntr* was inscribed much later, in different ink, and by a different hand. The scribal styles are not the same."

"Great." Zezi plopped down, cross-legged. "Now we have to hunt down two people instead of one."

"That's why you're here, isn't it?" Ty asked. "You hope to find the arsonist."

"Hatshepsut ordered us to come," Dendera said, "and we are using the opportunity to search for clues."

Annippe and Ty traded a determined glance. "You're not searching alone anymore."

❧ 14 ❧

THE DECORUM OF KNIGHTS

The following days each felt unlucky to Dendera. Ra dawdled across the sky, and her lessons dragged. When Khonsu's moon claimed each evening, she raced home to find Annippe, Ty, and Zezi anxious to spill what they'd seen or heard that day.

Annippe elaborated on the high priest's Decoramun lesson. "Hapuseneb said each of us should be a model of sobriety at temple feasts, due to the lack of restraint shown by commoners at the Beautiful Festival."

"You respect authority too much," Zezi said. Dendera agreed this was Annippe's greatest flaw, but Annippe was also as cunning as Isis.

"Let me finish," Annippe said. "Hapuseneb wouldn't light the fire for goddess offering." She eyed each of them in turn. "He never lights a fire. The arsonist, the killer, is unafraid of fire."

"Of course," Zezi scoffed.

"This is a good point," Ty said. "A lot of people fear fire."

"You're trying to prove who the arsonist isn't," Zezi said.

"It's someone who reveres Seth," Dendera said.

"Or came into possession of the amulet," Ty observed, "like you."

"Hapuseneb honors Seth." Dendera traced Seth's face on the amulet.

"He's too nice to kill innocent people," Zezi argued.

Annippe paced. "He couldn't have started that fire."

"Where is Hapuseneb's office?" Dendera asked.

"You're not allowed in Hapuseneb's office." Ty gave Dendera a stern stare. "The high priest is the only one who knows where it is."

"Hapuseneb has served Hatshepsut for many years," Annippe said with dignity, "and Father trusts Hapuseneb."

"Omari trusts Paheri," Ty added.

"But how did Paheri know my parents died in a fire?" Dendera asked. Of all the people at Karnak, Paheri was most adept with fire. Every morning, he lit fires at every shrine.

"I don't know, but my father would never…"

Ty touched Annippe's arm. "We know, but we need the rest of the story."

"I'll ask him," Annippe said, "but he talks as much as a beetle."

"Have you been in Hapuseneb's office?" Dendera

asked her brother. "You're his favorite."

Zezi shook his head. "I don't think he allows anybody in his office."

"Will you spy on him?" Dendera pressed.

"There's nothing to discover. He's devoted to Seth. He digs his strength," Zezi said and then quelled under Dendera's glare. "But I'll keep my eyes peeled."

"I think our best bet of discovering the arsonist is the *Book of Thoth*," Dendera said.

"You have less hope of finding the *Book of Thoth* than I do finding the Tincture of Isis," Annippe said.

"Omari removed the scrolls pertaining to the *Book of Thoth* on Pharaoh Hatshepsut's request." Ty scratched his head.

"Hatshepsut asked the scrolls to be removed?" Zezi asked.

"Trying to find the *Book of Thoth* is risky," Ty said. "Several Karnak priests disappeared on such quests."

"Father said the *Book of Thoth* isn't real," Zezi said.

"Oh, it is real," Annippe said. "My father…"

Dendera cut in with the prickliest question of all. "Can we trust Hatshepsut?" The pharaoh was good to her, but it was best to upturn every stone.

"About that stone…" Ty pointed at the vibrating amulet. "What powers does it have?"

"She can light fires with it," Zezi said.

"You can what?" Annippe asked.

"Tetisheri says the amulet has *heka*," Dendera said, "and I experiment with it, but I've only pecked the surface of what it can do."

"Did the amulet start the fire at your home?" Annippe asked.

The amulet caterwauled.

"Tetisheri found the cedar branch." Dendera rocked the stone back and forth to calm it. "They could have used the stone to light the branch though."

"Light a fire. Now." Ty pointed.

"I can do better." Dendera balanced the amulet on the tips of her fingers. "Flitniwet." The amulet levitated above her hand. Ty's leopard skin rose up from his back, floated through the air, and flopped itself over Zezi's head.

"Next, you'll be sprouting wings and flying yourself." Zezi threw the leopard skin.

Ty caught it, laughing deep and slow. "The day we met, you used the amulet to banish that crocodile, didn't you?"

Before Dendera could answer, Annippe asked, "Does the amulet thump at night? Is that what I hear?"

Zezi leaned his head back, laughing.

"It hisses and hiccups too, right?"

Dendera pulled a wad of cloth from her waist sash. "I wrap it to muffle it. Seth's amulet is a water clock that won't stop."

Drip, drip, drip, went the amulet.

Annippe stared. "I've never seen a stone with its own personality."

"We could ask Eshe to examine it," Ty said.

"She would confiscate it," Dendera said.

"And tell you some nonsense about not letting your heart be troubled," Zezi said.

Ty chuckled. "Does it bother you to keep it with you all the time?"

"Sometimes I want to chuck it in the Nile," Dendera said. Seth's amulet squealed until it skipped off her palm. "It always reminds me why I kept it in the first place."

Annippe picked up the stone with the tips of her fingers. "You do realize there's a powerful curse on this amulet." She dropped the stone on Dendera's palm.

"Perhaps a fatal curse," Ty said. "Your parents died while it was nearby."

"The amulet's curse didn't kill my parents." Dendera massaged her neck. "It was the fire."

"We need to find out if the same person set the fire and cursed the stone." Zezi leaned forward and rubbed Seth's amulet. "Call us the Curse Chasers."

"A code name." Ty nodded. "If someone asks why we spend our free time together, we can say we formed a study group on how *heka* works."

"Like the Knights of Kemet," Dendera said.

"Who are the Knights of Kemet?" Zezi asked.

"When the Dethroners began overthrowing Egypt's pharaohs, a group of priestesses formed the Knights of Kemet to protect them," Dendera explained.

"Where did you find a scroll about the Dethroners?" Ty asked.

"I asked the amulet for one," Dendera said, "and it appeared under my headrest."

"Dendera!" Annippe gasped.

Zezi's jaw dropped.

Ty touched Dendera's arm. "I wouldn't trust…"

"The scroll said the Dethroners were powerful magicians." In Dendera's mind, the threat of the Dethroners threaded itself into her hunt for the killer. She held up Seth's amulet. "Whoever cursed this stone excelled at magic."

"Ask Eshe her opinion on the Dethroners," Ty suggested.

"She'll say what you've said." Dendera sighed. "Who are the out-of-towners who visit Eshe?"

"Travelers often come to the temple for safety amulets," Annippe said.

Dendera pulled a scroll from her sash. It was the size of a fig. She tapped it with the stone. The scroll flew up in the air, fattened to the size of a goose, and flopped on her lap. She held the rolled scroll so that Ty, Annippe, and Zezi could see and then read the title aloud, *The Dethroners' Discourse.* "It says they wrote the *Throw Up Texts* which gives detailed instructions on how to depose pharaohs." She unrolled the scroll and flipped to a page near the middle. "It describes its members. They dress in black. They wear ivory amulets. The hippo is their sign. They disfigure themselves. Don't they sound the same as the men who visit Eshe?"

"The Dethroners don't exist," Annippe said.

"Right," Zezi said. "Except, what if they do?"

❧ 15 ❧

DESPICABLE

A dense and dewy fog covered the grounds the following morning as Annippe walked Dendera to the worst class at Karnak. The air swirled thick from the ground up to their knees, and Dendera felt like she was walking thick-legged through the soup Karnak's bakers liked to cook.

They reached the door carved top-to-bottom with the spiraling, undulating, slithering shapes that made Dendera's skin crawl. A rough-cut piece of papyrus, hastily sketched with hieroglyphs, was tacked to the outside of the door.

Wait INSIDE

Annippe kneaded Dendera's back and turned toward the Sanctuary of Song. Dendera lugged open the door of the Serpent House. Dendera didn't doubt

Hapuseneb spent his spare time honing Serpentology lessons to horrify her. Though the high priest doted on Zezi, he delighted in torturing Dendera. Despite her requests to join his weekly class, which included Zezi, his friend Shay, and the priestess Akil, Hapuseneb insisted on tutoring Dendera one-to-one.

As usual, Hapuseneb was not present when Dendera arrived. He relished any chance to make Dendera spend extra time with his precious snakes, knowing how she despised them. Half the morning passed as Dendera stood tapping her foot and listening to the rustling scales and incessant hissing of the Serpent House's plethora of slithering specimens from field and desert. She adjusted her waist sash. Seth's amulet was spewing odd sounds, and her single consolation was that the spitting snakes muffled her cranky stone.

When the heavy door burst open at last, Hapuseneb entered with a cobra coiled around his chest. Its tail pointed at Hapuseneb's Seth amulet. "Today, you learn mastery over the king cobra," he announced, gold head agleam, and beckoning. "Come and stroke its tail."

Keen to distance herself from the cobra, Dendera vaulted over the river running through the center of the Serpent House, even though it harbored asps and other water-loving snakes. Hapuseneb pinned the cobra's flared and hooded head between his palms. Dendera backed into the wall where snake skins and fangs were suspended in liquid-filled jars. It was the safest refuge inside the Serpent House. All the other walls were lined with covered bowls that rocked from whatever coiled within. She would face dead pieces of snakes over lives ones whether the day was lucky or not.

Hapuseneb advanced, holding the trapped cobra aloft, and smiled, his eyes two cracks slit in dry, black earth. "The cobra is the eye of Ra."

Ra, shmay, Dendera thought and placed both hands on the shelf behind her, steadying herself. "The serpent Apophis remains ever-ready to devour Ra." She recalled Omari's lessons and the etiquette tips Annippe sprinkled over their conversations. "With all due respect, High Priest, I wish to learn theory alone. I do not aspire to work with the temple snakes."

"At least taste its venom." Hapuseneb snatched an empty jar and hooked the cobra's teeth over its edge.

Tut, tut. Memories of Tetisheri scorning her snake phobia seared Dendera's mind, but she backed away, shaking her head. "You cannot make me drink that."

"The venom is poisonous when injected by the cobra's fangs into its victim." Hapuseneb coiled the cobra inside a turquoise bowl and placed a lid on top. "When extracted and drunk, cobra venom heals." He held out the jar filled with gooey-gold venom.

"I'm healthier than a chariot racehorse." Dendera edged toward the side door and prepared to sprint from the Serpent House. "I rely on herbs for healing, but thank you for the offer. I'm late for my next class."

Hapuseneb's eyes glinted like a viper's.

Dendera arrived for Mummification in a foul disposition. Distracted as she was by the snakes and

Hapuseneb, she'd forgotten to search for clues. She still considered the high priest a top suspect.

"I should have asked him to take me to his office," Dendera announced to Ty. "He'd be happy to lock me inside with a poisonous snake."

"He wouldn't take you to his office," Ty reasoned. "During your lessons in snake lore, you must remember the cobra goddess Wadjyt, The Green One, She Who Rears Up." Ty stroked the spotted leopard skin across his chest. "One day, you will rise up, Dendera. You are already my brave one."

"Zezi refuses to visit your Mummy Room." Dendera's anger bubbled to the surface. "Why can't I refuse to study snakes?"

Ty shrugged. "Hapuseneb makes allowances for Zezi. I admit he does favor your brother. Hapuseneb is not threatened by Zezi as he is by you."

"I'm not a threat!"

"I agree, but Hapuseneb knows Hatshepsut has expectations of you," Ty said. "Zezi came along for the chariot ride, so to speak. Hapuseneb is surprised by Zezi's abilities."

Wishing to forget Benu Brain and his slimy snakes, Dendera urged Ty to begin their lesson. "How many priestesses work in mummification?"

"Two at present, but Hatshepsut pushes us to raise the number of priestesses in every curriculum. You will make three." Ty opened the door to the Mummy Room, a silent sanctuary secluded at Karnak's west end. Dendera stepped inside the immaculate space, well-stocked with tools soaking in oil-filled jars, containers of all sizes, sharp stones, and syringes. Pungent herbs and spices spiked the air. The walls were painted with images of Ty's god Khonsu, ram-headed with the moon suspended between his horns.

With Ty teaching, mummification proved an interesting, tranquil experiment. Their current subject was an elder priest who died of natural causes, and the full moon shining at midday indicated the opportune time to finish this stage of the intricate mummification process.

Dendera picked up a wooden mask that was carved and painted in the image of Anubis. "What is this for?"

"The chief embalmer wears this," Ty said and slipped the mask over his head. "Removing the brain is tricky." Ty inserted an iron hook into the man's left nostril. "It takes a moment to feel out the lobes." He wiggled the tool around inside the man's head, latched onto the brain, and slid it from the man's nose.

As Dendera watched, she imagined wrenching Hapuseneb's brain from his bald head. Brandishing iron tongs, she seized the brain from the end of Ty's hook. It squelched a little as she placed it on the table.

"Some sem priests throw away the brain," Ty said, "but I keep them. After it dries, we will preserve it in myrrh oil." He indicated a canopic jar sitting on the shelf. "Make incisions here and here." Ty dabbed red powder on the priest's abdomen.

Dendera gripped a sharp obsidian blade and extracted the specified internal organs. Ty favored myrrh for organ-preservation because "myrrh's smell pleases Osiris, god of resurrection," or so he said. Organs, after they dried, were suspended in these odorous oils, and then stored in canopic jars outside the body.

Ty placed his hand over the dead priest's chest. "We leave the heart in the body so that it can be weighed against Ma'at's feather."

"Who made the first mummy?" Dendera tonged the man's liver and placed it on the table to dry. She readied a canopic jar with frankincense oil, which she preferred since it was Mother's favorite.

Ty pointed to a painting of Isis, hovering with outstretched wings over Osiris's body. Tears dripped from Isis's eyelashes, but her lips spoke determined words over her brother-husband. "Isis gathered the parts of Osiris's body after Seth dismembered him." Wielding a syringe, Ty injected cedar oil into the priest's empty abdomen cavity. "Isis spread her wings over Osiris to conceive her son Horus. She then granted Osiris eternal life. His spirit lives. Only his form changed."

"Annippe calls it alchemy." Dendera lined up the dead priest's lungs beside his intestines on the table. "Do you believe the story is true or a legend?"

"True. Alchemy is metamorphosis. Mummification readies the dead to transform for the afterlife. Metal-workers refine silver and gold; they render them pure." Ty eyed Dendera. "Knowing the goddesses and gods changes us, purifies us."

Dendera smirked. "I want to know Thoth, or at

least read the *Book of Thoth*. Omari, I mean, your father, refuses to talk about it." She held out an amber bottle.

Ty's eyes widened as if an idea had slipped into his brain. "Ask Seth's amulet! It gives you other scrolls!" Ty grabbed the bottle of palm wine from Dendera's hand.

"I did," Dendera said, patting her sash. "The rock wailed NOOOOO all night."

Ty shook his head. "No one alive has seen the *Book of Thoth*. As I said, Hatshepsut purged the scrolls pertaining to the book from Karnak's library."

Something in Ty's tone tipped off Dendera. "You know something." She pitched forward on her toes, waiting.

Ty considered Dendera. "It is said that Isis, in Thoth's name, will bestow the *Book of Thoth* to one person, one who is worthy." Ty made a small cut on the priest's chest and poured in the palm wine, rinsing the inside of the priest's body.

"In other words, I have more hope of finding a live sphinx." Dendera snagged a wooden mallet, pounded myrrh gum into a powder, and smudged it inside the dead priest's abdomen.

Ty handed Dendera a jug of frankincense oil. "Saturate the entire mummy, head to toe." He grabbed another jar. "I will follow behind you with myrrh oil." When they finished drenching the mummy, Ty draped a linen sheet over the priest's body. "His body will cure for seventy days. Then we will swaddle him in cloth before he is entombed."

As Ty escorted Dendera from the Mummy Room, she pointed to the house with the jeweled door, the one near where she'd seen Ty and Annippe early one morning. "What is inside?"

"That is the Crystal House." Ty pulled a key from beneath his leopard skin and unlocked the door.

As Dendera stepped inside, sunlight spilled through the window, casting prisms on the walls and floor. In the shelves sculpted into the mud walls of the room, light danced on the multicolored rocks, crystals, blobs of gold, and silver nuggets stored there. Ty's earring twinkled teal blue.

"Do you know much of crystal healing?" Ty asked. "I mean, other than working with Seth's amulet."

Dendera shrugged. "I take Amulet Aptitude with Eshe, but I prefer herbs."

"You should try a crystal healing, at least once." Ty gestured to a cow-shaped couch, reminiscent of Hathor's sacred cows, and Dendera sat. Ipi bounded through an open window and perched on one of the cow's golden horns.

"Lean back and close your eyes." Ty placed a turquoise on Dendera's forehead. "Hathor is Lady of Turquoise. Perhaps she will bring you a message."

The turquoise stone rested heavy between Dendera's eyebrows. *Father would think this is an absolute waste.* Seth's amulet glowed with heat under her palm. Her eyes sank into her skull like two golden stones. *Off we go on another dream.*

Hathor slid Dendera's hand in her own. Dendera wriggled her fingers, intertwined with Hathor's. They walked to the Nile banks and dove to the river bottom.

"This is where secrets go," Hathor whispered, and bubbles blossomed from her lips.

A school of bolti fish circled Dendera. Hathor raised her hand, the river parted, and they rode a wave to the top. Hathor deposited Dendera on a fine cedar boat, kissed her forehead, and vanished. Dendera smoothed her linen sheath. She was desert-sand dry.

Pharaoh Thutmose leaned on the ship's railing. He extended his hand to Dendera. Streams of turquoise flooded the evening sky. Thutmose shifted and changed. He was Seth of the red desert, muscular man topped with crocodile head. He snarled and spat tongues of flame. Clouds rimmed in indigo moved across the sky and swallowed Seth.

Ty stepped on the boat beside Dendera, his leopard skin flapping in the breeze. They laughed together with brother-sister ease. Ty pointed to a temple on the far bank of the river. "I will tell you the secret of ages…"

A stiff voice jolted Dendera from her vision. Ipi screeched and bounded out the window. Ty stood from the couch. Hapuseneb repeated, "Get up. You have a visitor."

16

STORY OF DAYS

Ripples of heat poured from Hapuseneb's body as he wrenched Dendera from the room. His wooden Seth amulet banged his chest as he dabbed his sweaty, gilded mask. Zezi skulked behind the high priest. "What was that room, sis?" He wrapped a cat snake around his arm, a new pet confiscated from his last lesson.

"The Crystal House, it's a healing room," Dendera said. "Ty took me there after Mummification."

"The pharaoh wishes you trained in healing." Hapuseneb spat.

Zezi caught Dendera's eye and moved his eyebrows up and down. Dendera clamped her lips shut and walked on. She stretched her fingers, unnerved by the dream. She could still feel the warmth of Hathor's hand intertwined with hers.

Snap, snap, Seth's amulet sounded.

Hapuseneb glared. "What are you doing?"

Dendera snapped her fingers.

"Stop that at once," Hapuseneb said. "It annoys the energy of the temple."

"Forgive me," Dendera said. *Snap out of it*, she thought. *Hathor is a story. I'm dreaming of Hathor because Mother loved the idea of Hathor.*

The threesome traipsed past Karnak's main hall and veered onto a secluded walkway that shrouded the Pool of Sobek. Sacred crocodiles paddled through the lotus flowers that floated on the crisp water. A red granite statue of Sobek guarded the pool. Hatshepsut sat on a bench, observing the crocodiles from a safe distance. She scooted over to make room for Dendera.

Wispy willow branches rustled overhead, and Pharaoh asked Zezi how his studies were progressing before dismissing both he and Hapuseneb. When they were alone, Hatshepsut told Dendera: "Neferura has grown weaker, and my physicians bring her no ease. You must visit soon."

"Of course, Your Majesty." Dendera paused. "How do you feel about Senenmut spending time with Neferura?"

"Senenmut has cared for Neferura since she was born," Hatshepsut said. "Why?"

"Neferura seemed dazed the last time I saw her," Dendera said, testing her limits with the pharaoh. "Senenmut was with her."

"That is one thing Senenmut cannot help with." Hatshepsut touched her temple and then circled her hand outward. "When my daughter goes off in her own world, no one can bring her back." The strain of caring for a sick child for a lifetime lined her face. Dendera picked a lotus blossom and handed it to her.

Hatshepsut inhaled the lotus's perfume.

"Did you know it takes seven days for a lotus to bloom?" Dendera pointed to a small bud poking its head above the pool's surface. "The bud sprouts, it rises above the water, gangly stem climbs, skinny bud plumps, glossy petals stretch, it reaches skyward, it stalls. You lose hope and think the bud will never open. On the seventh day, it blooms. For one day. The next morning, the petals fall. It's done."

"All that work to bloom for one day." Hatshepsut twirled the flower between her fingers.

"Mother called them wonderblooms," Dendera said.

"Because you wonder if they'll ever bloom." Hatshepsut laughed softly and trailed her finger over the petals. "Do you know the Legend of the Lazuli Lotus?"

"It sounds familiar," Dendera said, remembering Mother's fingers brushing her cheek while she told the story. She couldn't remember the details of the tale. "Did you know lotuses are medicine? I will ask Tetisheri if root, stem, seed, or blossom might suit the princess's needs."

"You are growing in your abilities," Hatshepsut said. "I wonder if I might ask you...I had a dream last night. A dispute brewed within the borders of Egypt. Thutmose and Senenmut say it was only a dream."

"Dreams can help us see the truth," Dendera said,

thinking of *The Dreams of Isis* which Omari nagged her to study.

"Of course, Thutmose may be behind it all." Hatshepsut observed the orange sun, drooping in the sky like a pomegranate ripe for picking. "When he was young, he was happy for me to reign in his place."

"Why did you take the throne?"

"An uprising in Nubia threatened our borders," Hatshepsut said. "I was *only* a female regent. Thutmose was a child. The Nubians thought it was the prime time to claim Egypt's land and riches. Our people were afraid. I proclaimed myself Supreme Pharaoh to give them courage. I even had myself portrayed as a man so they would see me as king."

"I've seen the statues," Dendera said. "You carry it well, as a man or a woman."

Hatshepsut chuckled and continued her story. "I brokered a meeting with the Nubian King, and we signed a peace treaty."

"You are a wise leader," Dendera said.

"My father was a warrior-king," Hatshepsut said. "In those days, Egypt knew nothing but turmoil. I wanted to give our people, our home, a return to peace." She sighed. "Now, Thutmose grows older. He has the heart of a warrior, and he fears what is at stake."

"What is at stake?" Dendera scrunched her forehead.

"The return to matriarchy, my dear," Hatshepsut said, "and I brought you to Karnak to help me."

"The rule of women," stated Dendera.

"Yes," Hatshepsut said. "From the Dawn of Ancient through the Age of the Sycamore and until midway through the Age of the Cobra, queens reigned in a procession of peace and prosperity, Dendera. There were no wars." Hatshepsut's eyes filled with tears. "Then invaders came, and they killed Egypt's queen. They installed the first king of Egypt."

"Were they the Dethroners?"

Hatshepsut raised her eyebrows. "What do you know of the Dethroners?"

"There are whispers," Dendera said. Ipi leapt from a branch overhead and landed on her shoulders. "Strange men have been lurking around town."

"I know the men you speak of." Hatshepsut nodded. "Listen to the whispers. Help me."

"How?"

"Keep teaching Annippe," Hatshepsut said, "even if Hapuseneb gets angry."

Dendera froze.

"I have eyes all over Karnak, and still, I'm missing something," Hatshepsut said. "Dendera, we must strengthen the priesthood. Learn all that you can and teach all that you can."

"I will help you." Dendera touched the pharaoh's hand.

"That is enough for now," Hatshepsut said. "My dream from last night causes me unrest."

Seth's amulet lurched in Dendera's waist sash, goading her. She said, "Let's go look in the sacred pool. Perhaps Ipi can help us see your answer there."

As they walked toward Sobek's pool, Seth's amulet rattled, and Dendera picked up two sistrums. She handed one to Hatshepsut, making as much noise as possible. *Sing*, the amulet urged. To shut up the stone, Dendera chanted the hymn Eshe taught daily in the Sanctuary of Song:

This is the day Goddess made.
Mistress of Joy, we sing to you.

Her voice cracked on the tune. *This is the dumbest thing I've ever done*, Dendera told the amulet. Ipi squeezed her, and Hatshepsut blended her strong voice with Dendera's. The sacred crocodiles were trained to calm at the sound of priestess's music. The beasts sank to the bottom, and the Pool of Sobek became a watery maze of curves and ridges.

Seth's amulet spun against Dendera's waist. "Trutarem." She'd never heard the spell; it rose from her lips unbidden.

From a place deep inside Dendera, a Voice beckoned. It was high and ancient. She wanted to tamp down that Voice that was not her own, but it was impossible to push it away. The Voice became warm as Ra overhead, toasty as the sand underfoot. It soothed and urged until Dendera agreed to let Her use her voice. Thunder rumbled overhead. Out of Dendera's mouth came a crash of thunder and

Goddess' words: "I see a city where the priests do not honor Hathor, Lady of the Mountains. Her temple falters because their hearts are corrupt. She will step down from the turquoise sky and crush those who shame Dendera Temple."

When Dendera came out of her trance, Ipi screeched and hopped to a crooked branch overhead. Hatshepsut shook her. "Do you remember the words you spoke?"

"Yes." Dendera's knees buckled.

Hatshepsut caught her and lugged her to the bench.

Seth's amulet *blinked, blinked, blinked* against Dendera's waist. A hint of Hathor's presence lingered, soft and still, inside Dendera. This was the second time Dendera *felt* Goddess, and it seemed to her that Goddess' strength must be as inexhaustible as the Nile, ebbing and flowing, always available. *Was Father wrong about at least one of Egypt's deities?*

The outside world came into focus. Hatshepsut held her shoulders. "It is an uncommon gift to speak in visions and remember what you said." Hatshepsut studied Dendera as if she'd never seen an Egyptian girl before. "The stars have not sent such a magician in a long, long time."

"Magician?" Dendera whispered.

"You are the one I seek." Hatshepsut beamed and continued in a whisper, "When I mounted Egypt's throne, the court astronomer told me I'd find you during my reign. She said Djedi's successor would have powers I'd never seen in any other." The pharaoh grazed Dendera's pyramid mole. "By the Nile, you remind me of the olden stories of Djedi and his warrioress. They say he only trained girls, and for good reason. Your vision confirmed my instinct. My dream, too, was about the city of Dendera — that's where the dispute brewed. If it is Thutmose..." The pharaoh shook her head. "We must keep this our secret until you complete your training."

Djedi? I'm no 110-year-old magician. Omari said Djedi had power equaled by no magician before him or since. I have no clue how to reattach a goose's severed head to its body!

"The beasts only spit after the Pool of Sobek has released an oracle." Hapuseneb wiped crocodile saliva from the tip of his nose, along with a glob of gold makeup. "You used Sobek's pool without permission."

Hatshepsut rose from the bench. "Dendera answered a question of great concern for me."

"Majesty, Dendera is in training. She has no oracular authority." Hapuseneb pointed his nose skyward in an attempt to stem the flow of gold makeup slipping off the end. "Why did you not ask me, your high priest, for help?"

Dendera kept silent. Instinct told her that Hapuseneb hadn't heard Hatshepsut whisper that Dendera was the "magician" she was looking for. He would have been more livid.

"The girl's vision was true," Hatshepsut declared. "She confirmed the dream I had last night about the uprising in Dendera."

Senenmut stood behind Hapuseneb, bobbing his head. "Gracious Majesty, the sacred pool is to be used by a trained priest. A priestess-in-training is ill-equipped…"

Hatshepsut interrupted while Senenmut railed on. "Dendera shall be called 'one who has visions of the Lady of the Stars.'" Hapuseneb stood stony-faced. "We march to Dendera Temple to restore it to Hathor," Hatshepsut continued, surveying Hapuseneb and Senenmut as if they were dirt beneath her golden sandals.

"Sovereign of the Two Lands." Eshe stepped forward. "We all know Dendera is gifted." She bestowed a small smile. "Perhaps her vision is true, but if she is mistaken, you would not want to estrange yourself to Dendera Temple by accusing them of misdeeds before you have solid proof."

"Then you shall go to Dendera Temple for me, Eshe." The pharaoh took the stance of a warrioress, feet planted, hands on her hips, decisive as stone. "Tell them I require a full account of their activities. This will grant you access to the temple's records. Make a full report to me when you return." Her orders given, Hatshepsut strode from the Pool of Sobek and mounted her waiting chariot.

The crocodiles grew restless. Hapuseneb railed. "You are a mere child. How could you presume to use the sacred pool and Ipi?"

"I read about using the sacred pool in *Oracles to Remember*. Omari gave me the scroll," Dendera said.

"You read about it? Speaking in oracles requires

training from a qualified priest and years of practice." Hapuseneb snorted.

"It was instinct, Hapuseneb, and my desire to aid the pharaoh. I am sorry I offended you…"

"You're sorry?" Senenmut snarled, advancing on Dendera. "You overstepped the boundaries of the high priest. You defamed the priests of Dendera, a city that is sacred to Hathor." Senenmut's spit spattered Dendera's face.

Annippe, Ty, and Zezi gathered on the outskirts of the garden. Her Curse Chasers were here, but no one said a word.

Eshe stepped between Dendera and the two men. Facing Hapuseneb and Senenmut, she said, "Let not your hearts…"

Hapuseneb shoved Eshe aside. Behind him, the crocodiles reared up on their hind legs and opened their jaws. Hapuseneb's jowls quivered; Dendera had never seen him this furious, not even that time she refused his offer of homemade Asp Ale. "May Seth avenge the wrongs you wrought this unlucky day."

In the midst of the crocodiles, a crimson creature rose on two legs — half human, half crocodile — Seth's eyes burned. Dendera gasped. Hapuseneb called on Seth, and Seth appeared.

The amulet seared so hot it singed Dendera's waist. She was in danger. She needed to escape. The amulet's energy surged through her body. She had no choice but to obey.

She held both hands to the sky and screamed, "Shemzapsu!"

A lightning bolt streaked from the sky and split the ground between Dendera and Hapuseneb.

Seth vanished in a twirling sandstorm. Senenmut was blasted off his feet and landed in a crumpled heap on the grass. The crocodiles fell back in the pool, spouting waves high over the willow tree. Eshe ducked and flung both arms over her head as a wall of water drenched her. Crocodile water soused Hapuseneb's head, streaked his makeup, and rolled down his body. His eyes sparked red. Dendera turned from Sobek's courtyard and bolted through the open gates.

17

THE SHAMAN'S HUNT

Mud-brick granaries and storage huts blurred past as Dendera raced through the maze that was Karnak. When she reached the abandoned House of Sycamore she'd visited with Annippe, she leaned against the stone pyramid, gasping, and then collapsed under the sycamore tree. *What is happening to me? Did Seth's amulet just grant me the power to banish Seth?* Dendera hugged her knees to her chest. She tried to slow her breathing, but thoughts of *Hapuseneb hates me* and *Seth's meaner than a hippo* kept intruding. One thing was certain: Hapuseneb feared her, and why shouldn't he? She shot a lightning bolt at him!

Seth's amulet sizzled. *Don't get distracted.*

I know my mission, Dendera answered. She had to find the arsonist, the murderer, but how? All her hopes were pinned on a contrary rock and a magic book that she wasn't sure existed.

Everything at Karnak was unraveling. Hapuseneb despised her. Hatshepsut wanted her to be Pharaoh's Magician. She didn't even know what that meant, but she'd become a *prophetess*. She foretold doom on the priests and priestesses of Dendera Temple. How did she get herself wrapped in this mummy bind? It was the amulet. The stone goaded her toward the Pool of Sobek. Maybe Eshe would prove her wrong when she visited Dendera Temple. That was at least a hope, but every bit of this was the amulet's fault.

Stand.

Dendera was unsettled anyway. She didn't feel like fighting Seth's amulet. She stood and approached the pyramid. Her reading skills had improved since Annippe first brought her to this remote corner of Karnak. Circling the pyramid, Dendera deciphered the sign "djed" which was repeated on all three sides. It reminded her of the old magician Djedi, but "djed" meant stable, unmovable. She wished something in her life would stay put.

Standing near the House of Sycamore, Dendera remembered Hathor's voice outside the Pool of Sobek. She trembled. Goddess inside her was energy, peace, warm, cold. She ran her fingers across the smooth carving of Hathor's face on the door to the neglected shrine. She wanted to push Hathor away; she wanted to feel her again. She wanted help.

It was the song that called to Hathor at Sobek's Pool. Dendera pulled the Hathor sistrum from her sash, the one Annippe had given her when they met.

Play with intention. Focus, Eshe always says. Dendera shook the sistrum. Seth's amulet shook. They played back and forth until the air began moving around her, like the dreams she used to have about Hathor. Seth's amulet clicked, and the forbidden door to the House of Sycamore creaked open.

Dendera looked around. She was alone. She slipped through the crack and closed the door behind her. Amber light spilled in from a skylight overhead, and she turned in a circle, taking in the mud-brick walls painted with scenes of Seven Hathors, the ones who presided over human life and death. One of the Seven held a newborn, and she gazed on his face as if deciding which path his life would take. Prickles ran up and down Dendera's spine. Had Hathor decided Dendera's fate when she was a baby? Did Hathor set her on this path to lose her parents, to find Seth's amulet, and to hunt the killer? She rubbed her pyramid mole; it was aching.

An odd stone statue stood in the center of the shrine. Two colossal stone hands rose as if they'd grown from the dirt. The wrists were joined, and the hands opened up to lay flat. The stone palms held a dusty scroll tied with papyrus thread. The amulet purred, wanting her to read. The glyphs, *Instructions to Djedi's Heir,* were scribed on the scroll.

She unrolled the scroll to the first page:

I, DJEDI, MOST POWERFUL OF EGYPT'S
MAGICIANS, HEREBY APPOINT YOU MY HEIR.
IF YOU ARE READING THIS, YOU HAVE
ENTERED THE SHRINE OF SEVEN AND HAVE
TAKEN UP THE SACRED SCROLL OF
GODDESS. YOU WILL NOW TAKE UP MY POST.
THIS IS YOUR DESTINY. THIS IS YOUR SHAY. I
COMMAND YOU BY THE MIRROR OF SEVEN
HATHORS, TO KEEP THIS SCROLL WITH YOU
EVERMORE AND GUARD IT WITH YOUR LIFE.
READ ITS ENTIRETY. TAKE MY INSTRUCTION
TO HEART. COMMIT THE SPELLS HEREIN TO
YOUR MEMORY. ARMED WITH THESE
LESSONS, YOU ARE DESTINED TO BECOME
MORE POWERFUL THAN I WAS IN MY OWN
TIME. I FORESEE THIS IS NECESSARY.
WITHOUT YOU, EGYPT WILL FALL...

*H*oly *hippopotamus*. Tetisheri was right. She never should have slipped her sandal inside Karnak. Hatshepsut wanted her to be Pharaoh's Magician. Now some dead magician wanted her to guard a dusty old scroll with her life. All Dendera wanted was to redeem her parents. How could she save Egypt? What in the name of the black land did it need saving from?

Dendera needed air. She stowed the scroll in her sash, stumbled out of the House of Sycamore, and ran past Ty's Mummy Storage. The sandy road turned to green grass, and she jogged until she reached the Nile bank, stopping to gulp in the breeze, green and alive like Nile algae. She rested her hand on a large rock beside the river but quickly jerked it away. The rock blazed with angry heat even though Ra's boat dipped below the horizon.

Swishing her hand through the cool water, Dendera saw mirrored in the ripples a man draped with black panther fur. Near the edge of the forest, Gazali waited. His cat eyes shined bright as the sunset. He beckoned. Zezi trusted Gazali and even said Mother wanted her to be friends with him. Dendera wasn't sure Gazali was worth trusting. She began wondering where Gazali's panther, Mudada, was when Gazali turned and walked into the forest. He looked back at her. Seth's amulet blew air on Dendera's wet palm to dry it. *Go*. Dendera flicked the last drops from her fingers.

As Gazali trekked deep inside the forest, he turned several times to be sure Dendera was near. He reached a circular clearing amidst a grove of ancient cedars. Dendera pushed through the waving branches and stopped at the sight of Mudada, stretched out on the grass, lifeless.

Dendera knelt next to the panther and placed her hand on his head. "He's dying." She looked up at Gazali.

"He is old." Gazali leaned over the panther's body, opened his hand, and scattered golden dust from his head to tail. "It is his time."

"Sakumenahba. Sakumenahba." Gazali hummed a foreign tune. The panther moaned. Gazali handed Dendera a bowl filled with glutinous black liquid. "Rub it across his forehead. Wish for his suffering to be over."

Gazali threw dust and rubbed oils and ointments, chanting and touching every part of the panther's body. Night fell. Since Gazali knew about Seth's amulet, Dendera took it out. She snuggled right next to Mudada, and holding her small red stone, touched Mudada's eyes and wished him peace. Gazali's hand passed over hers, and Seth's amulet shuddered. The panther exhaled. Dendera had never heard a living thing sound so utterly relieved.

Mudada's eyes fluttered. He stared straight at Dendera but didn't focus on her. His pupils, black as an Egyptian night, swirled milky white. Mudada saw something in the Beyond. He exhaled his last. Dendera caressed his head and closed his empty eyes. She sank her head into her hands, thinking of her mother and father, wishing she'd been able to hold them the night they died.

At least Mother and Father held each other. Rocking side to side, Dendera lost herself in the memory of the night her parents died. She remembered being in the forest, seeing the house on fire, running, hearing voices inside the home, getting on hands and knees, crawling inside, spitting black soot, searching for her parents, coughing smoke, passing out. A man's arms encircled her from behind. He dragged her body over and out a window, both of them covered in ashes, and deposited her under the safety of the tamarisk. That's where she'd first seen Seth's amulet. The stone jumped from the black loam and landed on her palm. The man closed her fingers over the rock, whispered, "Keep the stone. Let it guide you to the killer," and left.

She'd fainted. Against the backside of her eyelids, a burning image of Seth flickered and faded. She came around to the sound of Zezi's screams. He raced from the forest, stared in disbelief, and ran straight toward the burning house. Tetisheri hollered at him. Dendera's eyes fluttered open and closed.

Zezi stumbled toward Dendera and crumpled in the dirt, coughing smoke. He wrenched Dendera upright, leaned her against the tamarisk tree, and wrapped his arms around her. They leaned their heads together and watched black-crimson flames swallow their childhood home.

Dendera opened her hand. "It wasn't a dream." Seth's amulet hunkered down, settling onto her palm.

"No," Zezi said. "I wish it was. Our home is gone. Is there any way Mother and Father could have gotten out? Maybe they…"

"A man gave me this stone." Dendera turned Seth's amulet on her palm. The power of the stone broke through her shock, and wiping the stone clean of soot and ash, she searched out its secrets for the first time.

"What?" Zezi couldn't take it in.

Tetisheri was still staggering around the burning

house, tears falling in rivers, desperate for an open path into the inferno, looking for a way to save Ramla, her dearest friend. Dendera knew it was over. The moment the man told her to let the stone guide her to the killer, she'd accepted the truth. Her parents were dead.

Neighbors doused the fire with water from the garden canals Zezi had helped his father dig. Tetisheri collapsed beside Dendera and brushed ashes from her hair. "How did you get out alive?"

"A man pulled me out," Dendera answered. "I never saw his face."

"No one was here," Tetisheri said. "You must have crawled out, and your brain is addled by the smoke."

"I found this stone," Dendera said. "The man told me to keep it."

The look on Tetisheri's face gutted Dendera. It was shock, anger, regret, revulsion, helplessness, terror.

"Throw that blasted stone into the fire. Forget you ever saw it." Tetisheri lunged toward the stone on Dendera's palm. Dendera made a fist, hiding the stone, and rolled on the ground as Tetisheri grabbed her arm and pried her fingers.

Zezi rammed his head into Tetisheri's shoulder. "Leave her alone! Get off her!" Zezi banged Tetisheri's back with both fists. "She found a rock. So what? If she wants to keep it, let her keep it. What's wrong with you?"

"Fine." Tetisheri untangled herself from Dendera and Zezi, dusted off her arms, and smoothed her hair.

"Fine, but keep the stone *hidden*, and don't tell a soul you found it."

It was Zezi taking up for her, his reckless determination that Dendera should have the stone when he didn't even know why she should have the stone, that made Dendera decide she'd keep Seth's amulet whether the path it led her along was smooth sand or jagged rock.

The sound of Gazali dragging the panther's body deeper into the forest brought Dendera back to her surroundings. She sat up, hugged her knees, and flopped sideways again. Leaves and cedar branches cushioned her. Hathor floated on a cloud, holding her and singing in her ear. *Naos.* It was an ancient hymn Dendera remembered hearing eons ago but had since forgotten.

If Hathor was real, if Seth was real, could it have been Seth who pulled her from the burning house and told her to guard the stone?

Why would the Destroyer save you? Seth's amulet swayed.

The forest floor rustled. Gazali shook her awake as the first trickles of Ra's light fell in columns through the canopy of trees. "Mudada was a good companion." He held out the panther skin. "The magic we worked into his skin is meant for you." He smiled at Dendera's puzzled expression. "I've seen you in the fields, schooling the other priestesses about herbs. You will be a great healer, perhaps for the princess, perhaps for Egypt." He stretched out his arms, draped by Mudada's black fur. "Take it as my gift to you."

Dendera guessed that Gazali had tanned the skin by magic. There wasn't a drop of blood. She was half-touched and half-repulsed as she cradled the panther skin to her chest. "How do I use this for healing?"

"You will know." A tear escaped Gazali's eye.

❧ 18 ❧
JOURNEYWORK

Dendera staggered from the forest and followed the path alongside the Nile that was hidden amongst papyrus thickets. In a single day, she'd been called a magician by the pharaoh and hopeless by two men who hated her. She'd broken into a sacred shrine that no one had entered for centuries and taken possession of Djedi's secret scroll. Now she'd been named a healer by a man who worked magic into panther skins. She felt frazzled.

She needed someplace quiet to think. There was only one place she could go. At the outskirts of the temple, she reached Main Street in Thebes and veered onto the narrow Backstreet. She wished to pass through the city and arrive in the countryside without drawing attention to herself.

Near the flax fields where Scar and One-Eye made their camp, Dendera edged up behind a tamarisk tree and squatted down. The two men sat amid a mountain of bread, fresh-bartered from Birabi the baker. One-Eye leaned his head back, opened wide, and stuffed a lotus loaf into his mouth. Scar tore a wheat loaf in half and mushed his face into it, tearing hunks of bread with his teeth. They gorged like wild dogs.

Dendera dry-heaved and wiped her mouth. There was something shifty about those two: too much gold, too many amulets, and too much food. No matter what Ty and Annippe said, they dressed like Dethroners. She stole away, slipped past Dalila's house, climbed through the cedar thicket, and arrived outside a familiar mud-brick home. Tetisheri sat listless on a wooden stool in her courtyard. She and Dendera stared at each other, wide-eyed.

"What happened to you?" Dendera smoothed Tetisheri's disheveled hair and pulled up her torn shift to cover her shoulder.

"I'm only tired," Tetisheri said, wiping dirt from Dendera's caked face. "You're a mess." She stroked the panther skin and led Dendera inside.

Together, they sank onto a woven papyrus mat. Tetisheri didn't say a word. She listened. Once Dendera started talking, her story spilled forth like Nile water in the Inundation. "I'm in trouble at Karnak. Hatshepsut wants me to be her magician. Hapuseneb hates me. He hates that Hatshepsut trusts me. He's in league with Senenmut, and they're up to no good. They tore into me when I oraculumed for Hatshepsut, and none of my friends stood up for me, not even Zezi. It was Eshe who stood between me and the two men."

Seth's amulet yapped like a puppy. "And this stone prods me to perform magic! I called a lightning bolt to Karnak's courtyard and blasted everybody. I was so mad." Dendera described the House of Sycamore and held out Djedi's scroll. "Then, to top it all, Mudada died. Gazali gave me his skin." Dendera pulled the panther fur to her lap. Tetisheri was like a human treasure chest, and Dendera poured out her secrets, knowing they would be kept safe.

"I almost forgot. Hathor spoke the prophecy through me," Dendera said. "I nearly fainted."

"You finally felt her. She's loved you all along." Tetisheri rubbed the panther's head. "Gazali has been watching out for you and Zezi since before your mother died. Since you insist on keeping that awful rock," Tetisheri gave the amulet a dirty look, "I am glad you chose to wield it to give Mudada peace."

"That lightning bolt wasn't peaceful," Dendera said.

"The amulet protected you." Tetisheri looked as if it pained her to say it.

"Will you keep the panther skin for me?" Dendera asked. "I can't take it back to Karnak."

Tetisheri opened the lid of an old wooden chest, and Dendera lowered the panther skin inside. Ipi skipped through an open window and bounded to Dendera's shoulder.

"Blathering baboon," Tetisheri muttered.

Dendera went to wash her face. As Tetisheri sliced

rosemary bread, Dendera realized she hadn't eaten in a whole day. She was famished.

"I'm going to travel toward the northern mountains this afternoon," Tetisheri said. "I need to replenish my stock of thyme and fenugreek. Come with me. It will do you good to forget your worries."

"Hatshepsut asked me to tend Neferura. She has been ill again."

"You cannot heal another while you need healing yourself," Tetisheri said. "We won't be gone long."

For the next few days, Dendera walked the black lands alongside her mother's old friend. Even Seth's amulet turned placid. Ipi rode Dendera's shoulder while she gathered the wild herbs Tetisheri needed for her poultices and ointments. It worried Dendera that Tetisheri had grown puny and slow, but Tetisheri brushed aside Dendera's questions about her health.

Trying to pinpoint the killer likewise proved useless. Tetisheri didn't want to talk about Paheri, Hapuseneb, or anyone else at Karnak. They dined on dried figs and barley bread, and Dendera needled Tetisheri on how to heal Neferura. Tetisheri's diagnosis: "The darkness that looms over and around Neferura must be lifted."

While Tetisheri slept, Dendera unrolled Djedi's scroll to pass time. In a chapter entitled "Pell Mell Spells," the old magician explained Isis's healing trick: "You must learn the name of the illness and tell it to leave." Dendera thought this inadequate advice and leafed through the scroll looking for other healing spells.

Djedi proposed an exercise regimen to prepare his heir for the work ahead. It was quite similar to the Sema class she took at Karnak. Perhaps one of these would help the princess. Djedi wrote, "Do scorpion pose to draw near to Serket and open the spine; do plow pose to invoke Geb and..." Djedi claimed many of these poses had healing benefits, but Dendera couldn't imagine that frail Neferura could perch on her back and hike her legs over her head. She shuffled through a few more pages.

The scroll elucidated various incantations. Djedi proposed ways to undo curses, purify water, duplicate amulets, cast spells on unlucky days, and locate secret passageways. Dendera exited each chapter, maddened by Djedi's brevity. Where was the spell for finding a killer?

Dendera found it amusing that Djedi revered his pet baboon, and no matter where she was reading in the scroll, Ipi was adept at turning to the page with the baboon's picture. As Djedi had warned King Khufu, he warned his heir against searching for the *Book of Thoth*. "It will bring trouble in the form of its guardian Seth."

Djedi had a fascination with pyramids and repeated the phrase "People fear time — time fears pyramid" three times in the scroll. Though Dendera hadn't worked out what the saying meant, Djedi's pyramid obsession explained why the small pyramid sat beside the House of Sycamore. Dendera guessed Djedi had commissioned both the pyramid and the House to be built next to each other.

Perhaps Djedi even planted the towering sycamore tree.

She rubbed her pyramid mole and flipped to a chapter called "Strength's Stone." Djedi said his heir would come into possession of the stone when the time was ripe, and this mysterious rock would hold powers to help in dire emergencies. Djedi did not describe the stone nor tell where to find it. The old goat could have left it anywhere!

In "On the Spot," Djedi encouraged his heir to practice spontaneous magic. He wrote, "When a need arises, you will also rise up and find a way." This line made Dendera's stomach churn. She rolled up the scroll.

Tetisheri was snoring. Most nights, Dendera couldn't sleep on their bed of leaves and twigs, spoiled as she was by the comforts of Karnak, but this night, Seth's amulet trilled a lullaby her mother sang when she was young.

The moon sings a rocking song of delight
A tranquil melody that fills the night
Her circle embraces you and yours
A tender glow that listens, endures

If you have a question: Ask Mother Moon
Tonight, be brave; then listen to her tune
Her answer will come afar, quite clear
The moon croons for you, quiet and near

"Who's the killer?" was Dendera's perpetual question, but she didn't expect an answer. She wedged the scroll and the amulet into her sash and dozed off. A soft breeze rustled her hair. She entered a maze of pyramids, counting, counting, counting to one hundred. In the middle of the maze, a hundred geese squawked. *Snap.* As if someone snapped their fingers, every one of the geese heads fell off and rolled, grotesque, on the grass. Two men appeared in the middle of the severed geese heads as if they'd popped from the ground. Scar ate loaf after loaf of bread. One-Eye gulped jug after jug of barley beer. When fizz bubbled from his nose, he stopped. "Enough. One hundred."

Dendera jolted awake. Ipi was smack in her face. Seth's amulet asked, *See?* One hundred loaves and jugs — they stole Djedi's magic! They distorted it. They made it ugly and monstrous.

On the day they returned to Tetisheri's home, Dendera helped with the mundane tasks of grinding flour and lugging water from the Nile. She missed Karnak. She missed stretching her mind to learn new things.

"You do not belong at that temple." Tetisheri read Dendera's thoughts. "We must bring Zezi here, and you must both stay here with me. Karnak is cursed."

Cursed. Dendera missed her Curse Chasers. Seth's amulet flopped over on Tetisheri's table. Seth's finger on the stone pointed toward Karnak. She imagined Ty, Annippe, and Zezi had already looked for her at Tetisheri's. It was time to return and face Hapuseneb.

"That high priestess came here asking questions." Tetisheri stripped fenugreek seeds from the stalks and tossed them in a jar. "She brought more food and drink than I can use in a year."

"Eshe came to see you?"

"She wanted to know how your mother and father died." Tetisheri shook her head.

Seth's amulet rocked. *Relax; we'll go soon,* Dendera told the stone and stuffed it in her sash. "Eshe is Mother of Karnak, and she wants you to know she cares about us." Dendera's words were drowned out by grinding wheels in the courtyard. She ran outside.

Pharaoh Thutmose descended his chariot. "We have been searching for days. Where have you been?"

"Tetisheri needed my help on her travels," answered Dendera, pointing toward Tetisheri's house.

"Neferura's condition has worsened." Thutmose extended his hand. "Hatshepsut asks that you come right away."

Tetisheri stumbled outside. Thutmose caught Tetisheri by the elbow and walked her to a wooden stool.

Dendera poured Tetisheri a cup of water. Ipi chattered, and Tetisheri scratched his head.

"Tend to the princess," Tetisheri said. "Then come home."

"I'll visit soon." Dendera hugged Tetisheri.

Thutmose ordered his driver to go slow. Dendera tried to pat her hair into respectable shape. She had not had time to wash after her long journey with

Tetisheri. She asked the stone, *Why can't you do something useful like smoothing my hair?*

"Do not worry. I will have my servants attend you at the palace." Thutmose lowered his voice. "I must talk to you about Hapuseneb. Since the day Hatshepsut appointed you to the temple, Hapuseneb has been afraid you'd get his job."

Dendera sputtered. "I have no intention of replacing Hapuseneb. I am following Pharaoh Hatshepsut's orders."

"I know it's not your intention." Thutmose clapped Dendera's back, just as Ipi gagged up a hairball. Aghast, Thutmose shook his hand out the side of the chariot. Ipi's hair and other debris blew away on the wind. Seth's amulet snorted. Dendera moved Ipi to her lap and readjusted her sash to muffle the amulet.

Thutmose recollected himself. "Senenmut would be happy to help Hapuseneb, perhaps arranging for you to run away from Karnak. It's not safe for you to return to the temple." He pulled a papyrus stalk from his belt and began weaving.

"Why does Senenmut hate me? Neferura adores him. She says Senenmut has always loved her."

"I believe he does love her in his own way. We all love her, but her illness robs her of sense. She hides inside herself." Thutmose appeared lost in memory; his fingers worked the papyrus. "Senenmut has spoiled Neferura since she was a baby. He's kept her dependent on him. Senenmut can't stand it that someone besides him can help Neferura. The moment you held those berries under Neferura's nose, he couldn't stand you. He wants the throne, and he believes marrying Neferura will bring him power."

"You are Pharaoh, as well as Queen Hatshepsut." Dendera frowned. "He must know you're next in line to the throne." Seth's amulet whacked, and Dendera agreed with the stone's point: *Senenmut's plan, if this was his plan, lacked logic.*

"Senenmut has a twisted mind. He thinks I'm weak because I rule beside Hatshepsut." Thutmose paused, looking proud and wise. "While Hatshepsut takes care of Egypt's home front, I keep the borders safe."

"Egypt knows great peace under Pharaoh Hatshepsut," Dendera said.

"True." Thutmose nodded.

"Why don't you do something about Senenmut if he causes so much trouble?" Dendera asked.

"Neferura loves him," Thutmose said, "and I'm biding my time. Senenmut thinks I'll be easy prey when Hatshepsut is gone, but my army is prepared to ensure a peaceful transition of power when Hatshepsut dies."

Dendera's breath lodged in her throat. She didn't want to be caught in between Hatshepsut and Thutmose, and whatever quest for power existed between the two of them. She especially didn't want to imagine a time when Hatshepsut would not rule. Hatshepsut was strong and invincible. She was their queen.

"We all fear dying. Death is the Great Irreversible

in this world." Thutmose gazed from Dendera's face to the gray clouds hovering over Ra. "I cannot allow myself to shirk away from fear. As Pharaoh, I face my fears so I remain prepared for all things at all times. I've grown to see death as new life, a new-fashioned adventure, but enough of this." Thutmose took Dendera's hand and placed a miniature papyrus crown on her palm. "I know a way to help you out of your troubles with Senenmut and Hapuseneb."

Dendera was still processing Thutmose's death speech and had no idea what he was talking about now.

"Marry me and live at the palace, my pyramid girl."

The chariot wheels squealed to a halt in front of the palace. Before Dendera's mind could catch up with what Thutmose said, he ran his fingers through her matted hair, took her dirt-caked face in his hands, and kissed her.

❦ 19 ❦

KISSING PROBLEMS

Thutmose placed his hands on the small of Dendera's back and drew her toward him. She put both hands on his chest, and Thutmose took her hands one by one, kissed her palms, and wrapped them around his waist. He pulled her closer, put a finger under her chin to lift her face closer to his, and kissed her again. He was all muscle, solid as a mountain. She'd seen that in him. He didn't budge. He stood firm no matter what he faced. Though Thutmose had kissed many young women before, this was Dendera's first. She leaned her head toward his shoulder, and he shifted toward her, caressing her hair and running his fingers over her neck.

In those moments, Thutmose coaxed Dendera away from the single trail her mind usually walked, and for a time she let go of her quest. She felt dizzy, heady, as if the pull of the moon tides coursed through her blood, and she let herself flow with it. The touch of Thutmose's lips on hers made time pause, and her world spun with possibilities, breaking apart and shimmering in myriad directions. The enormity of all the what-ifs in her life settled like sand after a storm. Wrapped in Thutmose's arms, she might do anything or be anyone.

She was being kissed by a man she barely knew, kissed by a king. Steam escaped his taut skin like whorls from desert sands. *So, this is what this is all about.* Dendera had never considered being attracted to Thutmose before. How strange to think more strange thoughts than there were droplets of water in the Nile, and all the while, Thutmose kissed her still.

Pharaoh Thutmose is kissing me! Thutmose is betrothed to Neferura! Neferura is my friend! What have I done?

Dendera pushed him away.

Seth's amulet coughed.

Ipi hacked.

Thutmose looked over Dendera's head. His jaw tensed. "Neferura."

Dendera turned. Princess Neferura, weak as water, clung to Senenmut's arm in the doorway of the palace. Senenmut rubbed Neferura's hand, scowling at Dendera.

"How could you?" the princess whispered and staggered away, retching.

Senenmut sneered and spun to follow Neferura.

"She'll be fine," Thutmose soothed.

"You're betrothed to her."

He held Dendera's arm. "You will be Great Royal Wife."

"All of Egypt knows…"

"If I must, I will marry Neferura also, to secure the throne after Hatshepsut is gone, but Neferura will be happiest far from Egypt's royal court. She has no wish to rule beside me, but you could."

Dendera pushed his hand off her arm, leapt from the chariot, and ran to Neferura's room. Senenmut stood guard outside the door. "Leave. You've done enough damage," he said. The door opened and Neferura's attendant walked out. Dendera dashed under Senenmut's arm. Neferura lay curled on her bed, sobbing.

Senenmut stormed in the room. "The one day I coax her out of bed, you show up kissing that imbecile."

"Neferura, I'm sorry," Dendera shouted. Senenmut yanked her arm.

"Wait." Neferura sat up and brushed her cheeks. "I want to hear what she has to say."

The look Senenmut gave Dendera withered the lotus blossoms on the princess's table. He swooped from the room, head bobbing madly.

Dendera sat on Neferura's bed. "Thutmose was bringing me here to see you, and he surprised me. I …"

"Was it the first time he kissed you?" Neferura gulped.

"Yes," Dendera said.

The door opened again, and Annippe walked in. Relief washed her face.

Zezi followed. "Where have you been?"

"Tetisheri and I took a short journey to gather herbs," Dendera said.

"I'm sorry I didn't help you, Dendera," Annippe said. "When I saw Hapuseneb tearing into you, my mind froze."

"I'm working on Hapuseneb," Zezi said. "I'm trying to soften him up toward you."

"Are you wreaking havoc at the temple also?" Neferura asked with uncharacteristic venom.

"What has happened?" Annippe asked.

"She kissed Thutmose." Neferura crossed her arms and pouted. "You know, the man I'm supposed to marry." Neferura's eyes rolled up in her head. She slipped off her bed in a dead faint.

Annippe and Zezi pulled Neferura upright. Once again, Dendera pulled the juniper berries from her sash. Her hand grazed Djedi's scroll. Could she learn the name of Neferura's illness? Could Seth's amulet heal Neferura? She needed time to research, to think. Neferura was weak. Casting the wrong incantation might hurt instead of help.

Neferura's eyes fluttered open. "At least Senenmut wants to marry me."

"Neferura!" Dendera scoffed. "You don't want to marry that old man!"

"Thutmose does not want me." Neferura sucked in a breath. "When Mother makes ... *hiccup*... me marry him … *hiccup* … he will shut me … *hiccup* … away somewhere until I … *hiccup* … rot."

Annippe stroked Neferura's hair. "You're getting too worked up. Rest a bit."

"I'd better go check on Thut." Zezi edged toward the doorway. "See if he needs help with a chariot."

Dendera asked for an attendant to bring frankincense oil. Annippe massaged Neferura's feet. Dendera worked on her hands. "I know that Thutmose is intended for you, Neferura," Dendera whispered. "He took me by surprise. I should've had the sense to push him away. No man is worth losing your friendship."

Neferura answered in silence. She had fallen asleep. Annippe scooped the ostrich feather from her bedside table and placed it beside her. "Gentle Ma'at, bring her peaceful dreams."

In the side chamber, Annippe helped Dendera wash and dress in a fresh gown. Later that evening, Zezi returned carrying woven mats and spread them on the floor.

"Sis, when did you learn to shoot off lightning bolts? I've never seen Hapuseneb so angry."

Dendera glared. "It just happened. I was mad."

"It's my favorite spell so far," Zezi said. Dendera rolled her eyes.

"Look how Nut's gown sparkles tonight," Annippe said.

Dendera gazed out the window. "How can Nut be Seth's mother?"

"She gave birth to Strength," Annippe mused. "Part of that strength lives in you."

"Why didn't I stop Thutmose?"

"Priestesses are allowed to marry," Annippe said. "Would you marry Thutmose?"

"Bah." Zezi spit out the window.

"The idea never crossed my mind," Dendera answered. "I had no clue he was about to kiss me."

Annippe touched Dendera's sash. "You have one purpose." The amulet *thwacked*. "Neferura does not want Thutmose," Annippe said, "but she doesn't want you to have him either."

Dendera shook her head. "I never meant to hurt Neferura." She remembered Neferura kneeling next to her in the throne room and saying, *I've never had a girl friend before.* Dendera's stomach lurched. *What a friend I've turned out to be.* "I won't let this — this thing with Thutmose — happen again."

Zezi scowled and turned to Annippe. "Will you and Ty marry?"

"We are not so serious." Annippe yawned.

"Speaking of marriages," Dendera said, "Neferura needs to learn how to stand up to Hatshepsut."

"That's what Thut says," Zezi agreed.

"Has Neferura any interest in the priestesshood?" Annippe asked.

"She faints when she is on display," Dendera said, thinking of the debacle at the Beautiful Festival of the Valley.

"Perhaps she would do better in a silent sanctuary," Annippe said.

"When she is stronger, I'll ask her," Dendera said.

On Hatshepsut's command, Dendera, Annippe, and Zezi spent the next few days tending to Neferura, which was easy work since the princess mostly slept. Senenmut was out of their way because Hatshepsut ordered him to live at Karnak Temple for a few days to oversee the final installation of her obelisks.

The Palace Library, Dendera discovered, yielded little on the subject of healing. She hoped one of the scrolls would at least hint at the name of Neferura's illness. Still, she found *Queenly Quests* illuminating and figured that Hatshepsut followed the advice of the primitive queens when she took control of the throne years ago when Thutmose was young.

Neferura only awoke with emotional outbursts that upset her mother. To stay in Hatshepsut's graces, Dendera read *The Tales of the Cross-eyed Crocodile* to Neferura. It kept her quieter than a marshmallow's mouse. Thutmose stood outside Neferura's doorway, listening to Dendera read. When she finished, he took Zezi to practice archery and race chariots. Dendera wondered if Thutmose used her brother to get closer to her, but since it made Zezi happy, she let it be.

A few evenings later, after she'd given Neferura a myrrh massage, Dendera climbed into bed. Zezi was worn out, and Annippe also slept, her breath flowing in rhythm with the Nile.

Dreams claimed Dendera. All night, she walked through a field of golden grass, searching. She stopped, her feet teetering over the edge of Black Earth, her arms circling backward to balance, and turned. Ipi sat on his haunches at the edge of the field, prattling "Tetisheri" over and over. Mother patted Ipi's hand.

Dendera awoke, feeling trampled like the grass underfoot. She picked up Seth's amulet, and it echoed, *Tetisheri*.

TETISHERI'S TALE

Morning, clammy and raw, rushed the open chariot. Though Zezi drove faster than ever, the trip stretched to the Field of Reeds. Fat round raindrops began to fall.

"Tefnut is crying today," Annippe said, looking up into the gray clouds.

Dendera held out her hand. With every raindrop that fell, Seth's amulet said, *Tetisheri. Tetisheri. Tetisheri,* and rainwater puddled on Dendera's palm.

Wild grape vines twisted and twined up Tetisheri's front wall. Zezi hopped from the chariot, picked a cluster, and popped a grape in his mouth. He said, "Tetisheri is late picking these."

They slipped through the door and found Tetisheri on her woven floor mat.

Dendera rushed to her side and felt her forehead. "She's burning with fever."

Tetisheri stirred. Her eyes were glazed, her cheeks sunken. Dendera pressed Tetisheri's abdomen with her fingers. She'd learned an amazing amount of anatomy from her time in Ty's Mummy Room. "I think she's bleeding inside." Zezi and Annippe hovered nearby, looking helpless. "Tetisheri, what happened?" Dendera asked.

"Barley beer was bad." Tetisheri gestured toward a jug on her table and let her arm drop. "I knew you would come back. Your mother took care of me once when I was ill." Tetisheri closed her eyes and reached for Zezi's hand. "Zezi, you were just a babe crawling in the dirt. Your mother brought juniper berries and boiled them down to syrup. Dendera plucked one of the berries, rolled it between her palms, and plopped it in her mouth."

Dendera placed a cool cloth across Tetisheri's forehead. Tetisheri continued to mutter. "Ramla loved the city of Dendera."

"Yes." Dendera stroked Tetisheri's head.

"That's why she named you after it," Tetisheri rambled. "Ramla loved to visit Dendera."

"She wanted to visit," Dendera corrected. "She'd never been there."

"Yes, she visited once a month for a long, long time," Tetisheri said. "Then she traveled only on feast days. She saw too much in Dendera. The priests grew tired of her." Tetisheri continued raving, and Zezi whispered something inaudible. Dendera stepped outside the front door and pulled a twig off the rosemary bush. She rubbed rosemary needles between her palms, and held her scented hands under

Tetisheri's nose, hoping to bring Tetisheri to her senses.

"She's not in her right mind," Annippe said.

Tetisheri rasped at Annippe. "You remind me of your mother."

"How did you know my mother?" Annippe asked, but Tetisheri closed her eyes and gabbled.

"This is from the temple." Zezi stood to examine the jug on Tetisheri's table. *Hwt –ntr*.

"She was weak when we traveled to gather herbs," Dendera said.

"Do you think it was the same person who killed Mother and Father?" Zezi smelled the jug.

"No." Annippe clutched her heart. "Perhaps she refilled a jug you brought her with bad beer." Annippe couldn't think ill of anyone at Karnak.

As Ra's boat reached its pinnacle in the sky, Dendera boiled a poppy draught and spoon-fed Tetisheri to ease her pain and fever. Annippe and Zezi shifted Tetisheri on the mat to make her more comfortable. Tetisheri drifted to sleep while memories flooded Dendera's mind. "Last year, during Inundation, Mother visited family in Abydos. I asked to go, but she made me stay home with Father."

"I thought Mother would get washed away in the flood," Zezi said.

"Inundation is nothing to fear," Annippe said. "The Nile is reborn as Osiris was reborn, and Isis rejoices."

Zezi rolled his eyes.

"She left during the third month of the Inundation," Dendera said, thinking out loud.

"The Festival of Hathor is held in Dendera in the third month," Annippe said. "She would have passed by on her way to Abydos."

"Yes, Ramla loved to dance for Hathor." Tetisheri's voice was quieter than a butterfly's wing beat, and her chest caved to her ribs. She coughed blood.

"Mother danced for Hathor at home," Dendera said, confused.

"When Father was in the fields," Zezi mumbled.

"What does that matter now?" Dendera leaned her ear over Tetisheri's mouth. Her breath sounded different; it sounded the way Ty described the "death rattle." He once told Dendera, "Right before a person dies, their breath changes."

Dendera's stricken face told Zezi what he didn't want to know. He plunked cross-legged to the floor, cradling his head. "Not again. We already lost our parents."

"We could take her to the temple," Annippe offered. "One of the healer priests might be able to help her."

"I don't see how we can get her there," Zezi said. "There isn't room in the chariot to lay her down flat."

"Tetisheri hated the temple," Dendera said.

Zezi asked, "Can't you use the amulet?"

Dendera realized that Seth's amulet had been silent for its longest stretch since she'd found the stone. She pulled it from her waist sash. It sat solemn and still on her palm. It was no good.

"Tetisheri hated the amulet too. It would make it worse, but we need to do something quick." Dendera opened the wooden chest and pulled out the panther skin.

Annippe gasped. Zezi asked, "Where did Tetisheri get that?"

Dendera tried to drape the skin across Tetisheri, but Tetisheri grabbed her arm. Dendera stroked Tetisheri's cheek with the back of her hand. "Tetisheri, all will be well. Let me help you."

"Peace, children." Tetisheri's eyes flashed. For the first time that day, Tetisheri looked like herself, the wise healer Dendera knew. "Save the panther skin for the one who needs it."

"Where on Black Earth did you get that?" Annippe asked.

"A shaman from Punt …"

"Gazali?" Zezi asked.

As Dendera told them about Gazali and the magic they worked into the panther skin, Annippe's eyes grew as round as blue lotuses in bloom. "I've heard stories of this magic from my father. It is ancient. I've never known anyone who could perform it."

"Do you see why Mother wanted you to meet Gazali?" Zezi asked.

Again, Dendera tried to put the skin on Tetisheri, but Tetisheri put up her hand. "Save it, Dendera. My goddesses will take care of me." She exhaled and winced.

"Tetisheri, you're in pain," Dendera said. "I must help you."

"Get the cobalt bottle from the high cabinet," Tetisheri whispered.

"No." Zezi shook his head. "Another herb. Something. Anything."

Tut, tut. Tetisheri tapped Dendera's hand. "Khemepane alone will help me. Go."

Tears splashed Dendera's cheeks as Tefnut's tears had splashed her palms earlier. She climbed the stool and with trembling hands, lowered Tetisheri's cobalt bottle. She remembered the starlit night moons before she and Zezi entered the temple. They'd followed Tetisheri into the forest. She'd drawn three circles around a plant with a large, smooth sycamore stick which she called her "healing rod."

With circles drawn around the plant, Tetisheri faced the west and dug the root with her stick, singing a hymn to Hathor, Isis, and Nut called *Three Faces of One*. She cradled the root like a newborn child and carried it home. While Tetisheri boiled the root down to syrup, she explained that she cared for many ill patients who had no hope of recovering. When used correctly, khemepane soothed away the pain and eased a person's transition when it was time to leave their body and enter the Field of Reeds.

Dendera never dreamed she would pour the globby black liquid into Tetisheri's open mouth while Annippe supported Tetisheri's head. Zezi paced, running his hands over his braids.

With an effort, Tetisheri gulped the drink and took Dendera's hand. "This will bring me relief, Dendera.

You are a treasure from my goddesses." Her lips worked as if she had much to tell.

"Rest, Tetisheri." Dendera dabbed frankincense oil behind Tetisheri's ears. Zezi dropped to his knees.

Tetisheri exhaled, worn by her efforts to speak. "Leave the temple, Dendera … Zezi." Tetisheri eyed Annippe. "You leave too, girl. The Dethroners will come after you." Tetisheri locked onto Dendera, pleading. "Leave … temple … carry goddesses … with you."

"Dendera, do something!" Zezi swung his arms in a panic, banging Dendera on the back, and his braids flew out in all directions as if energized by lightning. "Don't let her die!"

Annippe wrapped her arms around Zezi and pulled him off Dendera. She held Zezi tight, held Dendera's eyes, and inclined her head.

Dendera turned to Tetisheri and held out Seth's amulet. "May I use it for peace, once more?"

Tetisheri gave a small nod. Dendera cradled Tetisheri's head, trailed her fingers through Tetisheri's mud-colored hair, placed her hand, with Seth's amulet, over Tetisheri's chest as it rose and sank. Tetisheri was her treasure chest, her secret-keeper, her teacher. *Peace, Tetisheri. I'll remember you. I won't forget...* Tetisheri's hand went limp and slipped to the floor. Hatshepsut's bracelet fell from her arm.

Dendera squawked as Tetisheri exhaled her life's last breath. She watched Tetisheri's *ka*, her essence, fly home to her goddesses.

❦ 21 ❦

FALLEN

Kissing Tetisheri's eyelids, Dendera slipped the bracelet into her waist sash, next to Seth's amulet and Djedi's scroll. She shuffled through the house, looking for a blanket. Annippe pulled off her cloak, and Zezi helped her drape it over Tetisheri's body.

"I never imagined death to be beautiful," Annippe said and held Dendera while her sobs flowed like Nile rapids crashing against ancient rocks. Zezi leaned into Dendera's side, and the three of them stood together, holding each other for the longest time, and Dendera had never felt closer to any two people. There was something about death that made you appreciate life and the ones you loved more than ever.

Wrapped up with Annippe and Zezi, there in Tetisheri's one-room house, Dendera realized she'd never cried after Mother and Father died. She'd felt sad. She'd accepted the loss. She'd moved in with

Tetisheri. She'd taken care of Zezi. She'd helped mummify Mother and Father. She'd helped entomb them. She'd never cried. The night of the fire, Seth's amulet took over her thoughts, directed her actions, seized control of her life.

Losing Tetisheri was losing another part of Mother, another link to Mother, and once Dendera allowed herself to cry, her grief over Tetisheri mingled with the loss of all the moments she would have had with Mother and Father. They died young. Mother should have been here to help Tetisheri. Maybe Mother would have known how to save her. Dendera sobbed harder when she imagined how Father might have looked, standing outside Tetisheri's doorway, with his hand resting on top of his favorite donkey's head. Old Kiki had run away during the fire, and she and Zezi never saw the donkey again. Father loved to watch Mother work her healing magic. "Find something good in everything, my girl." That's what Father would say.

Let it go, Seth's amulet told her. *Let it go and let it out, but you can't cry forever. You still have work to do.*

Dendera felt somewhat grateful for the rock. It stopped her tears and brought her back to herself. She guessed that was the good Father would want her to find. One of the reasons she'd never let herself cry over Mother and Father was that she feared if she started, she'd never stop. She wiped her eyes and turned to Zezi. "We have to go back to Karnak."

"You should stay away from the temple," Zezi

said. "Tetisheri was right. That place isn't safe for you."

"The temple is where we're going to find the killer." Dendera held out Seth's amulet. "Nothing's changed." She pictured Tetisheri's face like it was the first time she'd shown her the amulet, right after the fire. "Tetisheri knew something about this amulet," Dendera said, "and I never asked her. I was afraid to ask her. She wanted me to get rid of it. I should have asked her why."

"She didn't want you hunting a killer," Annippe said.

"You could ask Thut to help you find the killer," Zezi said. "He'd do it for you. We don't have to go back to Karnak."

"I don't want Thutmose's help," Dendera said. "I've already gotten too close to him."

"We're still a team, you know," Annippe said, pulling Dendera and Zezi to her sides. "Ty and I are with you."

"I need to go to Karnak to ask Ty to help me mummify Tetisheri," Dendera said, "and I need to keep searching the House of Life for clues." Hatshepsut's pronouncement by the crocodile pool and Djedi's scroll weighed heavy. Tetisheri was the only soul Dendera had told about Djedi's scroll. She didn't mind Annippe, Zezi, or Ty knowing about it, but now wasn't the time.

A short chariot ride later, the three made their way down the avenue of sphinxes toward Karnak. Another golden chariot parked by the temple doors.

Hatshepsut descended its steps and caught sight of Dendera. "What has happened?"

"Your Majesty, my mother's dearest friend, my friend, Tetisheri … she just died." Dendera stared at the ground. "She took care of Zezi and me when no one…" Annippe put her arm around Dendera. "Your Majesty, we tended Tetisheri in her last moments," Dendera concluded with a gulp.

Hatshepsut spread her arms wide. "Death is a sacred part of life. Let us thank Hathor for Tetisheri's plenteous gifts and for the loving care she gave Dendera and Zezi. May Ma'at tip the scale of life in her favor when she appears before the gods for the Weighing of the Heart, and may Tetisheri live evermore in the wondrous Field of Reeds and Beyond." Hatshepsut swept Dendera and Zezi into a fierce hug. "I am sorry for your loss, both of you."

Ty approached from the temple doorway. He wrapped his arm around Dendera's waist. "May I attend to Tetisheri's body for you?"

"Thank you," Dendera whispered.

Hapuseneb and Eshe waited inside the courtyard. Dendera hadn't faced either since the lightning bolt incident. Eshe rushed toward Dendera and grasped her hand. "Let not your heart be troubled."

The high priest chewed the inside of his mouth as if he were gnawing the tirade he wished to hurl at Dendera. Glancing at Hatshepsut's stern face, Hapuseneb inclined his head to Dendera. "I offer my condolences."

Hatshepsut said to Eshe, "Your trip to Dendera was swift. When did you return?"

"This morning, Majesty. I was on my way to give you my report." There was a hint of pleasure in Eshe's voice.

"Let us go to my office," Hapuseneb said.

Dendera looked like a startled deer. Hapuseneb's office, that's where she'd find clues. She needed to know where it was. She glanced at Ty, but he shook his head.

Seth's amulet vibrated, and Hatshepsut said, "Come, Dendera. You gave the prophecy and should hear Eshe's report."

Hapuseneb's stare scalded Dendera, but he led the way. Dendera followed Eshe and Hatshepsut out of the courtyard, and Ty, Zezi, and Annippe conversed in furious whispers, watching.

Hatshepsut wrapped her arm around Dendera as they followed Eshe and Hapuseneb across Karnak's grounds. Hapuseneb stopped at the statue of Sekhmet. He placed one finger near the base of the statue, pressed a toe ring on Sekhmet's foot, and proceeded straight toward a solid wall. A door swung backwards, and Hapuseneb seemed to step inside the wall. Eshe and Hatshepsut followed. Dendera stuck her head inside. Hapuseneb, Eshe, and Hatshepsut were ascending a long staircase. Dendera shook her head. She'd never learn all of Karnak's secrets.

Each of the tamarisk stairs rising to Hapuseneb's office was painted with a different scene. As Dendera climbed, she saw the story of Ra depicted by one of

Egypt's finest artists. On the first step, the sun god embarked on the same journey he made each day. In the form of a scarab beetle, Ra entered a golden sailboat, his Boat of Millions of Years. The evening sky glowed amethyst, and as the steps rose, silver smoke billowed. Seth appeared in the prow of the boat; he wore his hound's head.

Seth's amulet crackled like lightning. Dendera sneezed three times to cover the brattle, and then a lightning bolt struck her: Seth was not Destroyer here. In this story, Seth played Protector. He scanned the horizon, the murky shadows, for danger. His ears perked. Apophis, the serpent of chaos, rose from the abyss. Stranger still, Apophis was the abyss, a gaping black hole that threatened to gulp Egypt. Seth's power alone could throw back the darkness. He raised a bare hand and with one flawless stroke, slew the gargantuan snake. The curtain of gloom vanished. Hathor continued her reign. Ra rose in a blinding blaze of ginger and amethyst. A new day dawned. In order for the sun to rise, each day Seth must fight the same battle anew. Day after day, Seth conquered Apophis. The strongest of the gods never failed to protect Ra.

From the dazzling sunrise painted on the last stair, Dendera stepped into Hapuseneb's oval-shaped office. The high priest's walls were lined with shelves containing ancient scrolls. Myrrh gum sat unburned in an ivory bowl on a slender table that also held a merkhet, the star-gazing tool. Two rocks held open a scroll on his desk. Dendera read the hieroglyph for

Amduat which meant "that which is in the afterworld" before the high priest rolled up the scroll and stashed it from view. Her eyes couldn't scan fast enough to take it all in.

Hapuseneb pulled the high-backed chair to the middle of the room where a hippo-hide rug was stretched across the floor. He seated Hatshepsut in this chair of honor and sat behind his desk. Hatshepsut indicated that Dendera should sit in a chair by her side.

Eshe stood before Hatshepsut. "Let not your heart be troubled, Most Honorable Pharaoh. There is no uprising in the city of Dendera. The temple runs smooth. While I visited, the high priest Ufa held a ceremony to honor Hathor and offered bountiful gifts."

Hapuseneb arranged his gold-masked face with smug assurance. "You see, Your Majesty, Dendera had no authority to act the oracle in this temple." He was glad Dendera's vision was "wrong."

"Silence," Hatshepsut commanded.

"Your Majesty, perhaps Dendera acted in haste at Sobek's pool." Eshe glanced at Hapuseneb. "I believe she meant no harm. In light of the loss she has suffered with Tetisheri's death, let us not judge her with harshness."

Hatshepsut turned to Dendera. "What are your thoughts?"

Dendera had hoped Eshe would prove her prophecy wrong. She'd hoped Dendera Temple remained true to Hathor, but instinct told Dendera the priests only played the proper role for Eshe. Looking back on the vision Hathor gave her in the Pool of Sobek, it was pellucid. Hapuseneb's tomb-dark eyes burned into Dendera's head as she tried to gather her wits. "Your Majesty, I feel my vision from Hathor was true, but I will be grateful if I am wrong."

Hapuseneb sputtered.

Dendera turned to him, thinking of what Annippe might say. "Hapuseneb, I respect your position as high priest and seek reconciliation between your mind and mine. I wished to serve my pharaoh. That is all." There. If Hapuseneb had a fava bean of sense in his Benu Brain, he'd let it go. Seth's amulet guffawed, and Dendera scraped her sandal across the floor to make noise.

Hapuseneb's gold mask relaxed, and for the first time since Dendera entered the temple, the angry veil covering his eyes dropped. He looked mollified.

Hatshepsut rose. "I will keep my eye on Dendera Temple." She turned to descend the stairs.

Eshe stared arrows at Pharaoh's back.

Dendera craved a long look through Hapuseneb's office and bookshelves, but the high priest's glare changed her mind. Bowing to Hapuseneb, Dendera hurried after Hatshepsut, but by the time she reached the bottom of the stairs, Pharaoh had mounted her chariot. Ty, Annippe, and Zezi sat shoulder to shoulder on a bench. Each jumped up, grabbed Dendera by her arms, and trotted her from the courtyard.

In the gardens, Zezi asked, "What happened?"

"The Dendera priests held a special ceremony to convince Eshe they honor Hathor, but I feel uneasy about it."

"Any clues?" Zezi asked. "What was Hapuseneb's office like?"

"Like you said, he digs Seth," Dendera said. "If I had time to read through all his scrolls…"

"Put it out of your mind for now," Annippe suggested.

Ty placed his hand on the small of Dendera's back. "I've sent two junior priests to collect Tetisheri's body. I promise to take good care of her."

"That is disgusting." Zezi stuck out his tongue.

Dendera smoothed Zezi's braids. "Tetisheri isn't in her body. Her spirit is free."

"It's still awful," Zezi said.

Annippe asked, "How did Hapuseneb treat you?"

Dendera shrugged. "Fair." She felt the weight of losing Tetisheri pressing down on her shoulders. She wished for nothing but the soul-sister home she shared with Annippe and sweet, dark sleep.

When they reached home, Dendera fell into bed, and Ty placed a cool cloth across her forehead. Annippe tinkered in the kitchen and brought a stone cup full of golden liquid.

Dendera sat up and sipped. "I'm impressed."

"You should be," Annippe said. "You taught me to use chamomile for sleep. Drink and rest."

Zezi sat on the edge of Dendera's lion-carved bed. "Thutmose said you might not be safe here at Karnak." Zezi and Thutmose both wanted her to leave the temple. Tetisheri had never wanted Dendera to come. On her deathbed, Tetisheri had cautioned, "The Dethroners will come after you." She tipped off Zezi too, and even Annippe! What was that about?

Seth's amulet ticked.

I'm almost out of time, aren't I? I have to find the killer before...

Tick. Tick. Tick.

"The temple has become my home," Dendera said. "Besides, where would I go? Tetisheri's house is an empty shell. I'd be vulnerable to attack there if it's true that Hapuseneb or Senenmut want to hurt me."

Zezi said, "I'm not going back there."

"It would be no safer," Annippe agreed. "At least here, we can keep you close."

"I'll stand watch tonight," Ty said. "Tomorrow, we'll find a solution."

"My men will stand watch." Thutmose's stout figure filled the doorway, his nemes headdress falling in stripes to his shoulders. His stance suggested he was prepared for war. He walked to the bedside. "Six sentries are posted outside, and tomorrow we will move you to the palace."

"I must stay here," Dendera said, yawning from the chamomile. "How is Neferura?"

Before Thutmose could answer, Annippe said, "Dendera needs rest," and ushered Ty and Thutmose to the door. "Zezi can sleep on the floor."

"No, let me take him to our place," Ty said.

Dendera heard the four of them making

whispered decisions. It ought to interest her, but they sounded far away. Seth's amulet continued ticking.

All was black, silent.

Dendera parked Ra's Boat of Millions of Years. Her day's work was done.

Tetisheri scaled Khonsu's moon headpiece and slid down the curve of his horn. "I'm watching over you," she said.

Dendera climbed onto the back of a hippopotamus. The beast sprouted wings, and they flew away, navigating Nut's stars.

Ma'at, goddess of truth, meted out justice from her golden throne in the ebony sky. Ma'at upheld one slender finger on which she balanced a single ostrich feather. Behind Ma'at, Neferura glittered, a star in Nut's sky. The hippo swerved. Dendera waved to Neferura, but the wind they made stirred Ma'at's feather.

Dendera grasped with both hands, but the feather slinked through her fingers.

From Nut's nightline, Ma'at's feather descended to Dendera Temple. Dendera and the hippo plunged after it. Mother stood in the temple courtyard. The feather was a wisp away from Mother's clasping fingers when Eshe shoved her aside. Eshe's body bulged, morphed, scaled. Seth, a burning crimson crocodile, widened his jaws and devoured the feather. The hippo landed and Dendera hopped off, craning her neck. The star that was Neferura vanished with a bang.

MAGICIAN RISING

S eth's amulet made a galumphing noise. Dendera bolted upright from her sleep, her stomach twisting in a rope's knot. Neferura was in danger. A picture of a page from *The Dreams of Isis* swam into memory. The hippo in her dream meant death or destruction, and she, Dendera, was riding the hippo. Was it her fault that destruction chased the princess?

Tiptoeing so she did not wake Annippe, Dendera dressed and slipped out the door. It was the hour before dawn, and Thutmose's guards insisted on escorting her past the sleepy houses of the priests, across the fields, and to the Mooring Place of Pharaoh. Dendera ran down the stone pathway lined with frankincense trees.

"Dendera!" Thutmose jogged from a grass field where he and Zezi were practicing archery in Ra's first light. Thutmose handed his bow to an attendant and clasped Dendera's hands. "My pyramid girl."

"I must see Neferura," Dendera burst out, sweaty, windblown, and breathless.

Thutmose stroked her back. "I'll walk you inside the palace. Zezi, you may continue to practice."

"I'm coming," Zezi said. "Bad dream, sis?"

"What are you doing here?" Dendera asked. "Why didn't Ty take you back to the priests' quarters?"

"I couldn't sleep." Zezi shouldered his bow.

"He is ever-welcome." Thutmose dismissed the guards with a wave and led Dendera through the hallways. Zezi opened Neferura's door, and all three of them stopped cold.

Thutmose bellowed at the attendant, "Where is Neferura?"

The attendant emerged from her side chamber, rubbing sleep from her eyes. "The princess was sleeping when I left her." She cowered under Thutmose's gaze, and then peered under the bed and searched Neferura's bathroom.

Hatshepsut appeared in the doorway. "What has happened?"

"Is Neferura with you?" Dendera asked.

"No." Hatshepsut put her hands on her hips. "I will check Senenmut's room. He sometimes sings to her if she can't sleep." She walked away.

"Her clothes are gone," Zezi said, closing the drawer on Neferura's wardrobe chest.

"She took her perfume, her ivory mirror, even the vulture bracelet." Dendera traced the faded lotus blossoms that had fallen on Neferura's table.

Hatshepsut returned to the doorway, pale-faced.

"Senenmut's gone too. His room was empty except for this." She held up a vulture-shaped amulet carved from an ebony cowrie shell. The vulture amulet rumbled. The room shook. Hatshepsut's eyes rolled up in her head. She dropped the cowrie shell which shattered on the floor. Pharaoh crumpled. Tendrils of green smoke billowed up from the shell fragments.

"Blast you, Senenmut." Thutmose scooped up Hatshepsut as if she were a flamingo feather and carried her away.

Dendera started to follow, but Zezi grabbed her arm. "We found someone who casts powerful curses."

"I should have seen this coming." Dendera stared at the ground. This was a disaster.

Zezi cocked his head. "What should you have seen?"

"Neferura looked like she was in a trance the last time we visited, and Senenmut was in her room," Dendera said. "I thought Senenmut might be cursing her, but Hatshepsut trusted him so I let it go."

"You were right to let it go," Thutmose said as he walked down the hallway. "Her physicians are caring for her." He pointed back toward Hatshepsut's room. "Hatshepsut won't hear a word against Senenmut unless she says it herself. If you'd questioned Senenmut, you would have lost Hatshepsut's trust, Dendera, and she has absolute faith in you." He cupped Dendera's elbow. "You are not to blame. Senenmut did this."

For days, Hatshepsut thrashed in bed. Thutmose mobilized his army to search the four corners of

Egypt. After her dream, Dendera feared it was all for naught, convinced either Seth of the desert or the vulture Senenmut consumed Neferura. Hatshepsut did not wake to eat or drink. She slept in unrest, sometimes screaming, sometimes mumbling. Nothing her physicians tried helped.

Hapuseneb insisted Zezi return to his temple duties. Since Zezi was Hapuseneb's favorite, and Ty and Annippe agreed to watch out for him, Dendera believed her brother would be safe. Keeping busy in the gardens or with his chariots and snakes was the best thing for Zezi.

Dendera called Eshe to the palace, but the high priestess couldn't decipher the spell Senenmut placed upon the vulture amulet since it had shattered to pieces. Though her presence did not soothe the pharaoh, Dendera refused to leave Hatshepsut's side.

When Thutmose visited Hatshepsut's room, he rubbed Dendera's back, but she pushed him away. "What is wrong?"

"It is my fault Neferura left," Dendera said. "She saw you kiss me."

"You must not think that way," Thutmose said.

"Senenmut will devour her spirit," Dendera said. "He's more destructive than Seth."

"How do you know Seth will not use his strength to protect Neferura?"

Hatshepsut thrashed. Dendera soaked a cloth in rose water and bathed her forehead. "Pharaoh is burning up." Dendera moaned. Her parents, Tetisheri, and now Hatshepsut, had all fallen. Neferura disappeared. Was it because Seth's amulet was near? Was the amulet truly cursed? She touched her sash where Seth's amulet was double-wrapped for maximum muffling. It scorched her hand.

"Physician Puky says there is nothing to be done," Thutmose said. "He fears she will not recover." He brushed Dendera's cheek. "You never answered me, pyramid girl." He slipped a ring onto Dendera's finger. A pyramid, a lotus, and a crown were carved onto the ring's golden face.

Dendera held up her hand, gazing at the ring. "It's beautiful." She pulled it from her finger. "I cannot accept this." She put the ring on Thutmose's palm and gave the answer Annippe taught her. "My life is the temple."

"When I kissed you, you kissed me back." Thutmose gripped the ring. "I'll keep this until you're ready."

Seth's amulet swooshed, and Dendera felt all of the Nile's power surging through her stone. She asked it, *Are you in control here, or am I?* Her Curse Chasers were right; they were dabbling with the power of both Seth's amulet and Egypt's pharaohs. "Power is intoxicating," she said her thoughts out loud and looked at Thutmose. "You are a powerful man, but Neferura is my friend. I'm the reason she left, and I will not betray her again."

"Dendera, I will be Pharaoh when Hatshepsut dies, and you will be Great Wife."

"I believe Queen Hatshepsut will recover,"

Dendera said. "We have to keep trying. Surely you are not so eager…"

"I am not eager," Thutmose said, glancing at the frail queen in her bed, "but I am ready. Hatshepsut's dream of returning to a matriarchy will not come to fruition."

Dendera gasped.

"Yes, I know," Thutmose said, "she read me the stories when I was young though she probably thinks I have forgotten." Thutmose took Dendera's face in his hands. "The people want a king, conquests, new lands, and riches. I will give the people what they want, but what I want is to make you queen."

Dendera sensed that elusive magic rise up between them. A desert sandstorm whirled inside her stomach, near where Seth's amulet was now spinning, jumbled in cloth. She had allowed herself to bow to Thutmose's power once, but she was determined not to make the same mistake. She pushed him away and turned to Hatshepsut's bedside.

Thutmose once said that he and Hatshepsut ruled side by side, but now he sounded glad to think of a time without Hatshepsut. Dendera recalled the ancient story of Seth killing Osiris. They were family too. Seth claimed he loved Osiris, but he also wanted his power. While Hatshepsut lived, she would always outshine Thutmose. Did Thutmose covet Hatshepsut's power?

"I must speak with my army general." Thutmose tucked the ring in his belt and stroked Dendera's hair. When she remained silent, he left.

Glad to be alone with Hatshepsut, Dendera practiced the meditations she'd read in *Breath of Ba*. Ipi hopped through the window and vaulted to her shoulder. The way Ipi massaged her shoulder with his paws helped Dendera slow her breath and heartbeat. Inhale. *Akh. Ka. Sha. Ba*. Exhale. *Akh. Ka… You will know*. Gazali's words tumbled down like rain. If ever there was a time of need, this was it.

She asked a guard to take her to Tetisheri's. When she returned to the palace, Hatshepsut's room was still empty but for the pharaoh. Ipi looked solemn as Dendera unrolled the bundle she made from one of Tetisheri's old blankets. She stroked Mudada's soft fur.

Raising the panther skin in both hands, Dendera prayed to the only goddess who made a raindrop of sense to her. "Hathor, thank you for the gift Mudada left behind in his death. Help me to use it now to heal your daughter." Dendera pulled back Hatshepsut's bed coverings, placed the panther skin on top of her, and extended Seth's amulet. "Medineta!" Dendera knelt beside Pharaoh's bed. If this didn't save the queen, nothing would. With Gazali's help, she'd done what she could.

Hatshepsut stirred. "Thanks be to Amunet." She propped herself on her elbows, and Dendera threw her arms around her. "Child, how did you heal me?" Hatshepsut leaned back to look at Dendera.

"Gazali, the shaman Senenmut brought from Punt, gave me the panther skin and told me how to use it. I wanted to use it for Tetisheri, but now I know it was for you." Dendera wasn't ready to show Hatshepsut Seth's amulet.

"Did I misjudge the shaman after all?" Hatshepsut mused. "I certainly misjudged Senenmut."

"He brought the source of your healing to Egypt."

"Excellent point, but he also caused the illness in the first place," Hatshepsut said. "I must find a way to keep this from happening again."

"Senenmut's gone." Dendera touched Hatshepsut's arm. "It won't happen again."

"The whispers continue," Hatshepsut said. "Physician Puky saved me a few lucky days ago. Someone slipped a poison into my daily medicines. Puky is an expert on poisons. When he smelled the ruined medicine, he poured it out before it got to me."

"That is lucky," Dendera said, feeling queasy. *Was it Senenmut who tried to poison the pharaoh, or could it have been Thutmose?*

"I must become stronger," Hatshepsut said. "I am queen. My people must see me as invincible." She slipped the panther skin off her legs. "Dendera, you must help me in this quest. You helped Neferura with juniper berries; you understand that incomprehensible baboon; you have visions of the Lady of the Stars; you healed me with magic panther skin. Do extraordinary things always happen around you, even when you don't intend it?"

Dendera didn't see herself nearly as exciting as Hatshepsut described, but she did remember strange happenings even when she was young. She said, "When I was about two, Father locked me on the roof at nightfall. He thought I was in bed, but I was hidden under a blanket on the roof. It was amusing at first, but then I got scared I'd have to spend the whole night alone. I banged on the rooftop door to get inside, but Mother and Father didn't hear. When I wore myself out from screaming and hammering on the door, I sat down and looked up at the stars. I picked out my favorite one, a pinprick in the sky, and calmed down. The star floated down and came to rest here." Dendera touched her pyramid mole. "As I sat looking at the door, I imagined the lock sliding free. Then I stood up and tried the door again. It clicked and creaked open, and I ran downstairs to crawl in bed between my mother and father."

"When you are trained," Hatshepsut said, "your powers will be … I can't imagine how strong. I tell you again, you will be Pharaoh's Magician, and together, we will restore the matriarchy forever. Is there any news of Neferura?"

"None. Thutmose has his armies searching, but she is weak. Senenmut knows nothing of healing. I doubt they took marshmallow root or juniper berries or frankincense oil with them." All the worries and fears Dendera had been holding in tumbled out in a rush, and the mighty pharaoh wrapped her arms around Dendera like any common mother would hold a hurt child. She massaged Dendera's back the way Dendera's own mother used to do.

"You think Neferura has need of this panther skin?" Hatshepsut rubbed the ebony fur.

"She needs healing," Dendera said, "someway, somehow."

"Wherever they are, Senenmut will do his best to take care of Neferura. He fed her meals when she was a baby. Neferura always preferred him." Hatshepsut gazed out the window. "If I could go back in time and raise Neferura all over again, I would. I know so much better now. I wonder if every parent feels that way." She shook her head to clear it like a dog does after a swim in the Nile. "Rest assured, I will leave none of Egypt's sand unsifted. Neferura will be found." Pharaoh's power was returning in measured steps. "We may as well take care of another matter while you are here. It is time for your Priestess Test. You must prove yourself." She paused. "When you pass the test and time appoints itself, I will name you Pharaoh's Magician."

Dendera had forgotten the Priestess Test the same day Hatshepsut last mentioned it — the day she was appointed to Karnak. Looking for the murderer, temple lessons, visiting Tetisheri, taking care of Neferura, and dealing with Hapuseneb's tirades monopolized her time. Dendera craved lazy days to search the House of Life. She needed a clue on where to find the *Book of Thoth*. Djedi's scroll and Seth's amulet weighed heavier than Nut's sky. Droves of unanswered questions haunted her. "I'm not ready," Dendera said by way of summary.

"Do not be concerned," Hatshepsut said. "The Priestess Test is a practical one that indicates you are willing and able to undertake a lifetime of service and study. When you pass this first obstacle, we'll discuss the next steps. When you are a full priestess, Hapuseneb will have no grounds to complain when I ask you to oraculum for me. Are you ready to travel to the city of Dendera?"

"Dendera?"

"Most priestesses test in their home temple," Hatshepsut said, swinging her legs off the bed, "but I believe the city of Dendera calls you home."

CITY OF DREAMS

T hree days passed slower than a turtle paddling against the Nile current. On the fourth morning, Dendera awoke with excited anxiety. It was a lucky day. All her life, Dendera had walked the Theban countryside in homemade sandals. Never before had she left her home, boarded a boat, and sailed the Nile.

Ramla loved to visit Dendera. Tetisheri's words churned in Dendera's mind, slow and determined, as if being honed into shape on a potter's wheel. No doubt, the city held clues to help her discover who killed her parents. Seth's amulet was crabbier than usual. Dendera crooned to it, wrapped it tight in soft cloths, and stowed it in her sash.

She opened her leather traveling bag, a gift from Hatshepsut, and ran her fingers over the cornflower-blue lotus painted on the front before packing her linen shifts inside. The bracelet Hatshepsut had given her long ago rolled across her bed. She could still see it falling from Tetisheri's wrist.

"Ready?" Annippe drew the string on her packed bag.

"I hope." Dendera stuffed the bracelet in her waist sash. She couldn't bear to wear the bauble, but neither could she leave it behind. "What was your test like?"

"My Priestess Test? Easy. I sang hymns and played the sistrum for Eshe."

Dendera would have to demonstrate her healing abilities and scribal skills. *Sssssssss.* Seth's amulet egged her on, and Dendera cringed. Would there be a Serpentology exam?

"Dendera," Annippe said. "I think your only worry during this test is the *Book of Thoth.*"

"Why would that be a worry?"

"It's forbidden," Annippe said, "but Omari knows how obsessed you are with the *Book of Thoth.* If it comes up during the test, avoid it. They'll want to see that you can overcome your temptations."

Dendera frowned.

Thutmose had vied to accompany Dendera on her trip, but Hatshepsut appointed Annippe her travel companion. Dendera considered it lucky. Thutmose would have distracted. She wished Ty and Zezi could go, but Zezi needed to keep an eye on Hapuseneb at Karnak. Ty needed to mummify Tetisheri so they could entomb her next to Mother and Father.

When Annippe and Dendera reached the courtyard, Zezi shot Eerie Eyes at their packed bags.

Ty pulled an amulet from beneath his leopard skin. It was the turquoise stone that brought Dendera's dream in the Crystal House. Ty had carved a baboon on the stone and set it in gold. A tiny glyph for "Curse Chasers" was etched on the side. He winked and slipped the armlet around her upper arm. "May Thoth's wisdom be with you."

"Thank you, friend." Dendera ran her fingers over Ipi's tail and passed by Hapuseneb. The high priest had been a sand grain warmer to her since her speech in his office. He bowed, gold head aglow, Seth amulet swaying.

"Let not your hearts be troubled. My prayers for a safe journey go with you," Eshe said. "Excuse me. Temple petitioners are waiting." Scar and One-Eye stood nearby, watching the scene with interest.

Dendera and Annippe gave Zezi a double hug, but he pushed them away and ran toward the gardens.

At the riverside, Hatshepsut stood giving orders for the boat's captain and crew. They loaded baskets upon baskets of gifts for Dendera Temple. Hatshepsut handed Dendera an ebony box. The sides of the box were etched with hieroglyphs. Hathor held a star in her hand, offering it to Isis, and the sky goddess Nut arched overhead, her midnight gown sparkling with stars.

"Open it," Hatshepsut said. "You will present it to the high priest when you arrive in Dendera." As Dendera opened the box, a deep smoky scent rose.

"My gardeners at Djeser-Djeseru harvested myrrh gum for your trip." Hatshepsut fingered the jewel-brown resin. "May Hathor smile on your journey and your test."

"If you find Neferura..." Dendera said.

"I'll send word." Hatshepsut crossed her crook and flail over her chest, a pharaoh's gesture of blessing.

They boarded Hatshepsut's sailing boat, The Splendor of Maatkare. The vessel was long and thin, crafted of cedar wood, and carved with a rising lotus blossom on the stern. While they stood in the bow, the rowers pushed them into the Nile's strong current.

The vast complex of Karnak was visible from the river. Ty waved from the roof of the temple's largest storehouse, his broad smile sparkling against the cobalt sky. Zezi sulked beside Ty with a massive cobra framing his shoulders. Dendera ran her finger over the railing and the glyph, "Maatkare." Hatshepsut's name meant, "Truth is the soul of Ra." She remembered Zezi wishing for a ride in Ra's boat and promised herself there would be another trip that included Zezi.

As they sailed north of Thebes, the countryside grew wilder and the mud-brick houses sparser. A field of cornflowers framed the riverbank; the grayish leaves formed a perfect backdrop for the blue blossoms.

"The scribes make their blue ink from the juice of that flower." Annippe filled Dendera's mind with small details, anything that might help her pass the test.

"My mother taught me that long ago." Dendera basked on deck, and a gusty wind stirred a swarm of grass jewel butterflies along the shore. They were Egypt's smallest butterflies, and their tan silky bodies gave the impression that the desert sand had taken flight. She leaned over the side of the boat. The rowers slipped their oars through the Nile's shimmering ripples, their work made easy by the boat's ingenious sail and the northward flow of the river.

The Nile's breeze blew the worry from Dendera's mind. Ty and Zezi would continue searching for clues at Karnak. Hatshepsut's power would unearth Neferura. Dendera tried to prepare herself to face the unknown, the Priestess Test, but Seth's amulet's incessant throbbing told her clues waited at Dendera Temple. A baboon chattered nearby, and Ipi appeared, arguing with a sailor.

"Do you know this stowaway?" The sailor laughed, carrying Ipi in his arms.

"He is Karnak's sacred baboon," Dendera answered.

"And he adores Dendera," Annippe said.

"Then you're in charge of him, Miss." The sailor let go of Ipi, and the baboon sprang to Dendera's shoulder. After bleating orders to the rowers, the sailor said, "I am Captain Chuma, and I welcome you aboard, my ladies. Her Majesty has charged me to make it a pleasant journey, and so I shall." He bowed.

"Sir, how will we know when we have reached

Dendera?" Dendera asked. "I have never traveled outside of Thebes."

"By Ptah, that is easy," Captain Chuma said. "North at Dendera, the river cranks a wide bend 'round Ra's sunboat. We set shore on Dendera before the river sweeps us past the bend. From the bank itself, you will know the temple by the carven statues of Hathor that guard it."

By nightfall, the river brought an unfamiliar coldness, and the girls huddled together to keep warm in the tiny cabin off the main deck. The desert's heat was nothing compared to the frigid wind that cracked their bones. The rowers kept a steady nighttime rhythm, slashing their oars through the dense black water. The plop, plop of fish echoed in darkness.

"Can't you warm us up with that amulet?" Annippe rubbed her hands together.

"I can try." Dendera unwrapped Seth's amulet. Though sometimes hot to the touch, the amulet had adopted the night's chill. She said to it: "Khasinge." It burst into flames and Dendera dropped it with a yelp, counteracting the spell with "Netinumb." The amulet froze solid and blasted them with air more frigid than the night.

"Nice," Annippe said.

Dendera next used "Mekhat" which helped balance the two spells. The stone did not provide enough heat to suit either, but it knocked off the chill.

"I've been meaning to try this." Dendera crossed her legs and placed the amulet on the wooden floor.

"Pep mennem." Beside Seth's amulet, three amulets appeared. The original was recognizable due to its age. The newer stones were less battered, and they also lacked the images of Seth on the front and "Hwt-ntr" on the back. "Care to try one?"

Annippe accepted one of the stones. "Hapuseneb would be mortified that I am learning magic."

"Hapuseneb's not here," Dendera said conspiratorially.

Annippe repeated the Khasinge-Netinumb-Mekhat trio, and their secret scribal lessons paid off. Annippe understood the deeper meaning of the spells. With a few tries, she was able to balance the *heka* toward more warmth. After this, they heated all their stones and slept.

Ra's circuital journeys blurred one into another, and along the Nile, dull, sandy shores turned first to grassy banks, and then to forests of palm trees with branches waving in welcome. A vast, angular structure appeared, its flat roof supported by rows of pillars, each bearing Hathor's face.

"This is Dendera temple," Dendera said.

"Right you are." Captain Chuma turned to bark orders to his crew, preparing to pull into the quay. Dendera enjoyed her first trip on the Nile but was glad to set her feet once more upon dry land.

"Hatshepsut ordered the sailors to wait on the grounds until you return. The palm grove will provide a fine camp." Captain Chuma gestured to the trees. "I'll send a few men close behind to deliver Hatshepsut's gifts."

Ipi leapt to his favorite riding place, but Captain Chuma pulled him back. "You'll make a better impression without this beast." The captain shook his fist at Ipi.

Annippe and Dendera started down an uneven stone pathway. "Your mother named you for this place." Annippe patted Dendera's back and handed her the ebony box.

"Yes." Dendera couldn't put words to the nervousness she felt. It was more than her test, more than the queasy way Seth's amulet quavered against her waist. As she and Annippe drew closer to the temple, Dendera began clenching her teeth as if a horse's bit was being pulled tight in her mouth. The paint on Hathor's columns was flaked and worn, making Hathor's face look old and neglected, stars apart from the youthful goddess painted on Karnak's columns. At Karnak, artists worked daily to touch up paint, refresh old scenes, and create new ones. Even in the desert, at Djeser-Djeseru, Hatshepsut commissioned the reliefs of Punt moons ago, but they appeared painted afresh.

The more she looked, the more ashamed Dendera became of Dendera Temple. "Why did Eshe not report this?"

Annippe gave a slight shake of her head, her eyes trained on a knot of priests and priestesses lurking in the courtyard. Amongst the group were Scar and

One-Eye! They were talking with Eshe as she and Annippe were leaving! How did they beat them getting from Karnak to Dendera?

All the priests and priestesses of Dendera wore the same black garb and identical ivory amulets carved with red hippos. Likewise, each of the priests and priestesses in the group, excepting one, bore a grotesque facial disfigurement. The left side of one priestess's face had been burned off. Red-scarred humps dotted another priest's forehead.

Dendera guessed the priest in the center of the group with no deformities was the high priest of Dendera. She approached him and offered Hatshepsut's ebony box filled with myrrh. "A gift from Her Majesty," she said with a bow, but her eyes scanned a nearby pillar. Hathor's nose was chipped away.

"Thank you. I am Ufa." The high priest eyed Dendera's pyramid mole.

Annippe bowed and presented the priest with a basket of dried lotus pods.

Ufa accepted the gift. "Hatshepsut sent word with a Karnak priestess that you are to be tested. She has performed other duties for us here at Dendera and has come to administer your test."

Eshe emerged from the shadows between Hathor's pillars.

"Ah!" Annippe took a step back.

Dendera bowed to Eshe. "Thank you for coming, Mother of Karnak, but why did you not travel with us?"

Eshe embraced Dendera. "Let not your heart be troubled. I believe you will find many surprises at Dendera Temple."

"You have one hour before your test," Ufa barked. "Get it over with, Eshe."

✣ 24 ✣

UNDONE, UNDEREARTH

A short, plump priestess, Mariasha, stepped forward. Jagged scars lined her face: three down her left cheek, four across her right, five zigzagging her forehead. She wrung her hands. "Follow me."

Dendera took her bundle from Annippe, and Mariasha led them through the barren temple. No incense burned. No flowers refreshed the altars. No wab priests swept the floors. At the top of a stone staircase, Mariasha opened a door. "Eshe will come for you shortly. Be ready."

Dendera's stomach rumbled. She wished for a cup of barley beer and a slice of lotus bread, but Mariasha offered no refreshments. Annippe followed Dendera inside and closed the door behind them. "Something's wrong," she whispered unnecessarily. "Why are they all so anxious?"

"I was excited to visit my namesake city, but now

that I'm here…" Dendera shivered. "They were all dressed as *The Dethroners' Discourse* says they'll be."

Annippe sighed.

"You still don't believe in the Dethroners, do you?"

"I've been told the Dethroners are a lie all of my life, but when Tetisheri warned us about them…" Annippe shook her head. "I would have trouble doubting anything she said."

Dendera nodded.

"Temples do adopt unique garb so perhaps that is all this is," Annippe said as if hoping to convince herself. "You must put this out of your mind for now. Focus on the Priestess Test."

"I hope I'm ready for this."

"Hatshepsut believes in you." Annippe pulled her mother's oyster shell amulet from her neck and hung it around Dendera's. "I send Isis with you."

"I can't take this," Dendera said. "It is too special to you."

"Remember me during the test," Annippe said. "Remember I believe in you. Remember the power of Isis goes with you. She will protect you."

The number of amulets now stashed on Dendera's person was beginning to amuse her. She stored Seth's amulet, Dendera's Treasure from her parents, and Hatshepsut's Nut bracelet in her waist sash. Annippe's Isis shell hung around her neck, and Ty's turquoise armlet was wrapped around her upper arm. She hoped the combination of protections would suffice during the test. Dendera washed in the small basin and changed into a clean shift.

Annippe anointed her head with precious rose oil. "You are ready."

There was no sistrum on the table in this stark room, but Annippe wrapped her arms around Dendera and sang a hymn to Hathor, goddess who cares for each person as her own child. Having Annippe nearby was like having a little bit of Mother again. Dendera's thoughts heaped one upon another as mud-bricks stack upon a cornerstone. Mother loved Hathor. Hathor seemed real at Sobek's pool. Dendera needed help. *Ask.*

Bang! Dendera jolted from the house she was building in her mind. The door swung open. Eshe pointed a spidery finger. "Come." Annippe squeezed Dendera's hand.

At the ground level of the temple, Eshe opened a door and led Dendera down a hallway that reeked of trampled, moldy barley. They trekked down another set of stone steps, a hallway to the left, a sharp corner to the right, through an open door, and then descended flight after flight of stone steps. Dendera guessed they were in a secret chamber under Dendera Temple that few knew about. Perhaps it was only used for the testing of priests and priestesses.

Eshe stopped outside two heavy wooden doors emblazoned with the ram's head of Amunet, deep in the belly of the earth. One-Eye slipped a flask of murky liquid on the high table. Scar held open a door, and the two men left.

"Drink." Eshe pointed to the cup.

Dendera noticed with a gasp that Eshe wore a Seth amulet. It was an odd pairing: crocodile-headed Seth against the beaded menat necklace Eshe always wore as high priestess of Hathor.

"Where's the written test?" Dendera scanned the table for a scroll, feather, and ink.

"Your test is a practical one," Eshe said, "and you cannot begin until you drink."

Dendera raised her eyebrows. "Why are things so different at Dendera, Mother of Karnak?"

"Call me 'Mother' if you will. Test time calls for tough. Drink."

On the sides of the cup, the images of Seth and Apophis were painted with cornflower-blue ink. The images of the Destroyer and the Great Serpent did not encourage.

Dendera lifted the cup to her nose. It smelled like slime scraped from the bottom of the Nile and burned. Poppy seeds floated on top of the thick greenish-brown fluid. She took one sip and retched.

"All of it," Eshe ordered.

Holding her breath to avoid inhaling the putrid fumes, Dendera gulped the drink and banged the cup on the table. Her throat was on fire.

Eshe opened a heavy wooden door and stepped aside. "Go. Face what comes."

"Alone?" Darkness ranked alongside snakes in Dendera's mind. She clutched her throat, felt her way along the wall, and stumbled through the open door.

"Strange. Your mother asked the same question."

As Dendera turned in confusion, Eshe slammed the door. *I misheard her. Eshe never mentioned knowing Mother before.* She heard Eshe slide a wooden plank into place.

The tart taste in her mouth — that was lotus leaves. What else did the drink contain? She had read about priestess's rites where hallucinogenic herbs were used, but the priestesses chose which herbs would induce their vision. She hoped there was no cinnamon. Annippe's shell amulet tapped her chest. She forced herself to stand up straight.

The Nile's deep seeped through the stone walls, cold, dark, and damp. In the distance, a sliver of light wavered. Dendera slid along the wall. Creepy sounds of rats scurrying and beetles scuttling across the dirt floor gave her beetlebumps.

As she neared the torch, something slithered across the floor and reared up. A cobra slid its tongue in and out, smelling her. Hapuseneb's high-angst Serpentology lessons flashed in her mind. Zezi would have no trouble with this part of the test. Dendera spit some of the nasty taste out of her mouth.

Tut, tut. She recalled Tetisheri pointing a sycamore branch and scolding Dendera after she yelped at the sight of a sand boa. "Dendera, it smells your fear. Make yourself stronger than the snake. Look it in the eye."

Dendera looked back into blackness, but before her, light. All that stood in her way was the king of snakes. *Ty called you the brave one,* Seth's amulet prodded. Dendera inhaled and gazed into the cobra's eyes. The cobra flared its hood, stuck out its tongue, and beckoned, *come closer. See what I can show you.*

Not wanting to, Dendera knelt in the dirt and looked in the snake's eyes like Zezi would. The torchlight glowed in the snake's pupils, and in the wavering light, she saw her mother dancing in the courtyard of Dendera Temple. A bronze helmet replaced Mother's usual wig of loose curls, but there was no mistaking her eyes, as if she had drunk in all of Hathor's sky with one glance. She sang a hymn praising Hathor for the city. Mother said the name over and over — Dendera, Dendera. She was dressed in a priestess's shift and rattled a sistrum. Paheri watched Mother with unmistakable admiration. Eshe skulked in the background, glaring first at Ramla, and then Paheri. Why did Paheri look at Mother that way? And why did Eshe look jealous of the way Paheri looked at Mother?

The cobra slithered to a door at the end of the hall. The door swung open, and the cobra slipped through. Dendera seized the torch, walked through the doorway, and descended another set of stone steps. A narrow rock hallway led to another wooden door. She pushed it open and peeked inside. In the middle of the room, from the dull floor, a fiery-red sandstorm twirled upright.

Flecks of sand pecked Dendera's skin. Blinding wind flung her hair. The storm died down suddenly, and Seth stood radiant in his muscular human body topped with a crocodile's head. Crimson hair cascaded down his back. His eyes blazed. He cracked his jaws wide and spoke. "I know what you seek." He held out the *Book of Thoth*. "You deserve all the power of Egypt," he tempted. "Take it, Dendera. The secrets of the Nile belong to you."

Dendera felt a golden string pulling her to Seth, drawing her to the book. The book would tell her who killed her parents. Seth's amulet hissed a warning, *remember what Annippe said*, but Dendera ignored it. She walked enraptured until pain seared her foot. She looked down. An ebony scorpion arched its tail underneath her. "Fat-tailed scorpion." She matched the live scorpion to the picture on the *Dreadful Deaths* scroll she'd studied. "Fatal, Omari calls you." Her foot swelled to the size of a melon.

Seth chomped his jaws. "Ignore the pain. Come to me. Come."

Wind howled around Seth. He twirled, restarting his sandstorm. It lifted Dendera off her feet, catapulted her across the room, and spun her inside the eye of Seth's storm. The walls of the room blurred as Dendera spun sideways. The wind blew her about as if she were a dry leaf. She tucked up her knees and held on.

Annippe's oyster shell pounded her chest. *She will protect you.* A beautiful voice sang, "I am Isis, Mistress of Magic and Speaker of Spells. I am accompanied by my seven scorpions."

Whirling inside the twister, Dendera's mind clunked like a broken wheel. Annippe. Isis. Help. House of Life. Hymn Annippe wanted to learn. "O poison of Tefen, enter not into me, come fall upon the ground…" Dendera shouted into the wind, spinning, turning. She called upon Befen, Mestet, Mestetef, Petet, Thetet, and Matet. "In the name of Isis, Mistress of Magic and Speaker of Spells, go no further, come forth and fall upon the ground."

Seth's storm stilled, and Dendera fell in a heap. Dizzy and nauseous, she dry-heaved and was glad Mariasha hadn't offered any food. Her foot throbbed. In the far corner of the room, Isis glowed. Draped in a golden gown, Isis spread her silver wings, and the seven crimson scorpions perched on her lotus headdress each took a turn arching its tail so that her headdress looked as if a wave — a perverse, scorpion wave — was washing over it. Isis glided toward Dendera, hovering above the ground, circling, and arching her wings.

Seth planted his feet hip-width, hugging the *Book of Thoth* to his chest and grinding his crocodile teeth. He stared at Isis with hungry, red eyes, looking as hypnotized as Dendera felt. Isis removed a necklace from around her throat, a black stone on a golden chain. Isis dangled the stone over Dendera's foot. A single grain of black sand fell, and the pain ceased. Was this the Tincture of Isis which Annippe obsessed over?

Wings filled the room and covered the ceiling; Isis flickered amongst starlight. Dendera blinked. In the dungeon under the earth, Nut stretched her body over Dendera like a shield. For a moment, Seth disappeared, and all Dendera could see were the stars shining on Nut's nightdress and melding with Isis's wings.

In the midst of the stars, there on the ceiling of Dendera Temple deep underneath the earth, Hathor arose: The Lady of the Stars spread her arms wide, rattling her sistrum. The three mingled until Dendera saw One. *Mother and Annippe told me. Tetisheri sang it to me. Three Faces of One. Maiden Hathor, Mother Isis, Crone Nut.* Dendera's pyramid mole throbbed, and she traced the three sides of the triangle on her cheek.

Naos. Hathor sang and rattled her sistrum as she withdrew into Nut, and Nut's blue, star-strewn body faded until the ceiling underneath Dendera Temple looked like only a ceiling again. Isis lowered her wings and looked to Seth who was standing stock-still.

He killed and mutilated her husband. How does Isis stay so calm near Seth?

Isis extended her hand toward him, and the *Book of Thoth* floated from his hands to hers. "You may borrow it to learn what you must." Isis placed the *Book of Thoth* in Dendera's hands. "Be careful." The *Book of Thoth* differed from every scroll Dendera had ever seen. Large and square, its leather casing was etched with gold hieroglyphs of the benu bird and baboon.

Tell him to go. Seth's amulet leapt from Dendera's sash into her hand, and she stood. Isis moved behind Dendera and spread her wings. Seth killed Apophis for Ra, dispelled the chaos so Ra could rise, but Dendera wondered if Seth was also where chaos arose in the first place. "Be gone from me, Trickster." Dendera raised her hand and blew across Seth's amulet. When her exhale reached Seth, he vanished.

Caked with red dust and triumphant, Dendera turned to Isis, but she was gone. In Isis's place, a stone archway opened. Grabbing another torch, Dendera walked through and descended the staircase. She emerged in a diamond-shaped room.

A beautiful sphinx statue carved of ivory granite sat in a wall cove. The artist had sculpted a serene face for the sphinx. She rested on her haunches. Dendera strode across the room and perched the torchlight in a red bottle on a table. She walked to the sphinx statue and stroked the cold granite.

The sphinx's hair stood on end. Dendera jerked back. The sphinx sprang to all fours and circled Dendera. Neck down, she had an albino lioness's body: Powerful muscles rippled from her torso, along her back, and down her four legs. Her head was a woman of effortless beauty with smooth, ivory skin, amethyst eyes, and a crown of flowing, sandy mane. She leaned her head back and opened her ruby lips wide, revealing lioness fangs for teeth. The sphinx's roar ricocheted between the walls. Dendera covered her ears. The sphinx paced from one tip of the diamond-shaped room to another. Her voice hypnotized. "Dendera in Dendera: waited long and lost much, for you, we did." The sphinx's eyelashes fluttered.

"That's a statement, not a riddle." Dendera rubbed her throat. Eshe's awful drink made her dimwitted.

"One riddle, you want." The sphinx paced, calculating Dendera. "One answer, you know." The sphinx planted her paws and growled. "One whose name, written was, on these walls appears. Time allotted, falls. Truth, discovers she, chained for years. Corruption, dishonor: Her Majesty's fears. The priests and priestesses, plot they, they shame. Glorious power, crave they, they claim. Unfolds, her mother, her father, forgives. Arrives the daughter, Dendera lives." The sphinx pawed the sandy floor.

Dendera rubbed her temple. "That's another statement, not a riddle."

Whoosh. Flapping wings filled the staircase opening, and an ibis swooped through. Ipi rode its back. The magnificent, snow-feathered bird circled the room three times. Ipi vaulted to Dendera's shoulder. The ibis landed on the sphinx's back. Dendera latched onto Ipi's paw.

Ipi babbled, and Dendera heard the words underneath: The *Book of Thoth* deciphers the sphinx's message.

Use me, Seth's amulet said, resigned. *Remember Djedi's warning about the Book of Thoth: It will bring trouble…*

"…in the form of its guardian Seth," Dendera finished. She placed the stone on the *Book of Thoth*. The benu bird and the baboon on the cover moved. Dendera opened the book, and the pages turned of their own accord, a story in motion. Mural scenes flickered one after another. Images flashed by: Ufa and the other priests and priestesses hid in secret corners of Dendera Temple. They hunched over scrolls on a desk. They plotted and schemed. They defaced monuments to Pharaoh Hatshepsut. They wiped Thutmose's names from scrolls. They craved destruction. More, they coveted power. The story stopped on a page that showed Ramla kneeling before Ufa, beseeching him to stop.

Dendera's head buzzed as if a swarm of bees had taken residence. Tetisheri wasn't raving. The scene she'd seen earlier in the cobra's eyes was true.

Mother snuck away from home and came to Dendera to serve as a priestess. She uncovered the plot — the plot Hatshepsut dreamed about — and attempted to talk sense into Ufa. Were Mother and Eshe friends? Why did Eshe never tell Dendera she knew Mother? Did Father know? One thing was sure, Paheri knew. He knew Mother here at Dendera, and Mother visited him at Karnak. Did he help Mother, or was Paheri her undoing?

Ipi whistled, bringing Dendera back to her surroundings. The sphinx resumed her pacing.

"There is corruption amongst the priesthood here in Dendera." Dendera looked from Ipi to the sphinx.

Ipi inclined his head. *The plot has brewed long to overthrow Hatshepsut. The temple at Karnak is not blameless.* He placed his paw on Seth's amulet.

"Thutmose's army is powerful," Dendera said.

"Weakling, they believe him," the sphinx said.

"Because he rules beside her," Dendera finished.

Nonetheless, it would be quite a coup to overthrow two pharaohs with one swipe. Ipi pawed Dendera's ear.

"I must warn Hatshepsut. Ipi, do you know the way out of here?" Dendera's sense of direction was muddled by Eshe's drink and the maze of winding staircases and hallways. She wished for Annippe's steady sense of direction.

Ipi's mouth did not move, but Dendera heard his words. *Eshe's test is not over. Escape the sphinx.*

"Escape?"

Two parts to the sphinx, two parts to her test, Ipi said.

The majestic woman-cat paced the wall, shaking her mane. "Second riddle, she wants."

Dendera threw caution to the sands. "Lead me out of this temple."

The sphinx sat on her haunches. "For Your Majesty, a riddle: When she has more, fear less, she will."

A message for Hatshepsut: what would she need more of? She had gold. She needed Neferura, but how could that help her fear less? Dendera's mind moved slower than a beetle rolling its ball of dung. Eshe's drink drained her brain. She couldn't have answered if her life depended on it.

It might, Ipi told her.

"Answer, she won't, not now." The sphinx stretched her front paws until her front body was slanted, her rump high in the air.

"I'll pass along your message to Hatshepsut." Dendera bowed.

The sphinx yawned and flicked her paw at Ipi. "Out of the way, baboon."

She says this is your battle, but I'll stay close. Ipi

nudged Dendera. *Run. It's your best chance.* He hopped to a shelf on the wall and watched.

The last thing Dendera wanted was to go nearer the sphinx. She took a deep breath and stuck out a toe. The sphinx's lip curled into a growl. Dendera froze, head spinning. An image of her body, bloodied and motionless on the dusty floor, swam into focus.

The ibis circled over Dendera, rustling her hair, and soared back over the sphinx. The bird left a trail of turquoise smoke as it exited the doorway. Should she follow? Could she make it to the door? Would the sphinx let her walk out? Dendera took a tentative step. The sphinx sneered. She could reach Dendera in one bound. Dendera slid her foot forward. The sphinx bared her fangs.

Dendera had scribed "A Chapter for Being Swift-Footed" for Omari, if only she could remember the glyphs. She lost her nerve and bolted. Before she reached the staircase, the wind rushed. The sphinx snarled. A paw swiped her leg, raking flesh from her thigh. Dendera screamed. She turned, falling backwards, and extended Seth's amulet. No words came. She hit the dusty ground underneath Dendera Temple.

The sphinx slammed a paw into Dendera's chest and pinned her to the ground. It knocked the breath out of her. The sphinx leaned back her head in triumph and roared.

Dendera closed her eyes to shut out those long, curving fangs. She couldn't move, couldn't pull a breath into her lungs, and Eshe's drink played her worst memories in her mind. She remembered being in the Serpent House when Hapuseneb wrenched venom from a cobra's fangs. She felt sorry for the snake, now that she knew how it felt to have part of you stripped away. She clutched her leg. Hot, sticky blood soaked her hand.

Panic blackened Dendera's vision. *Naos*. She could still hear, and a song strummed inside her, that ancient hymn she used to know.

Crek. Dendera opened her eyes. The sphinx shrieked as her face froze. *Crak*. The sphinx raised her paw to strike and stopped midair. *Crik*. The paw changed from white to solid black. Dendera scuttled backward on two hands and one foot. *Crek, Crak, Crik* rang through the chamber. The sphinx transformed bit by bit, white to black, into a slab of ebony wood that appeared chiseled by a master sculptor. A scarlet bowl appeared on the sphinx's outstretched paw, a bowl brimming with smoldering ashes.

25

SEVEN HATHORS

Blood, warm and wet, puddled on the floor. Dendera cradled her leg. Hathor saved her from the sphinx. Naos was her song. Dendera considered the bowl on the sphinx's paw. Frankincense ashes continued burning, sending white smoke spirals into the air, and she remembered sitting under the grand fir trees outside the House of Life, scribing a lesson of a bird and an ancient spell. She blurted, "For she who knows this pure chapter, it means going out into the day after death and being transformed at will."

A flaming benu bird rose from the ashes and spread its wings. *Peep.* The baby bird hopped from its bowl perched on the wooden sphinx's paw to Dendera's knee.

Dendera brushed frankincense ashes from the hatchling's topknot. "Can you show me how to get out of the temple?"

Ipi jumped to the ground and cocked his head to the side, waiting for the bird's answer.

Do you think you are the reason Neferura left? The baby bird hopped from foot to foot.

"What? Neferura, I — yes, she was angry with me," Dendera stuttered and tried to gather her wits. "Neferura was jealous that Thutmose liked me, and I didn't see it. I should never have let Thutmose get close to me. He and Neferura are supposed to marry."

You take responsibility for your actions. The bird fluffed its feathers. *Let Neferura take responsibility for hers.*

Dendera felt weak and dizzy from her gashed leg, and Eshe's drink still muddled her mind. She scooped up the benu bird and cradled her against her chest. She pulled up her white gown which was soaked in red. The room spun. Dendera forced herself to look. Four long jagged lashes marked her thigh. The wounds were deep and perhaps magical. *I'm bleeding buckets. If you can help, now would be the time,* she told the amulet. She propped the *Book of Thoth* against the wall and leaned back on it. *Why can't I sing a hymn and scratch an answer onto a scroll? Why does this test have to be so hard?*

"Kraank. Kraank. Kraank." The bird sang, perturbed.

"I must find my way out of here." Dendera closed her eyes. "Hatshepsut must be warned." Ipi wrapped his paw around her elbow. Dendera stroked the benu bird's feathers. For some reason, it reminded her of Father, her simple, sturdy father.

A motherly voice spoke. "Baruti never understood your mother's desire to be a priestess, but Paheri did."

Dendera's eyes sprang open. "Eshe?"

"I see you met our sphinx," Eshe said and handed Dendera a wad of cloth.

"Thank you for helping me, Mother of Karnak." Dendera winced as she began wrapping her leg.

"Baruti supposed Ramla would be content to grind the barley and care for the garden." Eshe barked a short laugh.

Seth's amulet glowed with gentle heat, sending Dendera a secret: *Your father knew.* Father warned Dendera to stay away from the temple to protect her, but he accepted Mother, flaws and all. "Mother chose her own way." Dendera shifted her leg, trying to get comfortable, and pain shot up to her hipbone. "She didn't impose her needs on him."

"Did Neferura impose her needs on you?" Eshe asked.

"I suppose she did." Whatever herbs were in Eshe's cup weren't fading away. The effects were getting stronger. Her head swirled like clouds in a storm. Her leg throbbed. Dendera guessed this was all part of the test. She used to know a healing spell. What did Djedi call it?

Dendera leaned her head against the wall and closed her eyes. She and Neferura walked together along the riverbank, laughing and flushing a bevy of quail from the thicket. The birds soared into the emerald sky, free and weightless. Their relationship was unfettered. All their worries sank to the bottom of the Nile.

Neferura, where are you? The Neferura in Dendera's dream took her hand and led her around a wide crank in the river bend. They walked together, here in Dendera.

Dendera slid Seth's amulet to the *Book of Thoth* behind her back. She asked, *What is her illness? How can I heal her?* The amulet rolled over in her palm. It soothed her, and the spell came: "Na-Ma'at." Tell the truth.

More images spun through Dendera's mind. Senenmut rocked Neferura when she was a baby. He held an amulet over her and spoke words of dark power. Senenmut placed the black amulet on Neferura's forehead and said, "For your whole life, Neferura, you will be weak. You will be sick. You will depend on me. You will secure my place in Hatshepsut's confidence. You will marry me, fragile, helpless Neferura. Through you, I will claim the throne." Senenmut turned the black amulet on the baby Neferura's forehead so he could stare into the stone's face, carved with Seth's crocodile eye. He intoned another spell. "I place the WadEvil Eye upon you, Neferura. You belong to me."

Dendera's breath caught in her throat. *Senenmut enjoys causing pain,* Gazali had told her.

Eshe stood watching her. "The royals impose their needs on us all, Dendera." She teemed with hatred. "You have become too devoted to Hatshepsut. You have become too powerful to leave unchecked."

"I don't understand," Dendera said.

"The priests at Dendera will take the throne from Hatshepsut," Eshe said.

"Are they the Dethroners?"

"You have done your research, haven't you?" Eshe raised one eyebrow. "Or did the *Book of Thoth* tell you?" She reached behind Dendera's back and extracted the heavy golden book. Dendera clasped Seth's amulet. "The priests at Dendera are a fraction of the group. The Dethroners are scattered across all of Egypt. We have sufficient numbers to secure the throne."

"Hatshepsut wishes peace for all of the people in Egypt," Dendera argued. "She follows the way of the ancient…"

"Queens, yes we know." Eshe spat on the floor. "Hatshepsut wants to be glorified to eternity for returning Egypt to her queens."

"Is Senenmut in league with the Dethroners?"

"We have no need of his sorcery," Eshe said. "He had his own designs on the throne, but that is all for naught. Only our plan can succeed."

"What does this have to do with me or my test? I'm here to serve the temple and my pharaoh."

"You have to choose." Eshe knelt by Dendera. "I've worked so hard to gain your trust. You have inside knowledge of Hatshepsut's plans. You are close to her. You could gather information from her, be more useful to us than any other. Help us overthrow her. Help us contain Thutmose. The Dethroners will grant you powers you never dreamed of."

"I could never," Dendera stammered.

Eshe stood, towering over Dendera, and looked down. "You get out of the temple alive if you agree to join us." Her smile faltered, and then she hitched it back in place. "Those are my instructions from the Superbis, the leader of the Dethroners."

"Ufa?" Dendera's fingers tingled. She rubbed the face of Seth's amulet behind her back.

"No." Eshe shifted from one foot to the other. "Superbis is more powerful still."

"Where is this Superbis?"

"He resides at Edfu." Eshe shook her head. "Enough questions. Your time is up. Join us or die. Your drink was laced with a slow-acting poison." Eshe pulled a stoppered bottle from her belt. "I hold the antidote."

Dendera paled.

"Does it surprise you that I know as much of herb lore as you?" Eshe laughed, colder than Nile's night wind.

"I can't join forces against Hatshepsut," Dendera said. "Think of Hatshepsut's gifts to you, Eshe, the privileges you have as Karnak's high priestess."

"You are more foolish than your mother." Eshe raised the flask in her hand. "Let us toast your death."

"Wait." If there was no way out of the temple, if Dendera was going to die, she wanted the truth first. "Do you recognize this?" She extended her palm and revealed the throbbing stone that bore Seth's face.

Eshe smiled and squatted beside Dendera. "I feared it fell in the house and burned." Eshe snatched the amulet from Dendera's palm. "Did your friend Tetisheri know of the amulet? I gathered she knew too much when I visited her. I laced her drink with Slow Death, the same poison I used on you." She threw the flask to the floor, and the antidote splashed and sprayed in all directions.

A tear rolled down Dendera's cheek. *Tetisheri.*

"Let not your heart be troubled. Before you die, I will tell you a story." Eshe turned Seth's amulet on her palm. "There is a long tale behind this stone. I will make it brief. The amulet belonged to Djedi. He was the greatest magician Egypt has ever known, but he chose the wrong side. It was he who formed the Knights of Kemet to oppose the Dethroners. The struggle for power between the Knights and the Dethroners has burned ever since." Eshe nodded. "I discovered your mother had taken possession of the stone about the time I learned she too was a Knight of Kemet."

Propping the *Book of Thoth* on the floor, Eshe sat on it like a stool. "Perhaps, this part, I will show you." She pulled a jade stone from her menat necklace, held it to her temple, and spoke a word of power. "Memoramut." Eshe held the stone on her palm, and above her hand, images flared to life in midair, telling Dendera a story with moving pictures:

Shovel-cut canals carried water to the family garden. Eshe walked alongside Father's vines which were swelling with melons and grapes. She broke off a cedar limb and lit it with a torch she'd carried from Karnak.

Under the sycamore tree, Mother stretched her legs. She cradled a blue-bright bloom on her lap. A twig cracked. Mother wielded a crimson stone, whispered, and the lotus disappeared as if the wind swallowed. Mother jumped to her feet and ran toward the house. "No!" Flames licked the mud-brick roof. "Dendera! No!" She flung her skirt over her head and bolted through the blazing door.

Mother heard Father hacking, staggered toward the sound, and threw her arms around his neck. "She's coming," Mother said. "Is Dendera?"

"Dendera's safe. I sent her and Zezi to the forest." Father put his arm around Mother's shoulders, and they crouched low to the ground. He led her to the children's room. "We can climb out the window." Father coughed and covered his mouth. "Let's barricade the door first." Mother and Father pushed the beds into place and turned toward the window.

Eshe tiptoed behind them. She'd been hiding in a corner of the room, watching the scene. Eshe wielded a hawk-brown stone and uttered a spell. First Mother, then Father crumpled to the ground. Eshe wrenched the red stone from Mother's fingers. Eshe held up her hawk-brown stone and said, "Repetiteri." Mother and Father's voices began speaking as if from thin air, though their bodies were still, and their lips didn't move.

Smoke tendrils billowed up from Eshe's hand. Her storyboard dissipated.

Dendera's eyes flooded. Call me 'Mother,' Eshe had said to her face, knowing she'd already killed

Mother and Father, knowing she planned to deal Dendera a deathblow. The night of the fire, it wasn't life that stabbed Dendera in the gut; it was Eshe.

"Torching your home served a dual purpose." Eshe's eyes swirled cinnamon, like poison to Dendera. "I needed the stone. Ufa needed Ramla to stop blabbing his secrets at Karnak. It's lucky no one believed her. We raise young priests and priestesses on the belief that the Dethroners are an old fairy tale. It took the Superbis many years to locate the *Throw Up Texts*, which contains many secrets. It even told our leader you were the way to obtain the *Book of Thoth*." Eshe stood and extended her arms in triumph, Seth's amulet in one hand, the *Book of Thoth* in the other. "All power is ours. Overthrowing Hatshepsut and Thutmose will be effortless."

Heat surged from Seth's amulet. Eshe dropped it, wincing and holding her scorched palm. The stone bounced into Dendera's hand and blew, cooling itself.

In the center of the room, a swirling sandstorm arose, and at its center stood a muscular man with a crocodile head. Seth pointed, drew Eshe inside the whirlwind, and she began spinning. Eshe closed her eyes and hugged the *Book of Thoth* to her chest. The sandstorm blew the wig from Eshe's head. Her menat necklace fell and shattered. Seth's eyes blazed as he pointed at Eshe's chest. He gnashed his teeth. "Thief, you hold what does not belong to you!"

"Give him the book, Eshe!" Dendera pushed herself upright, balancing on one leg. She extended Seth's amulet and shouted, "Relinquinet!"

Eshe screamed, "Khepawae!"

The sandstorm died, but Eshe kept hold of the *Book of Thoth*.

Seth looked at the ceiling as though he could see the sky beyond it. He shouted "Ra!" Spit flew from his jaws, and he began whirling his sandstorm around himself. He flicked his wrist, unleashing a blast.

Dendera slammed into a wall and flumped unconscious. For one sweet moment, she had relief; all she saw was blackness. Then stars began popping on the backside of her eyelids, first one, then a few, and then all Dendera saw was white light. Her eyes slid open to temper the brightness. Eshe's flowing shift disappeared around the corner of the staircase. Dendera curled her fingers into a fist. Seth's amulet was gone. *Did Eshe take it, or Seth?*

A wooden plank slid into place.

What a mess I've made. Dendera curled up like a child and cradled her leg.

The benu bird landed next to her and brushed her cheek with its wing. Ipi fished in Dendera's sash.

"Leave me here." Dendera pushed Ipi away. "Go to Pharaoh's palace."

Ipi cawed. *No.* He placed something small, hard, and cold on Dendera's forehead. It was Dendera's Treasure, the ammonite she'd found walking with her mother and father.

"If Eshe got the *Book of Thoth* and Seth's amulet, the Dethroners will overthrow Hatshepsut." Dendera prodded Ipi. "Go. I'm not afraid. Hatshepsut is my queen. Warn her."

Where you stay, I stay. Ipi closed Dendera's eyelids.

Grains of sand stirred against Dendera's face. Wind rushed in the room underground. The breeze wrapped around Dendera, embraced her. *Hathor, help Hatshepsut. Protect her, protect Egypt.*

A voice on the wind said, "Those who love me, I love. Those who seek me, I find."

The benu bird flew to a stone perch on the wall. Beads rattled. Ipi pushed Dendera upright. *Look.* A sistrum was nestled in the wall. Dendera reached up and rubbed Hathor's face on the sistrum, Hathor's faces. Her head swam. She blinked. There was one sistrum with seven faces.

Seven faces moved away from the sistrum, spread along the wall. Below the faces, seven bodies were inked in as if a wall painting was being etched as Dendera watched. Dendera thought Karnak's finest artist could not have drawn a lovelier painting of Seven Hathors. Dendera still felt light-headed from the herbs Eshe made her drink, but she was sure the wall mural was moving. Seven Hathors were stirring along the wall. Was she about to see another story in motion?

This is no story, Ipi said.

One by one, Seven Hathors stepped from the stone wall and stood gazing upon Dendera.

Hathor was Light. She filled Dendera's field of vision as if Dendera had just glanced at Ra's sunboat. In that blinding light, a beautiful, feminine figure held up a mirror. She smiled at the reflections of her sisters, herself. She leaned over and held the mirror in front of Dendera's face. "What do you see, daughter?"

"You." Dendera could not tear her gaze from Hathor's face, not even to look in her mirror.

Ma'at caressed Dendera's leg as softly as Mother would have, and as Ma'at moved, the air swirled. Dendera wrenched her eyes from Hathor and turned to Ma'at. She was goddess made of air, from her wispy, blowing hair to her powerful, churning body. "She cannot see. Her leg hurts so." Ma'at loosened a feather from the benu bird's tail. She balanced it on the tip of her translucent finger and ran it along Dendera's thigh. "Medineta." The skin on Dendera's leg crawled and stretched, mending itself.

Dendera rubbed her thigh which looked as clean and new as baby's skin. "Did you give that spell to Djedi?"

Ma'at laughed and leaned toward Dendera's ear. "I whispered to him on the wind." Breeze twirled through the chamber. Ma'at was Breath-Ever-Blowing. A storm crossed her face. "Stronger winds approach, daughter."

Sekhmet stepped forward. Dendera's tongue lodged in her throat; she shivered and thought of the mauling sphinx.

Sekhmet's voice was the rushing river during Inundation. "Fear nothing, daughter." Sekhmet was Warrioress, Mother Fierce, womanly hourglass cloaked in red surmounted by a lioness's head framed with blue mane. "Prepare for battle. When the time comes, ask the night for help." Sekhmet threw back her head, parted her jaws, and roared.

Dendera's head spun. She remembered being on the rooftop, a young girl locked out. "I will come," Hathor sang.

And Darkness came. Dendera squinted in the black chamber underneath Dendera Temple. Nut was Night, an azure-skinned woman, a crone who grew ever-young and ever-wise. Her cobalt hair — dotted with moons, meteors, and planets — drug the floor behind her. Her eyes were stars that traveled toward Dendera's pyramid mole. A door opened in her mind. A younger Dendera ran toward the warmth of her mother and father. Goddess was with her that night on the rooftop when she was locked out and alone. "I am with you always, to the end of starlight." It was Hathor who sang, or Nut, All, or One.

The next Hathor stepped forward. She was Wadjyt, Life, dripping green, emerald hair braided with cobras. "Daughter, arise…*sssssssss*," and her hiss echoed around the chamber. Dendera would never disobey that voice. She stood on wobbly legs. Wadjyt uncoiled a cobra from her head. The snake wound around Wadjyt's arm and wiggled out of its old skin. Wadjyt stroked its tender new body with a green finger. "She is born anew." Instinct told Dendera to bolt; she forced herself still. *Hisssss*. The cobra licked the sistrum. A blue-bright bud was born; it peeked above the stone. The stem climbed. Petals plumped and stretched. The Lazuli Lotus bloomed.

Dendera traced the silken petals and looked into

the Light, into the aura blazing around Hathor, and the goddess inclined her head. Dendera plucked the lotus from the stone wall. Mother had this bloom the night she died. Dendera tried to pry from memory the story Mother told.

Seshat, the Law, stepped forward, her dress layers of papyrus whispering, whispering, whispering the answers to every question ever asked. Dendera wished she had until the end of time to do nothing but sit near Seshat and listen. Seshat bowed her head, topped with a seven-star-headdress, and blessed the lotus with the Scroll of Wisdom in her hand. "Use it well. The lotus can join with Strength's Stone for a short time. It will grant the power you need for this night."

Dendera bowed. "You wrote the *Book of Thoth*, didn't you?"

"Of course, daughter." Seshat stroked the benu bird. "It was my gift to Thoth."

"And Djedji's scroll?"

"I told Djedi what to scribe. He recorded as Ma'at blew," Seshat said.

At once, Sekhmet roared, Ma'at's breath circled the chamber, Wadjyt hissed, the sistrum rattled, and someone said, "Pull." *Click*. Dendera pulled the sistrum, and a door opened. Behind the door, a wide staircase rose, twisting and turning up and up, leading the way out of the depths of the earth underneath Dendera Temple. Dendera stumbled. The herbs in Eshe's drink worked still. She'd never be able to climb all those steps.

Isis, shimmering golden from her hair to her eyelashes to her sandals, stepped forward and spread her silver wings.

Good, Dendera thought. *I could use another drop of Tincture of Isis.*

"Wingwadi." Isis spoke the word of power.

Something tickled the insides of Dendera's shoulder blades. She shook her shoulders and stretched her neck side to side. Her back prickled as if feathers were brushing her, and beetlebumps popped up along her forearms. It felt as if something huge, bony, and soft was being pulled from between her shoulder blades. She looked over her shoulder, and wings — strong, soft, ivory wings wider than dreams — stretched from her shoulder blades, lengthened until they dusted the floor behind her. *Now this is alchemy*, Dendera thought.

"Heal yourself of the poison, and then be ready," Isis said.

"Seven Reflections of One." Hathor turned her mirror.

This time, Dendera looked. In Hathor's mirror, Dendera stood beside Hathor, and Hathor draped her arm over Dendera's shoulder. It was like looking at herself through Hathor's eyes. The both of them had copper hair and sand-gold eyes. Dendera looked away from the mirror and into Hathor's face which still shone like moonlight. "You are the pure chapter."

"And you know me, daughter." Hathor set down her mirror, pulled a red ribbon from her hair, and tied Dendera's hair with it. "I am with you always."

Hathor scratched the top of Ipi's head, and light danced around her fingers. She smoothed the benu bird's feathers, and the bird surged from hatchling to adult, sunset red with a gorget of white.

Kraank. The benu bird flapped her tail and flew up the staircase. Ipi hopped on the bottom step. Dendera transformed at will, a new being reborn. Her wings unfurled. Her wings were the strength, the determination of Isis.

Whaash. When the wings rose, they towered over her head.

Whuush. When they fell, they grazed her ankles.

Ma'at blew, and Dendera's own feathers dusted her cheeks. *Whaash. Whuush. Whaash. Whuush.* Dendera's feet lifted off the ground. She was flying! Higher and higher, Dendera flew up the stairs. *Whaash. Whuush. Whaash. Whuush.*

She'd spent all night wrenching pieces of a puzzle into different parts of her mind. Isis's wings whisked away all worry. Dendera didn't think; she soared. *Whaash. Whuush.* They reached a wooden trapdoor built horizontal against the land. The benu bird pecked at the wood. Dendera's wings rose and fell, *whaashed* and *whuushed*, keeping her aloft. Ipi jumped toward the trapdoor, shoved, and the door flopped open. The benu bird raced starward. Dendera flew past the last step, and Isis's wings vanished. Ma'at's breeze rushed to cushion her, and she landed in a field of rustling barley stalks. Dendera raised her head. On top of a hill in the distance, four dark figures waited.

❦ 26 ❦

MAGIC DUPLICATED

Dendera lifted her head and blinked. One of the figures raced down the hill, a woman in a flowing white sheath. Neferura! She would be reunited with Neferura here in Dendera. They would walk along the riverbank like they did in her dream.

As the woman drew nearer, Dendera realized she was running with more strength and agility than the feeble princess ever mustered. Dendera's disappointment evaporated when Annippe flung her solid, safe arms around her, cradling her head. She said, "You've been underneath the temple all night."

Then Zezi and Ty were hugging her and the other person, a man draped in panther skin, plodded toward her. A large black panther slinked alongside him. Gazali's green cat-eyes pierced Dendera's, and all went dark.

"She is ill," Annippe whispered.

"Poison," Dendera croaked. She wanted to look, but her eyelids felt heavier than two hippo's feet.

"I have rue," Gazali said, rummaging in his bag.

Ty swept his fingers over Dendera's eyebrows. "Hold on, brave one."

Ipi pawed her.

Annippe held her hand. "Why does she have a lotus?"

"Why is her gown bloody?" Ty asked.

Zezi opened Dendera's mouth, and Gazali placed a bitter leaf on her tongue. She gagged.

"When the leaf dissolves, swallow." Gazali covered Dendera in a heavy shawl and chanted in a foreign tongue. "Randeelongoo. Randeelongoo." Dendera smelled something animal. "Randeelongoo. Randeelongoo," Gazali chanted on.

Dendera's mind cleared as a sliver of Khonsu's moon peeked from behind a cloud. She was covered in Gazali's own panther skin. The live panther licked Dendera's hand. "Her name is Napata," Gazali said. "She is my new companion."

"We must return to Thebes." Dendera's voice rasped from the bitter herb. "I have to warn Hatshepsut."

"Did you find out who dropped the amulet?" Zezi asked. "Do you know who the murderer is?"

"Eshe."

"Eshe?" Zezi, Annippe, and Ty said at once.

"She and Ufa are Dethroners."

"The Dethroners are not..." Ty said.

"It can't be Eshe," Annippe said.

"Where is Seth's amulet?" Zezi interrupted.

Dendera sat up, and Ipi bounded to her shoulders. "With Seth or Eshe, and it was Djedi's. Seshat called it Strength's Stone. It holds powerful magic."

"Any fool knows that," Zezi said, "the way it thumps and bumps and carries on. Let's get it back."

"Dendera is too weak," Annippe said.

"I'll carry her to the ship," Ty said, scooping Dendera in his arms.

"Carry her to that pyramid we found," Zezi said. "She'll be safe there, and the rest of us can search for the amulet."

"There's a pyramid?" Dendera asked.

"It looks similar to the one by the House of Sycamore at Karnak," Annippe explained. "We found it when we were trying to find a way inside the temple from the backside."

"Show me," Dendera said, staving off Zezi and Gazali's complaints. "Put me down. I have strength for this."

Zezi pointed toward the temple. "The temple's on fire!" Clouds of smoke puffed low and wide across the landscape.

"It's the amulet," Dendera said.

"You're loopy!" Zezi yelled and took off.

The rest raced behind Zezi toward the wall of smoke. Eshe stood in the center of the crackling flames, wincing and shuffling the burning amulet palm to palm. Ufa stood to the side yelling instructions and flipping pages in the *Book of Thoth*.

Eshe's two henchmen, Scar and One-Eye, stood nearby, ogling the scene.

Dendera glared at Eshe, the kindest of her mentors at Karnak. She'd learned so much from her. *She left Mother and Father to burn. She poisoned Tetisheri.* She extracted the duplicate amulets from her waist sash, passing them to Ty, Annippe, and Zezi, and the movement caught Eshe's eye.

"No one will stop us now." Eshe aimed Strength's Stone, but the stone jerked her hand to the side. Eshe grasped the stone with both hands and targeted Dendera. A wavering string of flame erupted.

The Lazuli Lotus quivered in the wind, and Dendera raised it. "Quensu." The fire vanished with a wisp. Eshe gawked.

Ufa tucked the golden book under his arm and charged toward Dendera, but Napata sprang between them. The cat jumped high and kicked Ufa backward. Ufa slammed into Scar and One-Eye, and the three priests sprawled in a tangle on the grass.

Zezi, Ty, and Annippe hurtled toward Eshe. The curtain of smoke surrounding the amulet thickened, and a blazing sandstorm descended from the clouds. Ra's boat glowed in the morning sky, and Seth appeared for the third time. His human form was topped with a regal hound's head. Did Seth want the amulet or Thoth's book? Dendera had to choose between Eshe and Ufa.

Ty said Isis would give the *Book of Thoth* to one who was worthy, but Isis told Dendera to borrow the book, not keep it. Dendera wracked her brain. Djedi said Seth was the guardian of the *Book of Thoth*. She had to return it, but did Seth want Strength's Stone too?

She hesitated, and then rushed toward Ufa. Napata clamped her jaws over Ufa's forearm, and Dendera wrestled the *Book of Thoth* from his hands. Dendera turned and lobbed it. The golden book turned end over end, whistling through the air. Seth opened his snout and swallowed it whole. He then turned on the spot, and the air twirled crimson with him. He disappeared with a *narrrr*.

There. Seth's satisfied with the book, at least for now.

When Napata released her hold on Ufa's arm, the priest jumped up and ran. Gazali pointed. Ty and Annippe wrestled Eshe to the ground while Zezi tried to prize the blistering amulet from her fingers. Scar and One-Eye joined the fray.

Ipi bellowed. *Call it back*. Dendera's pyramid mole throbbed.

"Comnamun." Dendera extended the Lazuli Lotus to the amulet. "I am Djedi's heir." The smoking stone flew to her, and she soothed it until it rolled over on its back. Ty, Annippe, and Zezi were so shocked by Dendera's words that they loosened their hold on Eshe. She pushed her way free and hurried after Ufa.

One-Eye pointed to Dendera and shrieked, "It's her!" He and Scar jumped up and rushed in the opposite direction, heading for the countryside.

"Stop Eshe!" Zezi shouted.

Dendera regarded the amulet on her palm. She held the power to end Eshe, here and now. She remembered the spell from Djedi's instructions. She could avenge Mother and Father.

"The murderer came back." Zezi shot a warning with his eyes. "Your amulet said she would. Eshe tried to kill you under that temple."

Zezi was right. This was what Dendera had been searching for, planning for, waiting for. Eshe should burn. Dendera considered the stone which continued to emit a feeble stream of smoke. She closed her eyes. "Djedi wouldn't want me to use the stone that way. Mother wouldn't. Even Tetisheri told me to use it for peace."

"We could trap Eshe and Ufa," Gazali suggested.

"And turn them over to Hatshepsut," Dendera said.

"We need help," Ty said.

"We don't have time to get help," Annippe said.

Napata growled.

"Hold them, girl." Dendera wielded Seth's amulet. "Resenrage."

As Napata turned and bounded toward Ufa and Eshe, her legs began to stretch. Her body elongated from her head to her tail, and her tail grew longer to balance her powerful strides. Her belly bulged rounder. Her muscles swelled and rippled along her torso. Napata grew larger than a bull elephant. As her legs continued to grow, she ran faster and faster. She bounded higher and higher.

Zezi held his amulet aloft and shouted "Shemzapsu!" A bolt of lightning appeared in midair, sizzled and spit, and then split the ground in front of

Eshe and Ufa. Zezi punched the air. "That's my favorite spell!"

Eshe and Ufa swerved to run along the cleft in the earth, heading toward a grove of palm trees. Huge, hulking Napata nipped at their heels.

Annippe screamed, "Khasinge!" The palm trees burst into flames.

Eshe and Ufa were hemmed in on three sides by broken ground, flaming palms, and a super-sized roaring panther. They knocked each other to the ground in their desperation to make for the shoreline.

Call on Night. Sekhmet told her to ask the night for help. Dendera placed Strength's Stone in the Lazuli Lotus. The red stone rocked back and forth on the seed pod until it settled in the center. Dendera looked to the stars and picked out her favorite. "Mamma Nut, send help."

Ty looked from Dendera to the lotus to the sky. He pointed his amulet to the night. "Khonsumes."

Nut swung her skirt to the side. The full moon emerged from the clouds, and underneath it, the ram-headed god Khonsu. He stomped across the sky, carrying the moon between his horns, and thunder rumbled. He pointed with his spear, and Napata pounced. With her added girth, the panther had no problem pinning Eshe and Ufa to the ground. Khonsu fixed his gaze upon Dendera, and she knew what must be done.

Balancing the Lazuli Lotus with Strength's Stone nestled in its center, Dendera moved her palm through the air in a large moon-sized circle. The spell came: "Shenammanesh." A silver wisp escaped Strength's Stone. It swelled like a raindrop growing larger and larger as it flew through the air. It swirled silver like the moon, forming craters and ridges, and circled Eshe and Ufa, bulging rounder and fatter, and Napata lunged after them, still in the heat of the chase. It pulled all three up into the air, suspending them above the ground in a moving circle. *No.*

"What are you doing?" Zezi yelled and grabbed Dendera's arm.

"Napata!" Gazali screamed.

27

THE SECRET LIFE OF TWINS

"Wait! Wait!" Dendera pulled her arm free of Zezi, pulled the Lazuli Lotus close to her chest, and stared at Napata. *Free her.* The swirling moon shape boinged, pushing Napata out.

Napata sprang toward the ground, and the Moon Prison closed the gap where the panther escaped, clamped shut like a giant mouth around Eshe and Ufa. They pushed and kicked. The sides of the Moon Prison churned with silver eddies, but no matter what obscenities Eshe and Ufa screamed at Dendera, her spell held them tight. Napata bounded toward Gazali, shrinking in size as she ran, and returned to her normal size as she circled Gazali and ducked and flicked his hand onto her head, inviting him to scratch her ears.

"What did you do?" Zezi asked.

Ipi squeezed Dendera's shoulder, and she looked skyward. The moon slipped behind a cloud. Khonsu had returned to wherever it was he came from. Nut sparkled still. "Djedi called it the Loop of Limited Space," she said. "He never had to use it but told me I might."

"What do you mean, he told you?" Annippe planted her hands on her hips. "He lived and died many reigns ago."

"I found his instruction scroll." The amulet jumped from the Lazuli Lotus to Dendera's palm, bucking back and forth. "It's lucky I don't hate this thing anymore." She closed her hand on the stone, and it simmered.

"I still say that rock is cursed," Zezi said.

"Strength's Stone, and Seth, are cursed with protection." Dendera squeezed the amulet. "We need to get to Hatshepsut."

"What if they escape?" Ty pointed to Eshe and Ufa.

"The spell is temporary," Dendera said, "but it should hold them until Hatshepsut decides their fate."

Zezi frowned.

"Seth has the *Book of Thoth*, and we've got Strength's Stone," Dendera said. "They can't use its power. Eshe wasn't able to hold it the night she burned down our home, and she couldn't hold it tonight."

"Djedi meant it for you," Gazali said.

"Or for my mother. Eshe took the amulet from Mother the night she torched our home." Dendera looked into their confused faces. "Eshe said the

Dethroners discovered the secrets of the amulet. Scar and One-Eye hold some of Djedi's magic. That's how they eat so much."

"Maybe that's why they bought all those amulets from Eshe," Zezi said.

Dendera shrugged. "The details will unfold as we need them."

Annippe ran her fingers over the petals of the Lazuli Lotus. "What's its story?"

"I wish I could remember," Dendera said. "Mother told me once." Strength's Stone rocked. Dendera remembered Eshe using her jade stone to tell the story under the temple. It stung Dendera that Eshe was still teaching her, but she slipped the stone to the center of the lotus. "Will you tell your tale? Memoramut."

Ma'at's breeze rustled the Lazuli Lotus's petals, and a moving stream of images shot into the air, cradled by the lotus. An artist appeared to draw the scenes in midair, one by one, and Strength's Stone narrated:

In the age of the sycamore, a scribe traveled to the Field of Reeds so that he might record what he saw there before his time was due. As the scribe approached Hathor's sycamore, Goddess leaned from her tree of life, extended her fingers to the Nile, and plucked a lotus. The sky darkened, and Nut drenched the lotus bloom with night. Thus, the Lazuli Lotus was born of day and of night. Hathor loosened a

crimson stone from her necklace, planted it in
the center of the lotus, and handed the gift to
the scribe.

Z ezi gasped and pointed from the picture in
midair to the red stone tucked into the Lazuli
Lotus on Dendera's palm.

"You removed the stone and put it back," Annippe
said. "Why?"

"Seshat said they can be joined for a short time,"
Dendera said, "but they are only to be used together
on Hathor's command."

Strength's Stone sizzled and sparked. An image of
Hathor speaking to the scribe rolled through the air
above the Lazuli Lotus, and Strength's Stone spoke:
"Hathor gifted the Lazuli Lotus to the scribe and gave
instructions for its use. The scribe returned to the
temple, and following Hathor's advice, removed the
stone from the center bloom and planted the lotus on
the sand. Images scrolled. Where the scribe planted
the lotus, a sculptured pair of stone hands sprouted
from sand. "On the sculpture grown from sand and
lotus, the scribe will place a scroll to guide a future
one to the city where people fear time and time fears
pyramid."

Wind blew across the story board over the lotus,
and the images died. Dendera removed Strength's
Stone, clasping the lotus in her other hand. "Let's get
to this pyramid you found. We must warn Hatshepsut
about the Dethroners."

"Captain Chuma can take us back to Thebes."

Annippe rubbed Dendera's back. "You're still disoriented from the poison."

"The pyramid is a passageway," Dendera explained. "Djedi taught me all about it."

"She's jumped to the Nile deep." Zezi lolled out his tongue.

"My brave one…" Ty smoothed Dendera's hair.

"Trust me," Dendera said. "It's on that hill, right?"

Gazali eyed Dendera, took her arm, and led the way past the hill where Dendera had first seen the four of them waiting outside the temple. Napata edged her head under Dendera's hand, and Dendera stroked her while they walked. Gazali stopped short of the stone pyramid that stood just taller than Dendera.

Realizations dawned on Dendera the same as if one senet game piece fell and knocked down the others in quick succession. Djedi repeated it over and over in his scroll: "People fear time — time fears pyramid."

The pyramid had to be what Tetisheri and Mother called Three Faces of One, or Hathor, Isis, and Nut. Dendera ran her hand along each side of the pyramid, searching the hieroglyphs, and found the ones she knew would be there, the ones she'd read in Djedi's scroll. "People fear time — time fears pyramid."

But Sekhmet told her to fear nothing. People feared time because bad things happened in time. Parents died. Harvests were ruined. Hopes were dashed. Why would time fear pyramid though? That had to be because pyramid stood forever. Time had no power. If Hathor was real, she'd always be real, whether good things or bad things happened in time. The strange thing was that Father had it right too. He might've said kindness stood forever. Kindness meant living in peace when times were good and living in peace when times were bad. That was also what it meant to fear nothing. To know this truth was one thing, Dendera thought, to practice being fearless... that would take a lifetime.

"People fear time — time fears pyramid." Dendera outlined the pyramid mole on her cheek. "This is Djedi's secret passageway." Dendera was confident it would lead to where Seven Hathors were honored, where the sculpture of the stone hands used to hold the scroll that was tucked in her sash.

Ty, Annippe, and Zezi stood slack-jawed. Gazali said, "Lead the way."

Dendera stepped back and brandished Strength's Stone. "Portalis Waset."

One third of the pyramid melted away, leaving an open doorway. Dendera stepped inside and called back, "It's safe. It will lead us to Karnak."

As they stepped inside the dark corridor, the doorway behind them sealed shut. Space expanded. The triangular walkway's smallest point stretched above them. The pyramid swelled until it was large enough for all of them to stand side-by-side and walk arm-in-arm if they wished. Strength's Stone burned to give them light, and while they walked, Dendera told most of what she'd learned that night under the belly of the temple.

"She tried to kill you," Zezi said, shaking his head. "Eshe poisoned you."

"She did," Dendera said, "but the drink magnified everything that happened during the Priestess Test. It made me so dippy that I wasn't as scared of the sphinx as I should have been. It took Strength's Stone, the *Book of Thoth*, and Eshe's drink to help me understand how to heal Neferura, that Mother was a priestess, that the Dethroners wanted to overthrow Hatshepsut, that Hathor could help us stop them." She held up the Lazuli Lotus. "What Eshe intended for bad turned out good."

Dendera stopped and faced Annippe. "When my mother visited the temple, did your father make love-eyes at her or something? I mean, did he ever tell you he was in love with her?"

"No," Annippe said. "He treated her like any other petitioner."

Gazali feigned interest in his lined, calloused hands.

Zezi punched Gazali's arm. "What do you know?"

"Paheri might not want me to tell you this," Gazali said.

"But we have a right to know," Zezi said.

Gazali looked between Dendera, Zezi, and Annippe. "Dendera's mother and Zezi's mother was also your mother, Annippe."

Dendera looked into Annippe's startled eyes, Mother's eyes.

Annippe shook her head. "This cannot be true." Ty wrapped his arm around her.

"When was she born?" Zezi asked. "How did our father not notice that?"

Gazali shuffled his feet. "Annippe's father is Paheri, and Dendera's father is Baruti, but you two are twins."

Annippe and Dendera gasped at the same time and grasped each other's arms.

Gazali continued, "It is an improbable occurrence, but not impossible. Your mother's decision was difficult. Baruti needed her more. Paheri begged Ramla to let you be raised in the temple, Annippe, and he asked her not to contact you. He wished to protect you, and Ramla wished to hide the truth from Baruti. So Ramla agreed to keep her distance, but she caught glimpses of you each time she visited the temple. She also tried to keep her secret from Baruti by confining her priestess life here in Dendera."

"How could Mother keep this from us? She's my sister too." Zezi leaned into the side of the pyramid. "Wait. How did Mother know which girl belonged to which father?"

"Strength's Stone told her." Dendera clamped a hand to her mouth. The words had escaped involuntarily.

Zezi and Annippe stared open-mouthed.

"From what I've seen of that stone," Gazali said, "it's quite possible."

"How could Mother do that to Father?" Zezi asked.

"Your mother had two selves." Gazali put his hand on Zezi's shoulder.

"Father and Paheri must have loved two different parts of her," Dendera said. "I saw a part of her I'd never seen before."

"Can you show me?" Zezi asked.

"Not unless Isis loans me the *Book of Thoth* again." Dendera smiled. "But I can tell you what I remember." She planned to keep that part of her mother, the priestess she'd never known, in the naos of her heart, but for Zezi or Annippe, she would share.

"So, you think the goddesses and gods are real," Zezi said. "You agree with Mother and Tetisheri."

"Hathor is real to me." Dendera put her hand over her heart. Zezi scrunched his eyebrows. "Father was also right," Dendera said. "Kindness is religion. Father held true to no god or goddess, but he tried to help Mother until the end." Dendera put her arm around Zezi. "You decide for you."

They walked until they reached a dead end in the pyramid. Dendera focused on Karnak's House of Sycamore and Hathor's towering sycamore tree. She ran Strength's Stone along the stone wall and spoke the word of power: "Djed." The unmovable moved. They fell in a crack in the earth. It swallowed them up where they were and spit them back out where they wanted to be. The triangular door opened, and they stepped out of the pyramid and under the sheltering branches of Hathor's sycamore tree. They were safe at Karnak. Ipi vaulted from Dendera's shoulder and disappeared amongst the sycamore branches.

Gazali looked toward the temple complex and

rubbed Napata's head. "Dendera, the quality I admired most in your mother turned out to be her greatest flaw. Ramla always believed she could bring out the best in people. Instead of going to the Theban authorities with her evidence, the scraps of conversations she overheard among the priests and priestesses, she confronted Ufa. She was determined to make him see reason. Ufa pacified Ramla, told her he'd mend the rift amongst the temple, make the necessary changes, and give Hatshepsut her due. Instead, he ordered her murder."

Dendera's insides burned. "Eshe was the one who set fire to our home."

"I can't believe the Mother of Karnak…" Annippe clasped and unclasped her hands. "It didn't have anything to do with you or Zezi."

"This is all on Eshe," Ty agreed.

"Thank you." Dendera looked between Annippe and Ty. Her friends were trying to help.

"When someone burns down your home and kills your parents, it's hard not to take it personally," Zezi said.

Annippe rubbed Zezi's arm.

Dendera looked at Zezi. "Eshe wanted Strength's Stone. Ufa wanted Mother hushed up. They thought killing her was the only way to accomplish both." Was the stone the only reason Eshe killed Mother, Dendera wondered, or was her jealousy over Paheri's love for Mother another reason for her plan?

"Tetisheri asked me to keep this from you both," Gazali said. "She feared you would go after the priests if you knew. She tried to keep you far from the temple. She didn't want you to meet the same fate as your parents. Eshe and Ufa cared not that your father perished alongside Ramla." Gazali fixed Dendera with his cat eyes. "You would have burned too, had I not pulled you from the flames."

Understanding rushed Dendera. "It was you who saved me."

28

TRANSPLANTED

Dawn's light shimmered on the peaceful river. Dendera dangled a merkhet, the star-sighting tool, in front of her face, closed one eye, and aligned her merkhet with Ty's.

The year's first starlight twinkled on Ty's leopard-skin cloak.

Dendera cried in triumph, "Sothis!" and pointed to the star that signaled the Nile's annual flood. "She burns in the morning sky. Let us honor Hathor, Mistress of the Stream. She makes the river rise." Ipi whooped from her shoulder, Strength's Stone from her sash.

Pharaoh Hatshepsut beamed as Dendera initiated the ceremony of Wep-Renpet, the Opening of the Year. Annippe led a procession of younger priestesses. Shay, nibbling a barley stalk, stood guard over the grain offerings. Zezi danced with Jamila and Khay. Their voices and the jangle of their sistrums roused the geese from the sacred lake. The birds soared toward Ra's Boat of Millions of Years, their honks complimenting the harmony of Hathor's hymn. Only one priestess was missing from the ceremony at Karnak — Eshe.

Dendera returned the merkhet to Hapuseneb, and Pharaoh Hatshepsut bowed to her. "Will you show me the House of Sycamore, Dendera?" Hatshepsut tapped her crook on the walkway. "We must speak in private."

As they approached Hathor's shrine, Hatshepsut touched the sycamore bark. "Hathor is said to greet the dead at the edge of the Field of Reeds in a sycamore tree."

"She is the Tree of Life." Dendera gazed up into the labyrinth of branches. All the scrolls Omari foisted on her melded with the gifts she'd received from Seven Hathors underneath Dendera Temple. She straightened the red ribbon Hathor had tied in her hair.

Hatshepsut pointed to the House of Sycamore. "May I see inside?"

Dendera opened the door, and servants brought in the cake Dendera requested of Karnak's bakers for this lucky day.

"A crocodile?" Hatshepsut pointed to the cake. The saffron threads had even turned the cake red.

"A peace offering to Seth," Dendera explained, fingering Strength's Stone which snored on her palm. "I hope Seth will let me keep this amulet."

"Why should Seth get the stone?" Hatshepsut asked.

"Hathor made the amulet," Dendera said, "but I think Djedi inscribed Seth's image on the stone to invoke Seth's protection. Seth has been watching me since I found the amulet, in my dreams, in the desert, in the river, at Sobek's Pool, underneath Dendera Temple."

"Perhaps he's decided you're worthy to keep it," Hatshepsut said.

"I hope," Dendera said. She wondered who drew *Hwt-ntr* on the back. Was it Mother or Eshe? Perhaps one day the stone would tell her.

"Shall we cut off his head or his tail first?" Hatshepsut poised her knife over the crocodile cake.

Dendera laughed and sat on a bench carved like a lion. "If Djedi revered Nut's son, I can honor him too." But the thought of Seth led to Eshe.

After Dendera divulged the secrets of her Priestess Test to Hatshepsut, Dendera transported Thutmose and his army through the Karnak pyramid and to the hills outside Dendera Temple. Dendera used Strength's Stone to release Eshe and Ufa from the Moon Prison. Thutmose escorted Eshe, Ufa, and the other priests and priestesses of Dendera to a Nubian jail. Dendera had not asked if they were to be incarcerated or executed. She didn't want to know. Since Eshe told Dendera the Dethroners were scattered across Egypt, and that the Superbis frightened even her, Thutmose remained poised to crush further uprisings.

"Do you mourn Eshe?" Hatshepsut handed Dendera a slice of cake.

"Mourn her?"

"We all loved her," Hatshepsut said. "She was Mother of Karnak."

Mother of Karnak who killed my mother. Dendera couldn't untangle the knot Eshe had made in her mind. The best way to answer was to think like Annippe. "I mourn Eshe's decision to betray you, Majesty." For an Egyptian, to be banished to a foreign land was a penalty worse than death. Whenever Eshe, Ufa, and the others died, their souls were doomed to roam because their bodies were not anchored to a desert tomb.

"You are the daughter of my heart, Dendera." Hatshepsut paused. "A farmer near Edfu reported seeing Neferura."

Dendera gasped. "Where your troops search for the Superbis?"

"Yes, the farmer identified Neferura and Senenmut, but they've not been seen again."

Dendera sighed.

"My troops will not relent." Hatshepsut nodded. "I dreamed last night that you and Neferura walked a path along a river that snakes around a bend."

"It's the river at Dendera," Dendera said. "I had the same vision when I faced the ill-fated Priestess Test in the city."

Hatshepsut's smile broadened as she removed the blue crown from her head. "It was not so ill-fated. Did I not deem that you had passed, Priestess Dendera?"

"That's the truth if you've ever told it, Majesty." Dendera smiled. "When you find Neferura, I will heal her." She had already told Hatshepsut what the *Book of Thoth* told her about Neferura's illness — that Senenmut cursed her with the WadEvil Eye. From Djedi's scroll, Dendera knew that she could wield Strength's Stone, speak the name of the illness, and end it. All she needed was the princess.

"Senenmut will join Eshe in Nubia," Hatshepsut said.

Dendera grimaced. "Majesty, there was one part of my test I didn't tell. That sphinx I faced, she sent a riddle for you."

"For me?"

"She said, 'For Your Majesty, a riddle: When she has more, fear less, she will.'" Dendera lowered her eyes.

"Have more, fear less." Hatshepsut mumbled.

"I couldn't answer then, but I can now," Dendera said. "You may like it. You may not."

Hatshepsut moved her fingers through the air, figuring. "I give up. Do tell me."

"When you were ill, I healed you with the panther skin, and you told me you wanted to become stronger, invincible," Dendera said. "When you are stronger, you will fear less."

Hatshepsut leaned forward. "How do I get stronger?"

"In the stories of old, like the ones in *Queenly Quests*, the matriarchs all gained weight, lots and lots of weight. The more weight, the longer they reigned. To the people, the more a queen weighed, the more power she had in her queendom."

Hatshepsut arched her eyebrows. "You're telling me?"

"Come to think of it, even Djedi ate more and more the more powerful he became. Toward the end, he ate a hundred loaves of bread and drank a hundred jugs of beer every day."

"So, I've heard." Hatshepsut cupped her hand under her chin, thinking.

"To fear less, you need to weigh more," Dendera said. "At least, that's what the sphinx said, and I gather she's an image of Sekhmet, who is Warrioress. I can't imagine anyone more powerful than Mother Fierce."

Hatshepsut picked up the crocodile cake. "I suppose I can start by eating the rest of this."

Dendera laughed, and Pharaoh dug in. Hatshepsut wiped her mouth and said, "There is one thing I still don't understand. Why did you return the *Book of Thoth* to Seth? Isis gave it to you. Could you not have taken it from Ufa and kept it from Seth?"

"Isis gave me permission to borrow the book."

"But Seth…"

"Seth was in his role as Protector," Dendera said. "He appeared as hound, not crocodile. He slayed Apophis so Ra can rise, and he retrieved the book to return to Thoth."

"How do you know?" Hatshepsut asked.

Dendera pulled the Lazuli Lotus from her sash.

Hatshepsut gasped, pointing. "That's the Lazuli Lotus."

"Hathor gave this to me for that night. When I

held the Lotus, I wasn't afraid of Seth. I saw him as Hathor sees."

Hatshepsut leaned back against the bench and sighed. "That was your day to wonderbloom, Dendera." She stroked the lotus petals. "You understood all that you needed to on that one day. You blossomed. You shined."

"So now I can expect my petals to fall?" Dendera grinned.

"I hope not." Hatshepsut extracted a scroll from her belt. "Thutmose asked me to deliver this letter to you."

Dendera unrolled the scroll. A perfect papyrus finger-ring, topped with a papyrus pyramid, fell onto her lap. On the pyramid, Thutmose had scribed, "D + T."

MY DEAREST DENDERA,

FOR NOW, OUR JOURNEYS TAKE US IN SEPARATE DIRECTIONS. BUT IT WILL NOT ALWAYS BE THIS WAY. MY OFFER STANDS. AND I WILL NOT REST UNTIL YOU ACCEPT, MY PYRAMID GIRL.

YOURS,
THUTMOSE

"His scribal skills are primitive. His heart is

yours," Hatshepsut said. "Thutmose is betrothed to Neferura, but you may marry him also, if that is your wish."

"It is not my wish." Dendera rolled up the scroll and slipped the ring over the end.

"What is your wish?"

Dendera ran her fingers over Strength's Stone. *Can I be as noble a priestess as my mother? Can I be solid as a farmer's black land like my father? Will I use my talents to help everyone as Tetisheri did?*

When Dendera was a child, her father took a solid block of tamarisk wood and cut it into pieces. He then challenged Dendera to match the angles and curves, put it together, and make it look whole again. On that day, sitting in the House of Sycamore with her pharaoh, Dendera saw the pieces of her life scattered. She would pull herself together again, fit all the pieces of her life back together, recover from Eshe's betrayal, heal from losing Mother, Father, and Tetisheri. She would practice being as fearless as Sekhmet told her to be. But when Isis told her to heal herself of Eshe's poison, it was Zezi, Gazali, Annippe, Ty, and even Napata and Ipi, who healed her. She needed help. She wanted help. "I want to restore Hathor to her rightful place in Dendera."

Hatshepsut peered at Dendera and nodded. "I hoped you would stay in Thebes to become Pharaoh's Magician, but with your handy pyramid passageway, I suppose you can travel fast when I need you." Hatshepsut smiled. "One who has visions of the Lady of the Stars, I appoint you High Priestess of Dendera."

Hatshepsut placed a single finger on Dendera's pyramid mole. "Take Strength's Stone with you. Even should the Dethroners resurface in Dendera, you shall be unstoppable."

Hatshepsut paused. "You set out to redeem your parents, and in the end, you saved Egypt. How shall we honor them?"

Dendera thought of how Mother hid her talents. "Your Majesty, I would like to form a House of Life for priestesses at Dendera." Dendera didn't know what the future would hold for Hatshepsut and Thutmose. She wanted to be prepared. "We must train for the days ahead."

Hatshepsut struck the sandy floor with her pharaoh's flail. "It shall be called Ramla's House to honor your mother."

Dendera held Strength's Stone to her heart and imagined her father walking the fields of Dendera and stooping to run his fingers through the rich earth. "Father would have turned Dendera's barren lands into ripe farmland."

"Zezi will take on the task," Hatshepsut said.

"I'll need help with…"

"Annippe and Ty shall accompany you, of course." The pharaoh stood. "I must tell Captain Chuma to ready The Splendor of Maatkare for your journey. Work at Dendera Temple requires more supplies than we can carry through your pyramid passageway."

The river god Hapy sent Egypt his greatest gifts with the year's Inundation. The flooding of the Nile delivered new, rich soil from the riverbed onto the black land. Even with a Big Hapy, a high flood that rose toward the waving palm trees lining the riverbank, Annippe and Dendera traveled safe toward Dendera Temple because Captain Chuma chose the Day of Sound to set sail.

"Mother would want you to have this." Dendera slipped the Isis amulet from her neck. "Besides, it goes with your Isis headband."

Annippe smiled.

"Did you talk to your father?" Dendera slipped the necklace over Annippe's bowed head.

Annippe nodded. "He admitted that your mother is my mother. He said he didn't know how she came into possession of Strength's Stone."

"Someone from the Knights of Kemet passed it to her," Zezi chimed in. "They must have."

"Tell me a story of Mother," Annippe begged, looking between her siblings.

"Mother could coax a snake to sneak into Father's tool shed anytime she wanted," Zezi said, looping a baby viper around his fingers. "It scared him every time."

"We should make a snake our symbol for the Curse Chasers," Ty said.

"When baboons fly," Dendera said. Ipi barked, and Annippe laughed.

Where the river cranked its wide bend, Captain Chuma and his crew steered them ashore. Like the banks along the Nile River were being renewed by the Inundation, Dendera Temple was also being washed clean and built anew. Seven Faces of Hathor shone in truth as Hatshepsut's most skilled carvers worked to restore her glory. Inside the great hall, artisans painted scenes — Hatshepsut worshipping Hathor, the restoration of Hathor's temple. Dendera approached Hathor's shrine in the center room and made an offering of frankincense.

"We need a basket of sacred snakes next to the shrine." Zezi's braids sliddered down his back. "And a chariot parked outside." Chuckling at Zezi, Annippe delivered Hatshepsut's instructions to the artisans.

Dendera strolled across the barren grounds with Ipi riding his usual spot. Sweet smells of sunbaked earth rose in whorls. Gardeners sculpted new gardens and dug canals to carry water from the Nile. Dendera envisioned the young myrrh trees growing to tower above a garden bursting with marshmallow, chamomile, and juniper — all the healing herbs she wanted young priestesses to learn about in Mother's city of dreams.

She reached the small pyramid on the hill, Djedi's secret passageway. Ipi jumped to a fresh-dug stream beside a thicket of frankincense saplings. Seth's amulet *sloshed* like Nile waves. Dendera knelt beside Ipi, and he cupped his hand for a sip of water. She pointed Strength's Stone at the water. "Divinduum." The stream burbled, split, rose in two waves like twin gates to the unknown. Dendera pulled the Lazuli Lotus from her waist sash.

Ipi ran his paw along the blue-bright bloom. *Are you sure?*

Seth's amulet *clacked*.

"Positive." Dendera tossed the lotus. "Seven Hathors, I return what belongs to you." The lotus floated through the air, extending roots that slipped into the cracked earth at the bottom of the stream. The blossom bobbed as the waters swirled and closed. "For seven days, or seven years, or seven lifetimes, keep the Lazuli Lotus safe until Egypt needs her again." Strength's Stone thumped Dendera's palm, and she knew Hathor heard.

ABOUT THE AUTHOR

Laurie Chance Smith's deep love of mythology, archaeology, and history inspired her to write *Curse Chasers*, her first novel. She is a nationally and internationally published writer whose work ranges from poetic to insightful, and her first two books were colorful nonfiction. She lives in Texas with her family.

You may find out more about Laurie and her work at www.lauriechancesmith.com